ANYHOW

PRAISE HIM
ANYHOW

Vanessa

MILLER

Publisher's Note:

These short stories are a work of fiction. References to real events, organizations, or places are used in a fictional context. Any resemblances to actual persons, living or dead are entirely coincidental.

PRAISE HIM ANYHOW
Three-in-one collection of novellas including:
Tears Fall at Night, Joy Comes in the Morning & A Forever Kind of Love

Vanessa Miller
www.vanessamiller.com

ISBN: 978-0615842073
Printed in the United States of America
© 2013 by Vanessa Miller

Praise Unlimited Enterprises
13000 S. Tryon St. Ste F-228
Charlotte, NC 28278
www.praiseunlimitedenterprises.com

No part of this book may be reproduced or transmitted in any form or by any means, electronic or mechanical—including photocopying, recording, or by any information storage and retrieval system—without permission in writing from the publisher.

Other Books by Vanessa Miller
Better for Us
Her Good Thing
Long Time Coming
A Promise of Forever Love
A Love for Tomorrow
Yesterday's Promise
Forgotten
Forgiven
Forsaken
Rain for Christmas (Novella)
Through the Storm
Rain Storm
Latter Rain
Abundant Rain
Former Rain
Anthologies (Editor)
Keeping the Faith
Have A Little Faith
This Far by Faith

EBOOKS
Love Isn't Enough
A Mighty Love
The Blessed One (Blessed and Highly Favored series)
The Wild One (Blessed and Highly Favored Series)
The Preacher's Choice (Blessed and Highly Favored Series)
The Politician's Wife (Blessed and Highly Favored Series)
The Playboy's Redemption (Blessed and Highly Favored Series)
Tears Fall at Night (Praise Him Anyhow Series)
Joy Comes in the Morning (Praise Him Anyhow Series)
A Forever Kind of Love (Praise Him Anyhow Series)

Tears Fall at Night

THE PRAISE HIM ANYHOW SERIES

1

"I'm leaving you," Judge Nelson Marshall said, as he walked into the kitchen and stood next to the stainless steel prep table.

Taking a sweet potato soufflé out of her brand new Viking, dual-baking oven, Carmella was bobbing her head to Yolanda Adams's, "I Got the Victory", so she didn't hear Nelson walk into the kitchen.

He turned the music down and said, "Did you hear me, Carmella? I'm leaving."

Carmella put the soufflé on her prep table and turned toward Nelson. He was frowning, and she'd never known him to frown when she baked his favorite soufflé. Then she saw the suitcase in his hand and understood. Nelson hated to travel. His idea of the perfect vacation was staying home and renting movies for an entire week, but recently he had been attending one convention after another. And last week, he'd been in Chicago with her as she had to attend her brother's funeral.

Carmella was thankful that Nelson had taken vacation to attend the funeral with her, because she really didn't think she would have made it through that week without him. She and her younger brother had always been close, but after losing both their parents by the time they were in their thirties, the bond between them had become even stronger. Now she was trying to make sense of a world where forty-six-year-old men died of heart attacks.

Nelson had been fidgety the entire time they were in Chicago. She knew he hated being away from home, so she cut their trip short by a day. He hadn't told her he had another trip planned. "Not another one of those boring political conventions?"

He shook his head.

Nelson had almost lost his last bid for criminal court judge. Since then he had been obsessed with networking with government officials in hopes of getting appointed to a federal bench and bypassing elections altogether.

"Sit down, Carmella, we need to talk."

Carmella sat down on one of the stools in front of the kitchen island. Nelson sat down next to Carmella. He lowered his head.

"Nelson, what's wrong?"

He didn't respond. But he had the same look on his face that he'd had the night they'd received the call about his grandmother's death.

"Please say something, honey. You're scaring me," Carmella said.

He lifted his head and attempted to look into his wife's eyes, but quickly turned away as he said, "This doesn't work for me anymore."

Confused, Carmella asked, "What's not working?"

"This marriage, Carmella. It's not what I want anymore."

"I don't understand, Nelson." She turned away from him and looked around her expansive kitchen. It had been redesigned a couple of years ago to ensure that she had everything she needed to throw the most lavish dinner parties that Raleigh, NC had ever seen. Nelson had told her that if he were ever going to get an appointment to a federal bench, he would need to network and throw fundraising campaigns for the senators and congressmen of North Carolina.

So she'd exchanged her kitchen table for a prep table, and installed the walk-in cooler to keep her salads and desserts at just the right temperature for serving. The Viking stove with its six burners and dual oven—one side convection and the other with an infrared broiler—had been her most expensive purchase. But the oven had been worth it. The infrared broiler helped her food to taste like restaurant-quality broiled food, and the convection side of the oven did amazing things with her pastries. She'd turned her home into a showplace in order to impress the guests who attended their legendary dinner parties. She had done everything Nelson had asked her to do, so Carmella couldn't understand why she was now in her kitchen listening to her husband say that he didn't want this anymore. "We've been happy, right?"

Nelson shook his head. "I haven't been happy with our marriage for a long time now."

"Then why didn't you say something? We could have gone to counseling or talked with Pastor Mitchell."

Nelson stood up. "It's too late for that. I've already filed for a divorce. All you need to do is sign the papers when you receive them, and then we can both move on with our lives."

Tears welled in Carmella's eyes as she realized that while she had been living in this house and sleeping in the same bed with Nelson, he had been seeing a divorce lawyer behind her back. "What about the kids, Nelson? What am I supposed to tell them?"

"Our children are grown, Carmella. You can't hide behind them anymore."

"What's that supposed to mean?" Carmella stood up, anger flashing in her eyes. "Dontae is only seventeen years old. He's still in high school and needs both his parents to help him make his transition into adulthood."

"I'm not leaving Dontae. He can come live with me if he wants."

"Oh, so now you want to take my son away from me, too? What's gotten into you, Nelson? When did you become so cruel?"

"I'm not trying to take Dontae away from you. I just know that raising a son can be difficult for a woman to do alone. So, I'm offering to take him with me."

"That's generous of you," Carmella said snidely. Then a thought struck her, and she asked, "Are you seeing someone? Is that it? Is this some midlife crisis that you're going through?"

"This is not about anyone else, Carmella. It's about the fact that we just don't work anymore."

Tears were flowing down her honey-colored cheeks. "But I still love you. I don't want a divorce."

"I don't have time to argue with you. Just sign the papers and let's get this over with."

She put her hands on her small hips and did the sista-sista neck roll, as her bob-styled hair swished from one side to the other. "We haven't argued in years. I have just gone with the flow and done whatever you wanted me to do. But on the day my husband packs his bags and asks me for a divorce, I think we should at least argue about that, don't you?"

He pointed at her and sneered as if her very presence offended him. "See, this is exactly why I waited so long to tell you. I knew you were going to act irrational."

"Irrational! Are you kidding me?" Carmella wanted to pull her hair out. The man standing in front of her was not her husband. He must have fallen, bumped his head and lost his fool mind. "What are we going to tell Joy and Dontae? I mean...you're not giving me anything to go on. We've been married twenty-five years and all of a sudden you just want out?"

"Like I said before, Joy and Dontae will be fine." He picked up his suitcase again and said, "I'm done discussing this. I'll be back to get the rest of my clothes. You should receive the divorce papers in a day or two. Just sign them and put them on the kitchen table." He headed toward the front door.

Following behind him, Carmella began screaming, "I'm not signing any divorce papers, so don't waste your time sending them here. And when you get off of whatever drug you're on, you'll be grateful that I didn't sign."

After opening the front door, Nelson turned to face his wife. With anger in his eyes, he said, "You better sign those papers or you'll regret it." He then stepped out of the house and slammed the door.

Carmella opened the door and ran after her husband. "Why are you doing this, Nelson? How am I supposed to pay the house note or our other bills if you leave me like this?"

"Get back in the house. You're making a scene."

"You spring this divorce on me without a second thought about my feelings, but you have the nerve to worry about the neighbors overhearing us?" Carmella shook her head in disgust. "I knew you were selfish, Nelson. But I never thought you were heartless."

He opened his car door and got in. "You're not going to make me feel guilty about this, Carmella. It's over between us. I want a divorce."

As Nelson backed out of the driveway, Carmella put her hands on her hips and shouted, "Well, you're not getting one!"

She stood barefoot, hands on hips, as Nelson turned what had seemed like an ordinary day into something awful and hideous. He backed out of the driveway—and out of her life—if what he said was to be believed. Carmella had been caught off guard…taken by surprise by this whole thing. Nelson had always been a family-values, family-first kind of man. He loved his children, and she'd thought he loved her as well. The family had attended church together and loved the Lord. But in the last year, Nelson had found one reason after another for not attending Sunday services.

"Are you okay?"

Carmella had been in a daze, watching Nelson drive out of her life; so she hadn't noticed that Cynthia Drake, their elderly next-door neighbor was outside doing her weekly gardening. Carmella wiped the tears from her face and turned toward the older woman.

"Is there anything I can do?" Cynthia asked, as she took off her gardening gloves.

"W-what just happened?" Carmella asked with confusion in her eyes.

"Come on," Cynthia said. She grabbed hold of Carmella's arm. "Let me get you back in the house."

"Why is everybody so obsessed with this house? It's empty, nobody in it but me. What am I supposed to do here alone?"

Cynthia guided Carmella back into the house and sat her down on the couch. "I'm going to get you something to drink." She disappeared into the kitchen and came back with a glass of iced tea and a can of Sunkist orange soda. "I didn't know which one you might want."

Carmella reached for the soda. "The iced tea is Nelson's. I don't drink it."

Cynthia sat down next to Carmella. She put her hand on Carmella's shoulder. "Do you want to talk?"

"Talk about what?" Carmella opened the Sunkist and took a sip. "I don't even know what's going on. I mean… I thought we were happy. I had no idea that Nelson wanted a divorce, but evidently, he's been planning this for a while."

"You need to get a divorce lawyer," Cynthia said.

"I don't want a divorce. I don't know what has gotten into Nelson, but he'll be back."

"You and Nelson have been married a long time, so I hope you're right. It would be a shame for him to throw away his marriage after all these years."

Carmella put the Sunkist down, put her head in her hands and started crying. This was too much for her. Nelson was the father of her children. He was supposed to love her for the rest of her life. They had stood before God and vowed to be there for each other, through the good and the bad, until death. How could he do this to her?

"Here, hon. Dry your face." Cynthia handed Carmella some tissue. "Do you have any family members that I could call to have them come sit with you for a while?"

"My parents have been dead for years and my only brother died last week," she said miserably.

"Oh hon, I'm so sorry to hear that."

Carmella lifted her hands and then let them flap back into her lap. "I just don't understand. I thought we were happy."

Sitting down next to Carmella, Cynthia said, "I've been married three times, and honey, trust me when I tell you that you'll probably never understand. Men don't need a reason for the things they do."

They sat talking for a while, and Carmella was comforted by the wise old woman who had taken time out from her gardening to sit with her in her time of need. When Cynthia was ready to leave, Carmella felt as if she should do something for the kindly old woman. She ran to the kitchen and came back with the sweet potato soufflé that she had lovingly fixed for her husband. She handed it to Cynthia, and said, "Thank you. I don't know what I would have done if you hadn't helped me back into the house."

"Oh, sweetie, it was no problem. You don't have to give me anything."

"I want to. I made this sweet potato soufflé for my husband. But since he doesn't want it, it would bring me great joy knowing that another family enjoyed it."

"Well, then I'll take it."

After Carmella walked Cynthia out, she went to the upstairs bathroom. She lit her bathroom candles, turned on the hot water and then poured some peach scented bubble bath in the water. She got into the tub, hoping to soak her weary bones until the ache in her heart drifted away. The warm water normally soothed her and took her mind off the things that didn't get done that day or the things that didn't turn out just the way she'd planned. Carmella enjoyed the swept-away feeling she experienced when surrounded by bubbles and her vanilla-scented candles. But tonight, all she felt was dread. She wondered if anyone would care if she drifted off to sleep, slid down all the way into the water and drowned like Whitney Houston had done.

The thought was tempting, because Carmella didn't know if she wanted to live without her husband. Tears rolled down her face as she realized that as much as she didn't want to live without Nelson, he was already living without her.

2

"You better be glad we're friends, Jasmine. Because I would have to charge you for making me carry this heavy headboard if we weren't," Joy Marshall said. She put the headboard down and massaged her arm.

Jasmine Walker grinned. "You know I appreciate you, girl."

"Well, I would appreciate this mystery man of yours, if he showed up to do the heavy lifting."

Jasmine poked her bottom lip out. "He's at work, Joy. Come on, help me load this stuff on the truck, and I promise I'll make him take everything off the truck."

They picked up the headboard and made their way to the truck. "So, I'm finally going to meet this mystery man who swept you off your feet, but never bothered to pick you up for dates." Joy rolled her eyes. "I truly don't understand why you've kept on seeing him. For as long as I've known you, you've never let a guy treat you so cavalierly."

They placed the headboard in the truck, and then Jasmine said, "Well, he's made up for it now, hasn't he?"

"I don't know, Jasmine… renting is temporary. If he were really serious, he would have bought the house and bought a ring."

Jasmine put her arm around Joy's shoulder as they walked back into the house to get the rest of her things. "You'll see, Joy Marshall, my man loves me, and he's going to prove it to the world."

Joy didn't respond. Jasmine had been secretive ever since she started seeing this mystery guy. In her gut, Joy knew the man was married. That had to be the reason Jasmine was sneaking around all the time. Joy's parents were Christians. They had done their best to instill good moral values in their children, so Joy couldn't condone what her friend was doing. But she and Jasmine had been friends since they'd

13

been assigned as roommates during their freshman year of college. After graduating college, they'd both decided to attend law school.

Since Joy was a child, she'd dreamed of the day she would finish law school and then work in her father's law practice. Her father had changed the plans a bit when he became a judge, so now Joy and Jasmine planned to become partners in their own law firm. Their plan included five years of clerking or doing the grunt work at a respected law firm so that they could learn the ropes and network. The Honorable Nelson Marshall had given her plan two-thumbs up, so Joy knew that she and Jasmine were on the right track.

"I hope this guy you're moving in with understands that you and I are going to be business partners, and that we will need to stay in touch with each other."

"Oh, he knows. And believe me, he understands about business, so he won't get in our way."

It seemed strange to Joy that she and Jasmine never said her boyfriend's name. The one time that Joy had demanded that Jasmine tell her who she was going out with, just in case the guy was a serial killer or something, Jasmine had claimed that his name was Charles Riley. But Joy didn't believe that. The name had sounded fake to her, and anyway, if his name were Charles, Jasmine would have referred to it every once in a while. But she had kept him strictly in the second-person category. The lawyer in Joy understood that Jasmine was trying not to slip up and say something she wasn't supposed to, but what?

After they'd packed all of Jasmine's bedroom furniture in the U-Haul truck, Jasmine jumped behind the wheel and Joy got in on the passenger's side. As they drove down the highway toward Jasmine's new home, Joy said, "Troy and I would like to take you and your man out to dinner next week. Do you think he would be willing to go somewhere with your friends?"

"You act like I'm moving in with Shrek. I promise you, Joy, my man is not an ogre."

"That's good to know, girl. I just want you to be happy," Joy said, and then leaned back in her seat.

"I am," Jasmine said. She exited off the highway. "He makes me so happy... I honestly can't believe that he chose me. I really think you'll be happy for us once you see how good we are together."

Joy hoped that Jasmine was right. She had worried about her friend getting too wrapped up in a guy who wouldn't even pick her up for dates, but made Jasmine meet him, as if he were too busy to drive a few blocks out of his way. Joy wouldn't have been able to put up with a man like that. She thanked God every day that her fiancé, Troy, was just like her father: considerate, responsible and loving.

"We're here." Jasmine pulled the U-Haul truck into the driveway of a spacious two-story home.

Joy's eyes widened as she looked at the house. From the looks of the outer structure, Joy figured the house had to be at least four thousand square feet. "Are you sharing this place with another couple or something?"

Jasmine laughed. She then shook her head. "No, he likes to entertain, so we needed enough room to be able to host parties."

"You sound like my mother. She's always hosting one party or another for my dad. You need to go take some cooking lessons from her so you can really do your parties up right," Joy suggested.

"Girl, please, I don't plan to do any cooking. That's what caterers are for," Jasmine opened the truck door and got out. Joy opened her door and followed Jasmine into the house.

Standing in the foyer, Joy was once again struck by the expansiveness of the house. The white marble floors, spiral staircase and the upstairs balcony that overlooked the foyer—all gave the house a feel of importance, as if someone with stature and influence lived there. "How can your guy afford to rent a house like this?" She knew it was rude to ask, but the question was out of her mouth before she could stop herself.

"Girl, just help me get those boxes out of the truck and stop being so nosey," Jasmine said with a good-natured grin on her face.

"I just can't believe this place, Jasmine. Troy and I sure can't afford anything like this."

They headed back out to the truck. "Once the two of you put your money together," Jasmine said, "I'm sure you'll be able to afford something nice, so don't sweat it, Joy."

"Please. After we get married, we'll probably spend the next five to ten years paying off our student loans. After that, we'll be able to start saving for a house like this."

Jasmine pulled a box out of the back of the truck. "I'm trying not to think about my student loans. At least your parents paid most of your tuition. But what I didn't get in financial aid, I had to cover in student loans."

Joy grabbed a box, and as they walked back to the house, she said, "Yeah, just when I started feeling grateful about not having so much debt to pay back after college, I met Troy and it seems like his middle name is debt."

"See, if you would have listened to me, you would have hooked up with an older guy who'd already paid off his debt. That way he would be able to take care of you in style."

They set the boxes down in the foyer and as they turned to go get more, Joy said, "I'm happy with Troy. Besides, my father had a lot of school debt when he married my mom, but they worked together and paid everything off. They're living pretty well now."

Jasmine didn't respond. She grabbed the next box and took it into the house. They followed that same process until all the boxes were unloaded.

Exhausted, they sat down on the floor next to the boxes. Joy said, "I don't think I want to be your friend anymore."

"I understand. I'm so tired; I don't want to move from this spot."

The two women sat on the floor, exhausted and breathing hard for a few minutes, and then Jasmine said, "You're right, he should have helped me move this stuff. But don't worry; I'm going to make him pay for our labor."

"Now you're talking like the Jasmine I know." Joy rubbed her hands together in sweet anticipation. "I wish I could be a fly on the wall when he gets what's coming to him."

Jasmine stood up. She held out her hand to help Joy up. "Come on," Jasmine said. "Let's order a pizza and watch Lifetime. I'll get my mystery man to take you home when he gets here."

"That's the least he can do," Joy said, as she stood up and headed toward the family room with Jasmine.

After Jasmine called the pizza in, they sat down and started watching a stalker movie on Lifetime. Halfway through it, the doorbell rang. Jasmine and Joy looked at each other; neither wanted to move now that they had found a comfortable spot on the sofa.

Jasmine finally got up. "All right," she said. "It's my house, so I've got to start doing the work around here."

When Jasmine came back with the pizza, Joy grabbed a slice and then leaned back against the sofa again. She took a bite. "This is good."

Jasmine savored the ham, sausage, pepperoni and cheese. She swallowed and agreed, "Sure is. It tastes just like that three-meat pizza we used to order during freshman year."

"You mean it tastes like the three-meat pizza I used to order. And you and our other roommate used to beg me for a slice."

As soon as the words were out of her mouth, Joy wanted to take them back. Jasmine hated when anyone referred to how impoverished she had been during their first few years of college. Things were going pretty well for her now, so Joy thought she had gotten over her issues with growing up in a single-parent household, with food stamps and government cheese. But the look of embarrassment that she saw in her friend's eyes made Joy want to put the pizza down and eat her words instead.

"I'm sorry, Jasmine; I didn't mean to upset you."

Jasmine waved off Joy's apology. "Stephanie and I made our way through college on scholarships, financial aid, and work programs that helped pay for those expensive books. We didn't always have extra money for pizza."

Joy grabbed another slice and lifted it in the air in a toast, and then said, "But you do now."

"Oh, I intend to have a lot more than pizza money, believe that," Jasmine said with a self-assured grin on her face.

"I have no doubt. I've always believed that you would succeed. I certainly wouldn't be thinking about starting a law firm with someone I thought didn't know what they were doing."

"I forgot to get something to drink. We have lemonade and iced tea in the fridge."

"I'll take the lemonade."

Jasmine stood. "I'll be right back. Do you need anything else?"

"A pillow. I'm about to crash." Joy pulled out her cell phone. "I'm going to have Troy come pick me up. Your man is taking too long."

"Suit yourself, but he should be here any minute." As if on cue, the doorbell rang. "Can you get that for me, Joy? I'm going to go get our drinks."

"Sure," Joy said. She got up and headed toward the front door. Before she could get to it, the doorbell rang again, and then the person on the outside started pounding on the door. Joy was walking as fast as she could, so whoever was so anxious would have to wait. She was too tired to move any faster.

By the time she got to the door, the doorbell rang for the third time. Joy was tempted to stand there a little longer and let the person on the other side of the door suffer a while longer. But when she looked through the peephole and saw her father, she immediately swung the door open.

As Nelson Marshall stepped into the house, he said, "I lost my key again."

Joy didn't hear him because as he was talking, she asked, "What are you doing here, Dad? Did Mom send you after me or something?"

Nelson swung around to face his daughter. His eyes widened. He stuttered, "Wh-what are y-you doing h-here?"

"I'm helping Jasmine move into her new house," Joy told her father. Then with a look of confusion on her face, she asked, "If you didn't know I was here, why did you come to Jasmine's house?"

Before Nelson could respond, Jasmine walked into the room carrying two glasses of lemonade. She handed one to Joy and then walked over to Nelson, kissed him, and then handed him the other glass. "You're late. What took you so long to get home?"

18

Nelson stepped back and turned toward his daughter. "I-I can explain."

But Joy was figuring things out all on her own. Jasmine's mystery man was her father, and the two of them had been sneaking around for over a year. "The person you need to explain something to is my mother," Joy declared, storming into the family room and grabbing her purse.

This was too much for Joy. Her father wasn't a cheater. He was a good man who went to work every day and attended church on Sundays with his family. But as she walked back into the entryway and saw the smirk on Jasmine's face, Joy began to believe what her eyes were telling her.

"You did this on purpose," Joy accused Jasmine. "You wanted me to know that my father was cheating on my mother."

Jasmine put her arm around Nelson and said, "It's time you knew the truth."

Nelson stepped away from Jasmine again. "This isn't how I wanted to tell her, Jasmine. You had no right bringing Joy here without letting me know."

Tearfully, Joy said, "What are you doing, Dad? This is going to break Mother's heart."

Nelson tried to put his arm around Joy. She pulled away. "Your mother already knows that I want a divorce. I'm surprised she didn't tell you."

Joy asked, "Why didn't you tell me? I spoke to you last night, but I don't recall you saying anything about divorcing my mother, so you could move in with someone young enough to be your daughter."

"I'm a grown woman," Jasmine said, "and Nelson and I are happy, despite our age difference."

Joy turned her back to Jasmine and held up her hand. "Don't speak to me ever again. I am not interested in anything you have to say." With that, Joy headed for the door.

"Don't go like this, baby-girl," her father said. "I really want to help you understand why I decided to leave your mother."

Joy opened the door and then shot back at her father, "Oh, I know exactly what was on your mind." She walked through the door and slammed it behind her. Joy was so angry that she wanted to hit something. She had looked up to her father almost to the point of worship for as long as she could remember. Nelson Marshall had been a man of integrity… someone she, her brother and her mother could count on.

Tears rolled down Joy's face as she walked away from her father's new home. She heard the door open behind her, but didn't stop or turn around to see who was coming after her. She wanted nothing to do with her so-called best friend or her dishonorable father.

"Baby-girl, wait! Jasmine said that you need a ride home. Don't walk off like this."

She kept walking.

Nelson caught up with his daughter and grabbed her arm. "Let me explain."

"Get away from me."

"Don't act like a child, Joy. You know how life works."

Joy wiped the tears from her eyes as she swung around to face her father. "I sure do know how life works. Men who claim to love their wives turn around and cheat on them every day. But I never expected you to be one of those men." She was disgusted by her father. At that moment she was ashamed to call this man her father and the tears flowed again.

"Don't cry, baby-girl. Come on, let me take you home."

Joy backed away from her father. "No, I don't need you to take me home. You need to go home to your wife."

"I can't do that."

"Then leave me alone."

"I can't just leave you out here like this, Joy. I'm your father. It's my job to protect you."

She laughed at that. The man standing in front of her had just destroyed her belief in humanity, but he was talking about protecting her. "I'll call Troy. He can come get me."

She pulled her cell phone out of her purse and dialed her fiancé. When he answered, she explained that she needed a ride, and Troy promised to come and pick her up. She hung up the phone and turned back to her father. "There, I don't need you, so you can go back to your little girlfriend and continue tearing our family apart."

3

In the kitchen with her radio tuned to 92.7, her praise station, Carmella was busy baking cakes for her neighbors. Her way of saying thanks for the things they'd done for her in the past month: like mowing the law, trimming the bushes, coming by to check on her and just being kind to her. Dontae was still away at football camp, but would be home in two days. So, this was Carmella's way of letting her neighbors know that she appreciated them.

Cooking was a love of Carmella's; she could get in her kitchen and lose herself amongst the pots and pans and flour and sugar. She also loved listening to her praise music while she cooked or baked. Smokie Norful was lifting her spirit by telling her that God saw what was going on in her life and He understood when she felt like giving up. Then Smokie began encouraging her to keep moving forward, one more day, one more step.

Carmella was feeling it and was about to break out into a praise dance right in her kitchen, but then Joy walked in and killed the mood.

"Mama, why didn't you tell me that Daddy left you?"

Carmella had hoped not to have that discussion at all. She had prayed that Nelson would come to his senses and move back home where he belonged, before the children found out about his mid-life crisis. She'd thought he'd get the message when she didn't sign the divorce papers, but mailed the shredded document back to him. But Nelson had just sent her the document again. "Joy, this doesn't mean anything. Your Dad is just going through a mid-life crisis. He'll be back home soon enough."

Joy's eyebrow went up and she sat down at one of the counter seats. "You'd take him back after he moved Jasmine into his new house?"

Carmella took two lemon pound cakes out of the oven, closed the oven door with her foot and placed the cakes on her prep table. "What did you say, dear?"

Joy got up, walked further into the kitchen and stood next to her mother as she looked her in the face and said, "Daddy is living with my best friend, Jasmine."

She dumped the cakes out of the baking pans. "Don't say things like that, Joy. Where in the world would you get an idea like that?"

Joy put her hand on her mother's shoulder. "Listen to me, Mother. It's true. I saw it with my own eyes."

"Your father wouldn't do anything like that to us. He's a God-fearing man and he loves us." Carmella hadn't been feeling much love from her husband lately, but she didn't want to discuss any of that with Joy. Her daughter was a daddy's girl through and through. She hadn't even wanted Carmella to tuck her in at night when she was a child. Joy always asked for Nelson, to the point of hurting Carmella's feelings at times.

"Mom, come sit down with me in the family room." They walked out of the kitchen and made their way to the family room. Joy waited until her mother sat down on the sectional. Joy sat next to her and took her mom's hand in hers. "I helped Jasmine move today. She told me that her boyfriend had gotten a place for them. By the time we finished with moving things around in the house, Daddy showed up. I thought you had sent him to get me because I was taking too long, since I had called and told you that I would be coming over for dinner. But that wasn't why he was there."

Carmella was silent as she listened to her daughter. This doesn't seem like my life, she thought. Certainly doesn't sound like my husband, the man I married and promised to spend the rest of my life with. Nelson had been so sure that he would become a success in life and Carmella had just been grateful that he'd wanted her to be a part of what he was destined to create. They had spent a lot of nights praying for Nelson's career, his judgment and their finances. And just as Nelson had expected, their life had turned out great, with all the trimmings: a beautiful home, exotic vacations, college and mutual funds, the works.

"Dad admitted it to me, Mom. He said that you two were getting a divorce and that he was now with Jasmine."

"But that doesn't sound like Nelson," was all Carmella could fix her mouth to say. And then she thought, maybe it wasn't Nelson. Maybe some demon had come out of the pits of hell and climbed into her husband's body and was doing the slimy things that Nelson Marshall never would have dreamed of doing, if he wasn't under demonic possession.

"Mom... Mom. Where did you go?"

Joy was waving her hands in Carmella's face. "I'm still with you, Joy. I was just wondering if we should find a priest to perform an exorcism on your father or something." She then lowered her head and laughed hysterically.

"Mom, this isn't funny. Stop laughing."

But Carmella couldn't stop. Her husband had left her for a twenty-three-year-old recent college graduate, whom she'd fed numerous times in her own kitchen. If she didn't laugh, she'd cry until she drowned in her tears.

"I'm going to call Aunt Rose," Joy said as she jumped up and ran for the phone.

Rose had been Carmella's best friend since they roomed together in college. The two women had both married the year after graduating college. Their kids were born around the same time. They celebrated holidays and vacationed together. But even with all that, Carmella still hadn't called Rose to tell her that Nelson just up and walked out the door.

Rose made it to the house within fifteen minutes. The three women went into the kitchen. Carmella turned off the praise music and Joy and Rose helped her put icing on the cakes. "I need to get these to my neighbors. They have been so wonderful this past month and I want to show my appreciation."

"Hon, why didn't you call me? Why are you going through this alone?" Rose asked as she put the cream cheese frosting on one of the cakes. "And when did you have time to bake all of these cakes? There has to be at least twenty on the table."

"I have nothing but time," Carmella told her friend. "My husband no longer comes home and Dontae is still away at camp." She pointed towards Joy with a butter cream filled knife. "Joy has been staying in an apartment with Nelson's girlfriend down by the college."

After saying that, Carmella put her knife down and then punched a hole in the cake she just frosted. "Can you believe such a thing? My husband has a girlfriend."

Rose came around the table and pulled Carmella into a hug. As they pulled apart, Rose said, "Why don't we just go kill him?"

"Hey, I may not like him very much, but he is still my father," Joy said as she objected to where the conversation was going.

"You just put frosting on that cake and let me talk to Rose." Carmella threw a warning look in her oldest child's direction and then turned back to Rose. "Since Nelson is the father of my children, do you think we could just put him in the hospital?"

"Mom!"

"Hey, she wanted to kill him." Carmella pointed at Rose.

Rose pointed towards the cakes, giggling so hard, she could barely get a word out. When she finally collected herself she said, "Remember that movie, The Help?" she asked and then doubled over with laughter.

"Yeah, I remember The Help. You and I went to see it together. I'm still mad about that outhouse mess."

"Speaking of mess…" Rose said as she came up for air.

"Aunt Rose, I know you aren't suggesting that my saint of a mother bake a cake full of poo for my dad?"

Carmella put her hand over her mouth and her eyes widened as she began to understand what her friend was trying to tell her. "Rose, you are crazy, girl."

"What? You said you wanted to put him in the hospital. Don't you think eating a dung filled cake would do it?"

"Girl, I have too much respect for cakes to treat one so harshly."

"Well you're the one who wanted to put him in the hospital," Rose reminded her.

"By running him over or something like that, not by ruining one of my beautiful cakes."

Joy stepped away from the prep table. "I'm going to my room." As she walked out of the kitchen, she threw back, "And I hope I won't be testifying against my mother any time soon."

Carmella and Rose laughed, then Carmella got serious and said, "She's right. The man is my husband. I've been married to him for twenty-five years. I shouldn't be talking like this."

"He asked you for a divorce, Carmella. It's time to fight, girl. Do something," Rose told her as she bounced around the kitchen as if she were getting ready for a boxing match.

"I don't know how to fight," Carmella confessed. "All I've ever done is be Nelson's obedient pup, run his errands and take care of his house. I haven't even put the degree I worked so hard to get to use in over twenty years."

Carmella sat down on one of the stools in the kitchen, laid her head on the counter and cried like tears were rain and she was doing her part to end an all consuming drought.

***

Another day, another problem. Two days ago she'd cried on Rose's shoulder and then went door to door passing out pound cakes to her neighbors. This morning she was awakened out of her fitful sleep by the ringing of the phone. Carmella had tried to ignore it and sleep on, but it seemed as if it would stop ringing for a moment and then start back up again. Somebody wanted to speak with her, and they weren't going to give up until she answered the phone.

With her head still on the pillow, Carmella reached over to her night stand and took the phone off the hook. She put the receiver against her ear and mumbled, "Hello."

"Hi, may I speak with Mr. or Mrs. Marshall."

Her voice was groggy as she responded, "This is Mrs. Marshall. Who's calling?"

"This is Rita from Wells Fargo. We're just giving you a friendly reminder call concerning your mortgage."

That woke Carmella. She popped up in bed and asked, "What about my mortgage? What's wrong?" She'd never received a call from her mortgage company before; why on earth were they calling her so early in the morning?

"We haven't received the payment this month and we just wanted to remind you that it was due on the first."

The first was two weeks ago. They were almost halfway through August. Had Nelson been so busy playing with his girl-child that he'd forgotten his responsibilities? "I'll check into this and get back with you." Carmella hung up the phone.

A hot flash was overtaking her body, reminding her that she was forty-seven and pre-menopausal. She fanned herself with her hand, but that didn't help, so she opened the window and then realized it was August and hot as Hades outside. So she put the window down and turned the ceiling fan on. Just as she was cooling off, the phone rang again.

Carmella picked it up, but didn't say anything. A recording asked her to wait for a very important message. The message was about the payment on her Lexus SRX 400 being past due. "Oh, I know he done fell and bumped his head now."

She dialed Nelson's office, not caring that he would need to be on the bench within fifteen minutes and was probably handling some last minute judgeship stuff. She needed to speak with her husband and nobody was going to stop her. So when Laura, his long time secretary answered the phone, Carmella said, "Good morning, Laura, I hope your morning is going well."

"It is, Mrs. Marshall."

She noticed that Laura didn't ask how her morning was going. No doubt Laura already knew about Nelson's mistress. So she was probably worried that Carmella would break down on her and tell her all sorts of horrid things about her boss. "Listen Laura, I need to speak with my husband. I know he's probably busy, but I don't care about his schedule right now. I'm having a crisis and I need him on the phone ASAP."

"I'll put you through this instant, Mrs. Marshall." Just before transferring the call, Laura mumbled, "I'm sorry."

Carmella heard her and appreciated that she would let her feelings be known in the slightest way. But when Nelson picked up, she had no time to dwell on that kindness. "Why haven't you paid the mortgage or my car note?" she screamed at him.

"Good morning to you, too, Carmella. How are things going?" he asked in a calm manner as if everything was right with the world and the sun was shining down on him alone.

"I was awakened by bill collectors this morning, Nelson, so I'm not having a good morning. But I bet your little girlfriend was able to sleep soundly this morning."

"Jasmine doesn't sleep in like you. She has a job to get to every morning."

Carmella was livid. She had worked her fingers to the bone, making a home for her family and being the perfect hostess for Nelson. "How can you be so cruel as to disparage the work I've done for this family? Being a housewife is no longer good enough for you, I guess."

"No one is belittling what you did for our family. But don't you think it's time to get a job and handle your own bills?"

"No, I do not!" You're the one who left this family. And we have depended on your income for over twenty years now, right after you stopped depending on my income to get you through law school. And I guarantee you that any judge in this town would agree with me." She was out of her bed pacing the floor. "You are not going to get away with this, Nelson Marshall. If you want to live a double life, then you darn well better find the money to pay for both of them."

"Sign the divorce papers and then I'll make sure you get a decent settlement."

"In your dreams," she said and slammed down the phone. She was just about to throw it against the wall, when her bedroom door opened and Joy and Dontae rushed in. She'd totally forgotten that Joy was picking Dontae up from the airport this morning. Had he heard her? Oh God, she prayed not.

"Mom, why are you in here screaming about Dad living a double life? What's going on?"

Prayer wasn't doing her a bit of good lately. She fell back onto her bed and began screaming and crying—anything to avoid answering Dontae's question.

28

"Come on, Dontae; let me talk to you in the other room," Joy said as she watched her mother fall apart."

"B-but, what's wrong with Mom?" He went to his mother and tried to calm her. "Did I upset you, Mama? If I did, I didn't mean to, so please stop crying."

"It's not you, baby," was all she could say before the tears came again.

Joy pulled Dontae out of the bedroom and then Carmella sat up in the middle of the bed. She grabbed one of the fluffy pillows on Nelson's side of the bed and held it close to her chest, while resting her face in it. The pillow still smelled of his cologne. Carmella inhaled deeply. She'd always loved the way the Dolce & Gabbana pour Homme fragrance smelled on Nelson. It was woodsy and masculine. The fragrance was not for daytime wear because it could be a bit overpowering, so Nelson only wore it during evening events. When she stopped and thought about it, she realized that he had stepped out a lot of nights without her in the last few months.

She should have been more suspicious… paid more attention to what was going on right under her nose. She threw the pillow across the room, as the fragrance she used to love was now making her stomach curdle. She had been played for a fool and now she had to figure out how she was going to pay bills that Nelson had always assured her that she need not concern herself with.

She had graduated with a bachelor's degree in Art. But she never received her teaching certificate or attended graduate school so that she might be able to teach art in elementary or even at a community college. She'd married Nelson six months after graduation and then she'd had to work temp assignments and receptionist positions so she could bring money into the home while Nelson went on to law school. Once he'd finished school, she'd had their first child and he'd asked her to stay home and raise their children.

Funny thing was, Carmella had always thought she'd gotten the long end of the stick. While Nelson was forced to go out and work for a living and deal with the rat race, she had been able to stay home with her children and concentrate on keeping her home happy. But now that she was unemployable in this new economy, it hurt like a son of gun to realize that she'd actually gotten the short and frayed end of that stick.

"He did what?" Dontae exploded. "How come no one called to tell me any of this? Why am I just now finding out that my father has been sleeping with your best friend for a year?"

"You think I knew any of this was going on?" Joy got defensive.

"Well, she is your best friend. And you did let her live with you."

"She was a roommate. And we are no longer best anything. The woman used me the whole time and threw her relationship with Daddy in my face." Joy plopped down on the sofa and began crying.

Dontae went to his sister, put his arm on her shoulder and said, "I didn't mean that. I know it's not your fault."

"I just can't believe any of this is happening. Daddy and Mommy always seemed so happy. They went to church together for goodness' sake." Joy was simply outdone over the things that had transpired over the last few days. Her father's betrayal had shaken her core beliefs and she was now having second, third, fourth and fifth thoughts about her upcoming wedding. On paper Troy was a good man…a good catch. But would that paper be tarnished twenty years from now?

"We've got to do something. We can't just sit here and let Daddy get away with this. I've never seen Mama cry like that."

"I know Dontae, but what can we do?"

"Let's go talk to Daddy," Dontae suggested.

Joy folded her arms around her chest. "I don't have anything to say to that man."

"Well I've got a lot I want to say, so if you're not going, I'll just drive myself." Dontae grabbed the keys to the three year old Mustang his father bought him on his sixteenth birthday and headed out the door.

Joy went into the kitchen, spread some vegetable cream cheese on a wheat bagel, poured orange juice into a glass and grabbed a banana.

31

She then took the light breakfast to her mother's room. As she placed the plate on the night stand, she told her mother, "I'm leaving for class, but I need to make sure that you're going to be all right."

Carmella struggled to lift her head from her pillow and then flopped back down. "I'm just tired, Joy."

"I know you're tired, Mother. And I understand. But I don't want you getting sick over this."

"Let me lay here for a little while longer and then I promise I'll get up and eat something." Carmella closed her eyes and appeared to shrink back into her bed.

Joy couldn't bear to see her mother like that. And knowing that her father caused the pain was crushing. She didn't want to see him, which was a problem, because she worked for her father. Three days a week after school, Joy made her way to Judge Nelson Marshall's office to clerk for him. Her father wanted her to see what working lawyers did all day as they came in and out of the courthouse. Joy was in her last year of law school, with only two more classes to go before graduation. But at that point, she was so confused that she didn't know what to do.

She had picked her major because her father had been an excellent lawyer and was now an incredible judge. But the fact that he turned out to be such a lousy husband outweighed it all. So, even though she went to class like a good little law student, she absorbed absolutely nothing of what had been taught that day. Instead of going to work, she went back to the apartment that she had all to herself and typed up a resignation letter for her father, the judge.

She then walked around the elegant, two bedroom apartment that had been her home for the last two years and simply waved goodbye to the rooms. She had enough sense to realize that every action deserved a reaction. She was going to quit her job, so her father wasn't going to be in the mood to continue paying her rent. And besides, he now had a girlfriend and a wife to take care of, so the twenty-three-year-old daughter would just have to fend for herself.

Her cell phone rang. She sat down on her sofa and pulled the phone out of her Gucci bag, saw that it was Troy calling and answered, "Hey babe."

"Hey yourself. I was just calling to check on you. I haven't heard from you in a couple of days and just wanted to make sure everything was all right."

She kept meaning to return his calls, but then something else in her suddenly dysfunctional family life would happen. "I'm sorry. I haven't been ignoring your calls, it's just that my mother is really having a tough time dealing with what my father has done and I've been spending my time with her."

"I understand that." Troy paused and then asked, "Have you talked to your father?"

"No, and I don't plan to either," Joy quickly remarked.

"Joy, I don't want you to get upset with me, but he is still your father. You can't ignore him forever."

She rolled her eyes. Men... they were all in cahoots together. Joy was quickly learning that you couldn't trust them. Who knew what Troy was doing behind her back? And then she wondered just what type of behavior Troy would expect his children to accept from him. "So, I guess once we have children and you do me dirty, you think they should just continue giving Daddy a hug and kiss, never mind what you did to their mother."

"Joy, where is this coming from? I don't have plans on doing you wrong. Our children will never have to decide between their mother and father, because they will always have both of us."

She harrumphed. "That's what you say now. But just let me have two or three children, and gain a few pounds, then we'll see about that wandering eye of yours."

"What wandering eye?" Troy sighed. "Look Joy, I can see that you're going through a difficult time. But I need you to understand that I am not your father. My name is Troy Anderson and I love you."

She didn't respond. She wanted to, but for the life of her, Joy couldn't fathom the appropriate response. Love seemed like this empty word people loosely threw around. Because what did love really mean anyway? It certainly didn't mean that the person would stay with you through sickness and whatever else came your way.

"I'll talk to you later, Joy. Just give me a call when you feel like talking, okay?"

"All right, Troy. Thanks for calling," she said as if responding to a caller who had just given condolences for the death of a family member.

She put her cell phone back in her purse, stood, and got ready to leave her apartment when the house phone rang. She rarely received calls on that line. Only family and Troy and Jasmine knew the number. She stepped over to the phone and recognized the number as one that was coming from the county court system. But it wasn't any of the numbers associated with her father's office so, being curious, she picked it up.

As she said, "Hello," Joy was informed that she had a collect call from Dontae. What in the world is that boy doing calling me collect? Couldn't he have gone back over to Daddy's office and made the call rather than using one of the pay phones? She accepted the call and then asked, "Boy, don't be calling me collect. I am a poor college student and I can no longer afford such luxuries."

"Sis, I need your help. I'm in jail."

"You're where?" She was shouting, but she couldn't help it. The last thing she ever expected her studious and athletic brother to call and say to her was that he was in jail. Lord, help them all. "What happened?"

"I don't want to talk about it. Just come and get me, okay? I don't want to spend the night in this place. They say I can be bonded out for five hundred dollars."

She loved her brother, but she had just spent all of her money on her annual end of summer shopping spree and didn't have five hundred dollars to her name, or on either one of her credit cards. "I'll get you out, Dontae. I'll be there as soon as I get my hands on the money; don't you worry."

The minute she hung up with Dontae, she picked the phone back up to call her mother. But then she thought better of that. Her mother was already dealing with so much that Joy didn't want to bother her with this. She dreaded what she was about to do, but she had no other choice than to call her father.

When he picked up the phone he said, "There you are. I was wondering why you didn't come to work today."

She didn't respond to that, instead she said, "Daddy, Dontae is in jail and I need five hundred dollars to get him out."

"I know where Dontae is," he said calmly.

"Oh, so have you already paid his bail?"

"No, and I don't intend to. He can spend the night in that cell and think about what he did," Nelson responded.

"Excuse me?"

"That brother of yours came to see me this morning. I took him to lunch and then gave him the address to my new house and asked him to come by this evening so we could talk some more." Nelson let out a frustrated sigh before he continued. "Instead of waiting until I got off work, Dontae went to the house and threw rocks through the window. He even busted out the windshield on Jasmine's car."

"Okay, but why did you call the police on him?" Joy asked, her temperature rising by the second.

"I didn't call the police on him. Jasmine did. But I was in total agreement with her. No son of mine is going to get away with acting like that."

"Oh, so you have no mercy for Dontae, but you think your actions deserve a get-out-of- jail-free card?"

"What's that supposed to mean?" Nelson asked.

"Are you going to give me the money for Dontae or not?" She was done with their conversation.

"I told you. I'm going to do what's best for Dontae and let him sit and think about his actions."

Click. She slammed the phone down so hard, she hoped that her father's eardrum burst on impact. But people like Nelson Marshall never found themselves in harm's way. They just somehow always found ways to hurt others.

Joy hated disturbing her mother with something like this. But she had no other choice. She picked the phone back up and dialed her mother. The line was busy. Joy waited ten seconds and then dialed again… still busy.

She didn't have time to sit there and wait for somebody to help her. Joy left her apartment and raced to her mother's house. She dialed her number twice from her cell phone while en route, but the line stayed busy.

She pulled up to her mother's house and jumped out of the car. She unlocked the front door and rushed into the house. It was five in the evening. Her mother was normally in the kitchen, cooking up something good at that time of day, but she wasn't there. It didn't seem as if the kitchen had seen any activity the entire day. Joy left the kitchen and took the stairs two at a time, headed to the master bedroom.

Joy knocked on the door and then opened it. Her mother was snoring like a hibernating bear. She looked over at the nightstand and noticed that the phone was off the hook. Joy shook her head as she hollered, "Mama... wake up, Mama." She put the phone back on the hook.

Carmella jumped up and screamed, "No! Take the phone back off the hook, they won't stop calling."

"Who won't stop calling?"

"Bill collectors. They harassed me so bad this morning that I had to take a nerve pill."

Now her mother was on nerve pills. Thank you again, Judge Nelson Marshall. "You've got to get out of bed, Mama. Dontae vandalized Daddy's new house and now he's in jail."

"What? Who's in jail," Carmella asked, looking out of it and like she was ready to fall back to sleep.

Joy pulled the covers off of Carmella. "Stay with me, Mama. I need you to focus."

Carmella stretched, yawned and then swung her feet to the floor. "I'm focused. Now, what's going on?"

"Dontae is in jail. We have to bail him out."

"What? My baby is in jail?"

"Yes, so please put some clothes on so we can go pick him up. His bond is five hundred dollars, and I don't have it."

"I can get a cash advance on my Discover card." Carmella jumped up and went into her walk-in closet. She threw on a white tee-shirt and a pair of jeans. While she was putting on a pair of sandals, the phone rang. "Don't pick it up," she warned Joy.

"Mother, I've never known you to be afraid to answer your phone." She shook her head and picked up the phone. "Hello."

"May I speak with Mr. or Mrs. Marshall?"

Feeling ornery, Joy said, "Who is calling and what do you want?"

"I'm calling concerning a personal business matter. Is Mrs. Marshall in?"

"What is this personal business matter?" Joy demanded.

Carmella rushed out of her closet, took the phone away from Joy and hung it up. "Didn't I tell you not to answer?"

"Daddy stopped paying the bills?" Joy's mouth hung slack as she began to understand what was going on.

Carmella was embarrassed, but she shook her head, confessing that, "He won't pay anything until I sign the divorce papers."

"You need to clean him out," Joy said angrily. "Take every dime he has."

"One thing at a time, Joy Marshall." Carmella grabbed her purse. "I need you to drive me downtown so I can get your brother out of jail. When we get back, then we can work on ways to get the money out of your father."

5

"I can't believe that girl had the nerve to have my son arrested after she stole my husband," Carmella said as they arrived back at her house with Dontae in tow.

"I'm sorry about getting arrested, Mama. But I'm not sorry about busting out their windows. They deserve that and more."

"Stop talking foolishness, Dontae. That arrest could destroy your chances for getting into Harvard."

"I don't even want to go to Harvard anymore, anyway. So, who cares," Dontae said as he sulked off.

"Another dream Nelson has stolen," Carmella said of her son no longer desiring to go to Harvard. She lifted her hands to heaven and turned toward the kitchen. "Let me get dinner started. At least we still have some food around here."

Joy sat down on the sofa and turned on the television.

Carmella opened the fridge and started pulling out mushrooms, onions, and garlic before even thinking about turning on her radio as she normally did whenever she walked into the kitchen. She pulled a stainless steel pot down and filled it with water. She placed it on the stove, turned on the fire and then turned around to grab the rest of her ingredients for the pasta dish she was about to fix. But that's when she noticed that the faucet was dripping again. She'd asked Nelson time and time again to fix that faucet and he'd ignored her just as he'd ignored everything else she'd asked him to do. Well, he wasn't getting away with it this time.

She pulled open one of the kitchen drawers and took a pair of pliers out, then grabbed her car keys and headed for the door.

Joy jumped up. "Where are you going?"

"To get your daddy," Carmella said, not breaking her stride.

"Whoa, whoa, whoa." Joy put herself between her mother and the front door. "You can't go over there. Jasmine already had Dontae arrested. What do you think she'll do to you?"

"I wish that twig would say something out the way to me. I'll break her scrawny little neck."

"That still sounds like jail time to me, Ma." Joy held onto the door. "I can't let you do this."

"Girl, get out of my way." Carmella's eyes were wild as she shoved Joy out of her way and bulldozed through the door. Joy had told her where Nelson was staying the day she'd come home upset about his love nest. So now, she jumped in her car and raced over to the place where her husband's heart now resided. But she didn't care about any of that right then. What Carmella cared about was the fact that Nelson Marshall had stood before God and two hundred other folks and made promises to her. She now knew that Nelson wasn't an honorable man, but he was going to have to scrape up some honor that night or she was going upside his bald head.

As she stood in front of the house that her husband now shared with his mistress, she gagged as she tried to hold down vomit that threatened to spill over. She pressed her finger on the buzzer. When no one answered the door, she leaned on the buzzer. Someone looked out the blinds and then quickly closed them. "You might as well open the door," Carmella started screaming, not caring who heard her. "I want my husband out of this house right now."

When they still didn't open the door, she turned and started shouting towards the neighboring houses. "That's right, everybody. You've got an adultery-committing judge and his slimy teenaged slut living in this house right here." She pointed towards Nelson's house. "My husband's girlfriend used to come to my house with my daughter for evening and holiday meals. So if you women on this block know what's good for you, you'll watch your men, and you won't let this hussy in your house for sugar or a crust of bread." Carmella was jabbing a finger toward Nelson's door with every word.

The door opened and Nelson rushed out. "Now that's enough, Carmella."

She swung around to face him. "I just got started, so don't get in my way unless you want me to get in my car and run your no good, cheating behind over."

"Why are you doing this in front of our home?" Jasmine asked as she stepped out of the house but kept her distance from Carmella.

Carmella's arms were swinging wildly, the pliers in her hand almost connected with Nelson's jaw as she told Jasmine, "Oh, so you can come to my house and steal my husband, but I can't come over here and let the people know who they have in their neighborhood."

Jasmine's hand went to her hip. "Why do you think anyone would care that you can't keep a man?"

"Oh, I can keep a man. I kept him for twenty-five years, until you brought your man-stealing self to my house." Carmella pointed at her as she walked toward her. "You're just as bad as a pedophile. People ought to put your picture on their refrigerator and warn their men not to walk past this house."

"Shut up, Carmella. You're making a fool of yourself," Nelson screamed at her.

"Better I do it, than continue to let you do it," she told him as she swung back his way. She was just about in tears, but standing her ground.

"What do you want, Carmella?" Nelson asked as he turned and spotted the neighbors peeping through their windows and the ones who were bold enough, were just standing on their porches watching.

She handed him the pliers, and said in an almost begging tone, "I want you to come home so you can fix the faucet. It's dripping again."

Jasmine let out a great big belly laugh as she swung her long hair around and then said, "You're pathetic. No wonder Nelson doesn't want you anymore."

"Don't you talk to me!" Carmella screamed as she lunged at Jasmine.

The lady across the street yelled, "Get her! I've got a baseball bat over here if you really want to break her from stealing."

Carmella pulled Jasmine down to the ground and grabbed hold of her hair.

"That's right. Pull that weave out of her man-stealing head," another woman said as she stood on her porch, punching at the air as if she were in the fight against the woman who stole her man.

"Help me, Nelson," Jasmine screamed as she tried to defend herself against each blow that Carmella sent her way.

"Now C-Carmella, s-stop acting foolish." Nelson tried to pull his wife off of his mistress, but failed miserably. He then stepped around the side of the house and turned on the sprinklers.

Carmella felt the water and thought it was rain. The grip she had on Jasmine's hair slipped and Jasmine got up and ran back into the house. But Carmella stayed on the ground, punching and beating it if as she were still on top of Jasmine. She had no mercy as her hands continued to punish the ground beneath her.

"Get up, Carmella. Stop this," Nelson yelled.

Someone was talking behind her, but she couldn't make out what was being said. All she knew was that the rain was coming down and the dirt was flying all around her head. Suddenly, when the rain stopped, Carmella sat back, looked around as if she were lost and searching for something or someone.

Nelson was standing behind her. Cautiously, he asked, "Carmella, are you okay?"

"Did you fix the faucet?" she asked in a hollow, out-of-tune voice.

He inched toward her.

Carmella looked down at herself. The dirt and mud mingled with the soft fabric of her off white cashmere sweater. It was one of her favorite sweaters. She began screaming, "Why is all this dirt on me? Did you push me?" she yelled at Nelson as she got up and began chasing him around the yard with a crazed look in her eye. "How could you? How could you? You've dirtied my favorite sweater."

She lunged at him, but he stepped out of the way. "What's wrong with you, Carmella? You're acting crazy."

"I'm acting crazy?" She found a large stick in the yard and picked it up. "You ruin my best sweater… one I probably won't be able to replace, and then you claim I'm the crazy one?" She swung at him.

"Stop this and go home, Carmella. Someone is going to get hurt," he screamed as he cowered on the other side of his silver Mercedes.

"Looks like you're the one who's going to get hurt, you cheating dog," the woman from across the street yelled, enjoying the show.

Carmella swung the stick. "Why aren't you home?" she asked as the stick missed Nelson, but connected with the hood of his car.

Nelson yelped as if he had been hit, and attempted to rub the dent away. But when Carmella swung again, he had no choice but to bob and weave and let his car take whatever blows came its way.

Sirens were going off as Carmella swung from left to right at Nelson's head. But Carmella hadn't heard anything. She felt like one of those women on Snapped, because she wanted to draw blood and she didn't care whose blood it was. All she knew was that somebody had to pay for what had happened to her life.

Nelson fell back, Carmella then stood over him, paying no heed to the officers that approached. Carmella went somewhere inside of herself, hiding from all the pain that loving someone who didn't love her back brought. She lifted her arm for one more go at batting practice.

One police officer grabbed her arm. Carmella tried to jerk it back. She yelled at the officer to leave her alone and let her finish. "Nelson needed discipline."

The officer swung her to the ground. Carmella didn't even feel the impact. She laughed, and kept on laughing because her mind had taken her to a happy place... a place of peace. A place where she, Nelson and the kids frolicked on the sandy beach and Jasmine was nowhere in sight.

6

Instead of being hauled off to jail for assault, the police officer decided to take Carmella to the hospital. Nelson had her placed on a seventy-two hour hold so she could be evaluated. But Carmella was in such hysterics when they brought her in that she had to be medicated. She was now despondent and only wanted to sleep... sleep her life away. Carmella had no idea how much time had passed since she'd first come to that place or what was happening to her. She was only slightly aware of the people that came in and out of her room. She couldn't focus. Carmella was powerless to do anything to help herself. So she woke in sadness, napped in sorrow and by night fall she had cried so much that she pretty much bathed in her own tears.

"I'm not going to just let you lay here and ignore us." Rose stood on the side of her friend's hospital bed with a take charge look on her face.

Someone was talking to her, but her head was so foggy she couldn't make out what was being said, or who was saying it.

Rose put her hand on Carmella's arm and shook her. "Snap out of it, girl. Nelson Marshall isn't worth all of this."

Nelson? Did somebody call for Nelson?

"What's wrong with her?" Dontae yelled.

"She's sad, Dontae. Haven't you seen how much she's been crying?" Joy asked, standing next to her brother.

"That's all she seems to do is cry. Why won't she talk to us?"

Rose shushed Dontae. "She can probably hear you, so watch what you say."

But Dontae wouldn't be silenced. He pointed towards his mother. "She's been lying like that for two days now. Why is she acting like this?"

"She doesn't feel well right now, Dontae, but she's going to get better. I promise you that," Rose assured him. She then turned to Joy and said, "Why don't you two go home and get some rest. I can hang out here with your mom for the rest of the day."

Joy put her arm around her brother as she said, "That's nice of you to offer, Aunt Rose. But she's our mother so I think we should be here with her."

"Have a seat, Dontae." Rose said as she grabbed Joy's hand and walked her out of the hospital room. They stood a few doors away from Carmella's room as Rose told Joy, "Listen to me, hon, your mom is going to get through this nightmare. But I don't think it's good for Dontae to see her like this."

"But what if something happens to her while we're gone?"

"Nothing's going to happen to Carmella. The doctors just have her over sedated, if you ask me. So the next thing I want you to do is to go to the nurse's station on your way out and demand that they hold off on giving Carmella any more medication until she climbs out of the fog they have her in."

Joy took a deep breath then nodded. "I can do that."

"Okay, now can you help me get Dontae out of here? And don't let him come back here until tomorrow."

Joy shook her head. "He won't agree to leave. He's too worried about Mama."

Rose grabbed hold of Joy's hand. "I promise you and your brother that even if I have to get on my knees and pray all night long, Carmella is going to be all right. Tomorrow is a new day. Dontae needs to see her then, but not now."

"Okay Aunt Rose, I think I have an idea to get Dontae out of here."

They went back into the room. Carmella was still lying motionless, with her face toward the wall. Dontae was seated with his head in his hands crying, the same way he'd cried when he was seven years old and his dog, Samhad died. Joy put her hand around his arm and pulled him up. "Come on Dontae, I need your help with something."

Joy headed towards the door, but Dontae stopped her. "We can't leave Mom. She needs us."

Joy shook her head. "Mom needs some rest right now. The best thing we can do is to allow her to rest without hearing us crying and talking back and forth over her head. Now, I've got some things I need to do at my apartment and you can help me with that."

Dontae looked back towards the bed.

"We'll be back in the morning to check on Mama," Joy assured him. "Now will you help me or not?"

He hesitated, then put his hands in his pockets and nodded as he walked through the door with his sister.

Joy peeked back in the room and told Rose, "Give her a kiss from me and Dontae and let her know that we'll be back in the morning."

"I'll do that," Rose said. Then as Joy closed the door behind her, Rose got on her knees and began petitioning God on her friend's behalf.

***

As Joy and Dontae headed out of the hospital, she made sure to stop by the nurse's station and requested that her mother not be given any more medication until she was alert enough to ask for it herself. She also explained to them that she was in law school and her father was a judge, so they knew how to file lawsuits if need be. She and Dontae then stopped by a local grocery store, grabbed a few empty boxes and then headed to her apartment.

"What are the boxes for?" Dontae asked.

"I'm moving out. I'll be staying with you and Mama for a little while."

Dontae's eyebrow went up as he questioned Joy, "Why would you do that? Dad pays your rent."

"In the back of my mind, I was kind of hoping that he would continue to pay my bills even though he's divorcing Mama. But after seeing her in the hospital like that, I don't want anything from that man."

"It's going to be pretty hard not taking anything from him since you work for him and he signs off on your paycheck."

She patted her purse and said, "Got my resignation letter right here. I will be mailing it off to him in the morning."

"You act like all of this is Dad's fault," Dontae said as they pulled up to Joy's apartment.

"Who else do you think I should blame? Mom didn't wreck our home; Dad did that all on his own." She got out of the car and grabbed a few of the flattened boxes.

Dontae grabbed the remaining boxes and followed her inside. As they were taping the boxes and placing them around the room, Dontae told his sister, "I blame Jasmine. She was always coming to our house acting all nice and innocent and all the while she was putting moves on our dad."

"Just remember, it takes two to tango."

Dontae threw a box to the opposite side of the room. "I know you're not defending that snake. It sounds like you still want to be friends with her, even after what she did to Mama."

"Stop throwing my boxes around. And no, I'm not defending Jasmine. And I certainly am not friends with her. I just think that Daddy should have known better. Jasmine obviously doesn't care who she hurts. But Daddy should have known that his actions would hurt the family." She stood up with two boxes in hand. "Let's box up as many of my clothes as possible and get them over to the house. I think I'm going to put my furniture on eBay, so I can earn a little money while I look for a job."

Dontae followed his sister around the apartment, doing as she instructed. After about two hours of boxing and moving things around so Joy could take pictures to post on eBay, they finally left the apartment and headed home.

As they pulled up to the house and noticed that their father's car was parked in the driveway, the brother and sister had two different thoughts.

"The nerve of him. He has no business being here," Joy said as she turned off the car.

"Maybe he's sorry for what he did and is ready to come back home," Dontae said as they got out of the car.

Joy rolled her eyes and ignored her brother. He was acting like a sap, wishing for something that simply wasn't going to happen. Because Joy knew in her heart that her father wasn't there looking for forgiveness. He was probably just trying to move more of his things out before their mom was released from the hospital. She stormed into the house, looking for a fight. Her father had been her hero. Now he was just the man who'd done them wrong. "What are you doing in here?" she asked, with hands on hips as she stepped into the kitchen and found her father tinkering with the faucet.

Nelson grabbed a towel and wiped his hands, then he closed the cabinets below the faucet. "Your mom asked me to fix the sink, so I came over to take care of it."

"Oh you're quite a prince, aren't you?" Joy said with an exasperated expression on her face.

Nelson's finger wagged in her face. "Now look here, young lady, you might not like what I've done, but I'm still your father and you will respect me."

Joy scoffed at that and folded her arms around her chest. "Respect you? Are you kidding? I don't even know who you are."

"Stop yelling at him, Joy. Dad's just trying to make things right again." Dontae turned to Nelson and asked, "Isn't that right, Dad?"

"Of course I want to make things right between us, son." Nelson turned to Joy and said, "I want to make things right with you, too, Joy Lynn."

Her father used to call her Joy Lynn when she was a little girl, when he had seemed like Superman to her. Today she didn't want him to use her first name, let alone her middle name. "Is the sink fixed?"

"Yes, tell your mother that I took care of it." He shuffled his feet, looking uncomfortable in his own house.

Joy didn't say anything, just kept staring at her father with her arms folded and her lip twisted.

But Dontae piped up. "I'll let her know when we go back to the hospital in the morning, Dad."

"Thanks, son."

Joy rolled her eyes and shook her head. "Why are you sucking up to this man? He wouldn't even give me the money I needed to get you out of jail the other day… told me that you needed to spend the night in jail to teach you a lesson." Joy pointed an accusing finger at her father. "He's the reason Mama is in the hospital half out of her mind right now. If he would have given me the money, I wouldn't have even bothered Mama. She wouldn't have known that you had been arrested at all."

Dontae turned to his father. "Did you really tell Joy to leave me in that place?"

Seeing his one ally slipping away, Nelson hurriedly said, "I just wanted you to understand that there are consequences for actions, son. That's all."

"See what I've been trying to tell you, Dontae. This man—"

"Stop calling me, this man. I'm your father."

"Then you should act like it." Joy opened her purse and pulled out an envelope and handed it to her so-called father. "I was going to mail this to you. But since you're here, I might as well hand it to you now."

"What is this?" Nelson asked.

"My resignation."

He tried to hand the envelope back to Joy. "You don't have to do this. I already told my office that you need a little time off."

"I need a whole lot of time, Dad. I'm not coming back. Matter-of-fact, I don't think I ever want to see you again." There, put that in your pipe and smoke it, Joy thought as she glared at her father.

"Don't do this, Joy. Okay, I know that you're upset with me right now. But don't forget who I am. My relationship with your mom might be over, but I'll always be your father."

"You are such a hypocrite, Dad. You want Dontae to understand the consequences for his actions and you want me to forgive and forget. But you don't seem to care at all that you're bailing out on a twenty-five year marriage. So tell us, Dad, what are the consequences for your careless actions?"

"What do you want me to say to that, Joy?"

"I want you to answer me. What are the consequences for your actions? Do you even feel the slightest bit guilty that your wife is in the hospital because of what you did to her?"

Nelson stood in front of his children with eyes that were void of answers. When the silence became uncomfortable, he took his wallet and keys off of the kitchen counter and headed for the door.

"Dad, where are you going? I thought you wanted to make things right. You need to stay here with us. This is where you belong." Dontae was practically begging as he followed his father to the front door.

"Stop begging him, Dontae. He is not interested in us. He would rather be with a woman who only wants him for what he can give her, rather than stay with the woman who helped him get to where he is in the first place." The venom and contempt was laid bare in every word Joy spoke.

Nelson snatched open the door, but before he walked out, he turned back to his children and said, "Tell your mother that I have paid all of her bills and will continue to do so for the next three months. But if she wants to keep this house after the divorce, she'll have to find a way to pay for it."

When Nelson closed the door behind himself, Dontae turned to his sister, looking every bit the seventeen year old, rather than the grown man his height and muscles projected. "So that's it? He's just going to leave Mom to figure out a way to pay for this house?"

Joy wasn't about to let up on her father. She angrily pointed out, "And don't forget, this is the house that Daddy wanted in order to impress his peers. I guess he's decided that he doesn't care about impressing them, us or anybody else anymore. But you mark my words, Nelson Marshall will get his."

"How?" Dontae asked.

"Daddy isn't invincible, Dontae. And his job isn't secure at all. Judge Marshall has to be re-elected if he wants to remain a judge. Suppose it gets leaked to the papers that the so-called "family values" judge divorced his wife for his twenty-three-year-old mistress?"

Dontae rubbed his hands together. "Who can we call?"

Joy lifted her hands. "Hold up. Let's not be too hasty. Mom would never forgive us if we ruined her husband's career. But the minute he's not her husband," Joy shrugged, "all bets are off."

7

When Carmella woke the next morning, she didn't feel as if she was in a fog and couldn't think or make sense of anything. However, she was still in a bad place, mainly because she didn't understand why God had allowed all of this to happen to her. For more than two decades now she had loved and served God. Carmella had served in the choir, on the usher and greeter team and the marriage ministry.

Carmella thought that as long as she was handling God's business, He would, in turn, handle hers. But then her brother had a heart attack and died at the young age of forty six. She'd tried to deal with that tragedy by telling herself it wasn't God's fault that her beloved brother ate double and triple cheese burgers with bags of fries three to four days a week and was a hundred and fifty pounds overweight.

However, the problem Carmella now faced was that she was having a hard time not blaming God for the end of her marriage. It was His job to look after her, wasn't it?

Malachi 3:10 told her that if she gave her tithes to her church that God would pour out a blessing that she wouldn't have room to receive. But with the way things were going, it looked as if she had some extra room for some of them delayed blessings.

Her favorite bible verse came from Psalm 37:25: I have been young, and now am old; Yet I have not seen the righteous forsaken, Nor his descendants begging bread.

That verse always made her feel as if God had her back and that nothing could ever harm her or her children. But now that she knew God wasn't always on His j-o-b, what was she supposed to do now? Life had changed for her. But Carmella didn't know how to change with it. She didn't know how to live in a world where God no longer made sense to her.

50

For years she had projected the image of a super Christian who had it all together. Carmella had doled out so much God-centered advice to struggling Christians, that at times she wondered why she hadn't gone to school for counseling. But in her time of need, who did she have to guide or inspire her? Her parents were gone, her brother had recently joined them and even Nelson had left her. Carmella was searching for a reason to get out of the bed so she could leave the hospital. But the more she searched, the more she wanted to close her eyes and never open them again.

"Mom, you're awake!" Joy said as she and Dontae stepped into the room.

Carmella's eyes shifted towards the door, a brief smile crossed her lips as she watched her children walk into the room. "Hey, you two."

"Hey yourself," Dontae said as he walked over to his mother's bed. He bent down and kissed her forehead. "You had us worried yesterday. But you're looking more alert today."

Her teenaged son sounded so grown up, as if he had aged overnight. What was she doing with herself? Why was she lying in this bed and letting her children worry about her, when she should be the one worrying about them, like mothers normally do?

"Mom?" Joy's voice held concern after Carmella didn't respond to Dontae. "Are you okay?"

An involuntary tear rolled down her face as she said, "I'm trying to be."

"Dad fixed the faucet," Dontae told her in an upbeat tone.

Joy grabbed hold of her mother's hand and squeezed. "He paid the bills, too, Mom. So, you won't have to worry about that when you come home."

"Did he say if he was coming back home?" Carmella asked, hating herself for even needing to ask something like that, but she couldn't deny that she wanted her husband and her life back.

"He didn't stay at the house last night, but I'm sure he'll come back home, Mama. You just have to keep the faith, like you always tell us. Isn't that right, Joy?" Dontae looked to his big sister for support.

"Stop doing this to yourself, Dontae." She moved him away from the bed and told him to sit down. Joy then turned back to her mother and said, "Dad said that he's going to pay the bills for another three months, but after that you are on your own. I'm sorry to tell you this so flat out, but I don't want you to keep your hopes up for a man who may never come back to you."

"What else am I supposed to do, Joy? I've been married to your father for twenty-five years. My parents and my brother are gone… he's all I have."

Joy sat down next to her mother's bed and held onto her hand. "That's not true, Mama. You've got me and Dontae. And we will never leave you."

Tears sprang to Carmella's eyes. Her children brought her so much joy, and she never meant to insinuate that they weren't enough. As Joy and Dontae grew, she and Nelson made sure that they had all they needed and then some. From vacations to cars and education… you name it, her children had it, because Carmella required no less. She and her brother grew up in poverty. Carmella never wanted her children to experience the pain and embarrassment of being financially broke. But now she had allowed them to see her emotionally broken. As tears continued to fall down her face, Carmella wondered which was worse.

"Don't cry, Mama. I'm a dope. I shouldn't have said any of that to you today." Joy put her head in her hand and shook it.

"What Joy is trying to say is that we just want you to get better. Don't worry about what Daddy's doing. And you don't need to worry about the bills either because they've been paid," Dontae said.

There he was sounding all grown up again. Just two months ago she couldn't get him to stop playing his video games long enough to take out the trash, now he was admonishing her to keep the faith and encouraging her to worry less. Pretty soon he'd be leaving home, headed off to Harvard, his dad's alma mater. Carmella had imagined that she would convince Nelson to travel the world with her once Dontae was settled in college… she wiped away the tears, hating the fact that Nelson's betrayal hurt so much. "I'm sorry about losing it the way I did. Seeing your father with Jasmine just caused something to snap inside of me."

"It's been hard on you, Mom, we know that," Dontae encouraged.

But Carmella lifted a hand, stopping him from saying anything further. "I don't care how hard this is on me. I'm ashamed of myself for allowing you and your sister to see me like this. All I can do is apologize for what I've done and make a promise to both of you that once I get out of here, I'll never lose it like this again." Carmella had no idea how she would keep that promise, but she knew she had to say something to reassure her children.

The door opened and Rose walked in. "Well, don't you look alert this morning."

Carmella gave her friend a questioning glance. "Were you here yesterday?"

"You know it. The kids and I spent the day with you."

"Aunt Rose did more than spend the day with you. She sent us home and spent the evening in here praying for you," Joy told her mother.

"Is that true, Rose?"

Rose shrugged. "I didn't do anything that you wouldn't have done for me."

"I don't even remember anything about yesterday. Except that I felt as if I was in a fog and couldn't get out."

"That was because of all the meds they had you on. But Aunt Rose told me to make them stop medicating you," Joy told her mother. "We knew you'd feel better once you could think straight."

Carmella hoped that her daughter was right about that. After seeing Nelson with that man-stealing woman-child, and being laughed at for coming to get her own husband, Carmella had lost it. It was good to be able to lay there and talk with her children and her best friend. They spent the morning talking and then the nurse came in and told Carmella that she was being released.

"Thank the Lord," Rose shouted.

But Carmella didn't feel much like thanking the Lord, because she felt as if the Lord had let her down. Where had He been when Nelson was stepping out on her? Why hadn't the Lord allowed her to detect the clues that must have been there? And why had the Lord allowed Nelson to walk his narrow behind out of her life?

She didn't tell anyone how she was feeling. She just went home, climbed into her bed and lay there while Joy and Dontae fussed over her. The television was tuned in to the news and all of it seemed so depressing that Carmella couldn't take anymore. She began channel surfing, hoping to find something to put her in a better mood.

"Do you need anything?" Joy asked as she opened her bedroom door.

"I don't need anything, Joy. You just asked me that ten minutes ago. You and your brother need to chill. Go watch a movie or something."

"Okay, but if you need me, remember that I'm just downstairs." Joy looked anxious as she closed the door.

Carmella understood why her children were watching her like she was a kleptomaniac in a room full of fine china, but she needed time alone. She needed to think. Something she hadn't allowed herself to do much of since Nelson packed his bags and left. Carmella had been acting as if her life was over. But in truth, she still had a great deal to live for. Carmella just needed to find a way to let what she had left be enough. So far she hadn't figured out how to do that. But she was home and back in her right mind, so figuring out her new life would become priority number one, first thing in the morning. But tonight, she just wanted to veg out and watch television mindlessly for a few hours.

As she switched from channel to channel, she happened upon a Christian station, which reminded her that she hadn't been to church since this ordeal with Nelson began. Carmella didn't want to be preached at or feel convicted tonight, so she switched to the next station. It was another Christian station. But this one was showcasing a gospel concert. Carmella loved gospel music and would spend all day in the kitchen cooking and praising God while her praise music vibrated against the walls.

Recently though, when she'd gone into her beloved kitchen, it had only been to fix a quick meal, so she hadn't bothered turning on her gospel music. Nor had she bothered to praise the Lord while she went about her day. As she lay there watching and listening to the video of Deitrick Haddon singing Well Done, she realized that even after all that had happened to her, she still wanted to make it to heaven and wanted to hear God say well done.

As Deitrick asked, through song, if anyone wanted to see their loved ones again, tears dripped down Carmella's face as she thought of her parents and her brother, the loved ones she had lost and was positive that they had already heard the Lord say well done.

Carmella was amazed as she listened to the words of that beautiful song. But what disheartened her was the fact that the very same man who sang a song that could speak to the very heart and soul of the listener and cause them to want to do what's right in order to make it into heaven, had fallen short in his own life. But she prayed he would get back on track.

Nelson was awful for what he had done to her, but at least he wasn't a pastor or minister of the gospel. Just when she was starting to get angry, and plotting a beat down, rather than enjoying the song for the praise it sent up to God, the messenger left the screen and the song ended. Carmella knew that wanting to smash in the face of every man who ever had the audacity to cry out to God with the same mouth they asked for a divorce with, was not in any way, shape or form being Christ like. But she couldn't help how she was feeling.

She was about to turn off the television and close her eyes to try to get her mind right, when the host of the gospel video fest started talking and it seemed to Carmella as if he was speaking directly to her.

He said, "Life is strange in that we can be praising God one moment and falling into sin the next. Or if we aren't the one committing sin, we are so busy judging the ones who fall into sin that God finds no pleasure in us either.

"In Galatians 6:1 it says, If a man is overtaken in any trespass, you who are spiritual restore such a one in a spirit of gentleness, considering yourself lest you also be tempted.

"What am I trying to say?" the announcer asked after quoting from the bible. "Whether you are the one caught up in sin, or you're the one watching and judging it, we all need to pray. And one more thing…"

He pointed at the screen in a manner that caused Carmella to believe that he was once again only speaking to her, "When you're in the midst of trauma and drama, don't forget to get your praise on."

With that said the video of Praise Him in Advance by Marvin Sapp began playing. He was one of her all time favorite gospel singers. He had experienced so much tragedy in his life, and yet he still praised God. Carmella had much respect for Marvin Sapp. So when his video came on, she lifted up on her elbow and leaned closer to the television. Then Marvin Sapp reminded her that praise was her weapon against her problems, because it confused the enemy. She had forgotten how to praise God as she began going through this situation with Nelson. Carmella could picture the devil laughing at her right now.

She didn't know how or why it happened, but Carmella was clear on something now: she was in a spiritual battle and the winner would get her soul. When she gave her life to God two decades ago, it had been because she wanted to make it to heaven. She may have forgotten that simple fact over the last month, but in truth, Nelson's leaving hadn't changed her mind. She still wanted to see Jesus, her parents, her brother and everyone else that was walking on streets of gold. Carmella just didn't know how to get back to that place of peace she had once known.

Come to Me. My arms are open wide, waiting for you.

It was like a sweet whisper in her ear, but Carmella knew that God had just spoken into her spirit. She was going to win the battle, because she was going to start praising God even before the storm was through raging, as Marvin Sapp's song advised.

The next video popped up and Mary Mary started singing about taking the shackles off their feet, Carmella flung the covers off, got out of bed and started dancing around her room. She was just getting started as that video ended and the announcer declared, "You got problems, you got pain? Well praise God anyhow and watch Him bring you through it all."

When Yolanda Adams's I Got the Victory came on, Carmella lifted her hands and praised the Lord like she hadn't in a long, long time. Each one of the performers that night had spoken to Carmella's heart in a special way, but Yolanda's words emboldened her. She had the victory alright, and she wasn't ever going to give it back.

"You can't have my mind and you sure can't have my soul." She was shouting at the devil that tried to destroy her life and with each step as she danced around her room, she was stomping on that serpent's head.

Her door swung open and Joy and Dontae ran in. "What's wrong?" Joy asked, breathlessly.

"What happened?" Dontae asked as he came in behind his sister.

Carmella's turned toward the door as her children rushed in. They had these worried looks on their faces, like they thought it was time for another seventy-two hour hold. "Relax, you two. I haven't cracked up again. I'm just praising God."

"What for?" Dontae asked as if that was the most ludicrous thing he'd ever heard.

"You've seen me praise God before."

"Yeah, but that was when you had something to praise Him for," Dontae said.

Her children didn't understand her. But Carmella couldn't blame them. She had been walking around like a woman with no faith for over a month. She'd allowed Nelson to strip her bare—but no more. "For the rest of my life, I will praise God whether things are right or wrong... whether I'm happy or sad."

"If you say so," Joy said with a raised eyebrow.

"What do you mean, if I say so? God is good, Joy Lynn and it's time we started appreciating Him for His goodness."

Both Joy and Dontae looked at her as if she'd just stepped off a space ship and asked them to take her to their leader.

She didn't have time for unbelief. Carmella was on an uphill climb, finding her way back to her Savior and she wasn't about to let her kids get her off track. She put her hands on her hips and told them, "Either praise God with me, or get out of my room so I can finish my praise dance."

"I'm not going to dance around this room looking crazy," Joy said as she turned and walked out of her mother's bedroom.

"Count me out, too," Dontae told her as he also left the room.

Carmella smiled, turned up her television and kept dancing. Because she'd realized something... not only did she still have her children, but as Joy promised, they would never leave her. Carmella also knew that God was still on her side and that he would never leave her.

8

Things weren't all good in her life, but Carmella was in a praise-Him-anyhow kind of mood and she prayed she would stay in that frame of mind for the rest of her life. Her children were having a hard time adjusting to their new normal and Carmella blamed herself for a lot of their struggles. If she had handled the separation better, then maybe Joy wouldn't have quit working for her dad or lost so much enthusiasm for law school. Dontae had started cutting classes and being disrespectful to his teachers. Carmella was still praying about the best way to handle that. With Dontae, if she pushed too hard, he would just shut down and she wouldn't be able to reach him at all.

She'd tried getting Nelson to spend more time with Dontae, but the man seemed completely ignorant to the fact that his own son was hurting. Well today was pay up day, as far as Carmella was concerned. Nelson wanted a divorce and after three months of waiting for him to come to his senses, she had come to hers.

Carmella hired a lawyer to represent her interests. Her neighbor, Cynthia had given her Deidre Green's information, stating that the woman was a pit bull. Carmella was on her way to meet with Deidre, Nelson and Clark Johnson, Nelson's attorney. Carmella was prepared to sign the divorce papers, but she wasn't about to go away empty handed. Not after working to put Nelson through law school and then helping him with every step of his career. Nelson might not know that he had her to thank for the advances he'd made, but thank God, since speaking with Deidre, she knew her worth—and he soon would, too.

As they sat around the table, Carmella nodded to the man who used to be both their attorney, "Clark."

"How've you been, Carmella?" he asked, his discomfort evident.

"I've been better. But you live on and you move on, right?" Carmella had learned how to motivate herself in the days since she got her praise back. Whatever doesn't kill you makes you stronger, and she was living proof of that.

Clark smiled. "You've got the right attitude about all of this."

Nelson was sitting quietly, looking down at his fingers as she and Clark exchanged pleasantries. But Deidre piped up and said, "We just hope your client brought the right attitude to this meeting. And by right attitude, I mean, he needs to be in the spirit of giving."

"I've already given. I've paid the bills the last three months. But it's time for Carmella to get a job. I can't keep supporting her when I'm not even in the house anymore."

Deidre quickly responded, "You're not home anymore because your girlfriend wanted you to move in with her. But that's not my client's problem."

Carmella had been terrified about life after Nelson. She'd been even more terrified about facing him in a head to head meeting to discuss the terms of their divorce. But after meeting with Deidre and going over her worth after years of cooking, cleaning, child rearing and generally making life happen for all the other members of her household, she became more confident in her abilities. God is good, because she never knew she was worth so much. Nelson leaving didn't scare her quite so much anymore. Carmella thought, Just as the bible says, if the unbelieving, cheating, stanking, no good husband doesn't want to stay, then let him go on, and let him live a miserable life with his gold digger… well, maybe the bible doesn't say all of that, but it does say to let the unbeliever go. But on the day that she was finalizing a divorce she never wanted in the first place, Carmella felt entitled to a little adlibbing.

Nelson glared at Deidre and then turned to Carmella. "Why'd you have to hire an attorney? Why didn't you just sign the papers and get on with your life?"

Again Deidre placed a hand on Carmella's shoulder. "Because my client is no fool, Mr. Marshall. The agreement you sent to Mrs. Marshall basically entitled her to six months of living expenses and no more. But you seem to forget that Mrs. Marshall put you through law school and cooked, cleaned, bore your children and washed your dirty clothes for twenty-five years. So, I'd say that's worth much more than six month's of living expenses, wouldn't you?"

"Mr. Marshall isn't a wealthy man. But he is more than willing to bump that up to a year's worth of living expenses. That ought to be enough to assist Carmella with this transition. Wouldn't you agree?" Clark asked.

Deidre opened the folder in front of her. She took her time looking over the information, then once the suspense had mounted, she said, "Based on the research we've done on your client's financials," she paused, looking like a woman who enjoyed her job, "with your position as a judge and your consulting business, you've been consistently earning about three hundred thousand a year. We're going to be asking for half of that for a period of no less than five years."

"What!" Nelson exploded. He turned to Clark and said, "Do something."

"Fifty percent does seem a bit over the top, don't you think, Mrs. Green?"

"Not at all, Mr. Johnson," Deidre answered without giving it a second thought. "Carmella isn't the one shacking up with a teenager, she's just the woman left behind... the one who put her life on hold in order to make all of your client's dreams come true. He wants to be set free, fine. But he has to pay."

"But I can't afford it," Nelson glanced in Carmella's direction, his eyes imploring her to understand his plight.

She looked at the man who'd sent her flying over the cuckoo's nest, the same man who had broken her children's hearts, all because he was a selfish and ungrateful human being and she felt no pity for him. "Tell your girlfriend to get an after school job, or learn to live with less."

"Why should I live with less? You're the one who hasn't worked for twenty years."

No he didn't. She didn't even recognize Nelson anymore. The man she had been married to used to thank her for the way she contributed to their family. The monster seated across from her was all dressed up like Nelson Marshall, but he had to be an imposter. "I no longer feel as if I know you, and since I prefer not to talk to strangers, I'm going to ask that you address my attorney for the rest of this meeting."

"So, now I can't even talk to you? Some wife you turned out to be."

Carmella didn't respond to him. She turned back to Deidre and asked, "Can you please continue?"

"Certainly." Deidre glanced at her paperwork. Checked off a few items and then said, "We want to have the college fund for Dontae Marshall transferred into either Carmella's or Dontae's name immediately."

"Oh, so now I can't be trusted to manage my son's college fund?"

"You're a busy man, Mr. Marshall. We wouldn't want that college fund to fall into the hands of your mistress because you failed to keep an eye on it," Deidre wasn't about to let up on reminding Nelson that he was the one committing adultery in their marriage. As far as she was concerned he could sit back, shut up and start writing checks, because he was going to pay for the way he discarded his wife.

Nelson and Clark leaned close to each other and said a few words, then Clark said, "Since Dontae is seventeen and will be going off to Harvard next year anyway, Mr. Marshall has no problem with turning the college fund over to his son."

Whether Dontae would be going to Harvard or not was still an open question, but she wasn't going to tell Nelson that Dontae was on the fence about which school to attend the following year. That was the reason she wanted the money out of Nelson's care. She felt that he was in no position to dictate to her son what he should and shouldn't do. And Carmella knew that Nelson would try to use the money to threaten Dontae. If it was up to Nelson, Dontae wouldn't get a dime if he decided not to attend Harvard. She'd sleep better knowing that Dontae had the freedom to follow his own path.

"One more thing," Deidre said as she held up her hand.

"There's more? What do I owe you now...my kidney? I mean we are splitting everything of mine 50/50 right?" Nelson was beginning to sweat. He loosened his necktie as he shook his head in disgust.

Carmella almost laughed in his face. With what he owed her, she could buy a kidney if she ever needed one. She was so thankful that

Cynthia introduced her to Deidre Green. The woman knew her stuff and had opened Carmella's eyes.

"No, Mr. Marshall, we're going to let you keep your kidney. But we will take half of the two million that is currently invested in your retirement account. We will also be asking for half of your pension when you retire," Deidre told him with a sweet smile on her face.

"That is out of the question," Nelson barked. He looked at Carmella and asked, "How am I supposed to live? You're just being vindictive… I never expected this from you."

Clearly, Nelson hadn't expected Carmella to do anything but sign the divorce papers and let him go about his merry way. But her mom hadn't raised no fool. She knew how much was in every account they had, and after twenty-five years of service, if she was being set out to pasture, she was going in style. "I'm really not interested in hearing you whine. You want out, and I'm tired of begging you to stay. But you best believe that I am well aware of my worth. And I expect to get everything that's coming to me."

"Greed is a sin, Carmella. You know that, don't you?" Nelson glared at her.

"Starving to death should be a sin. Thank God I won't have to do that."

"Why don't you just get a job?" Nelson asked angrily.

"I had one, but it was stolen away from me," she shot back. Carmella was getting tired of this back and forth with Nelson. She felt her temperature rising and knew that anything else she had to say to him would not be Christ like, so she did her best to ignore him for the duration of the meeting.

Deidre passed the divorce paperwork to Nelson's lawyer. "I would advise your client to sign these papers. It's the best deal he's going to get."

"What about child support?" Nelson asked grumpily. "After I've given you all this money, are you going to then turn around and take me to court for child support?"

"Read through the documents. The child support is included in the fifty percent of wages we are asking for. Spousal support is slotted at thirty percent, and child support at twenty percent. Both will last five years, which is enough time to get your son through college."

"We will review it and get back with you," Clark said as he stood, tapping Nelson on the shoulder. Nelson stood and began walking out of the office with his lawyer.

Before they could walk out the door, Deidre added, "If I don't hear from you in a week's time, we will prepare for court. And at that time, we will ask the judge for fifty percent spousal support and twenty percent child support."

The door slammed behind them. Carmella hadn't realized that she'd been holding her breath, but as she released it, the tension in her neck and stomach began to ease. "Thank you," she said to Deidre. "I wouldn't have been able to get through this meeting without you."

"It was my pleasure."

"It looked that way. But I don't understand how you can enjoy meetings like this. Have you always handled divorces at your law firm?"

Deidre shook her head. "I didn't attend law school to become a divorce attorney. But fifteen years ago my father left my mother penniless, so he could marry his twenty-year-old receptionist. Mom killed herself right after my father announced his engagement." Deidre shrugged. "Ever since then I've been helping women get what they deserve out of these men who didn't deserve them in the first place."

9

In her kitchen with her praise music going and chocolate muffins in the oven, Carmella told Rose about her awful meeting with Nelson. She gave her a blow-by-blow account of how her husband had behaved.

"I'm proud of how you held up and fought back. Nelson is getting what he deserves. Only a slime ball would leave his wife the week after she had to bury her brother," Rose told her friend.

Carmella took her muffins out of the oven and began spreading her homemade icing on them. "It wasn't easy, girl. I was terrified to face him at first, but the more he opened his mouth, the more I enjoyed everything that was happening to him."

"Good."

Carmella brought a few of the muffins over to the counter island and sat down with her friend. "But you know, it did hurt when he questioned my Christianity. After what Nelson did to me, I had to struggle so hard to regain my faith and my praise, and then he had the nerve to say that I'm too greedy to be a Christian."

"I know you're not letting that adulterer make you feel bad about anything." Rose took one of the chocolate muffins off the plate and bit into it. The gooey goodness of it melted in her mouth and caused a lingering, "mmmm" to ooze out of her mouth.

"I know, I know… You're right. It's just that after the battle I just fought trying to restore my faith, I don't want to hear anyone deny my right to call myself a blood-bought Christian."

"I hear you." Rose swallowed the rest of her muffin and then pointed at the plate. "Can I have another?"

"I thought you were watching your waistline?"

"Let my husband watch it. I'd rather eat another one of these delicious muffins." With that said, Rose grabbed another muffin and swallowed it in ten seconds flat. Her head went back and forth as she licked her fingers and she sang, "Mmm, mm, m."

Laughing, Carmella said, "I'm glad you enjoyed it. Maybe I should set up a table outside and sell the rest of these muffins to my neighbors as they drive by."

"Now why would you want to do a thing like that, when we could just sit here and finish them off ourselves?" Rose jokingly responded.

"To earn money, of course."

"You don't need to earn money, remember? Nelson is going to be paying your bills."

"That's only going to last for the next five years. I'm forty-seven years old, so I don't want to be facing the job market in my fifties. I need to figure something out now."

"Didn't you major in liberal arts in college?" Rose asked.

Carmella nodded. "I was supposed to go to graduate school so I'd be able to teach or something. But Nelson needed me to work so he could finish law school, so I never even got my teaching certificate. Now I'm at a loss as to what kind of career I can realistically expect to have."

"Well we both know that you love to cook. So, maybe you should be selling your muffins. Oh and don't forget about your cakes—and the pudding you make is to die for, too." Rose snapped her fingers, swung around in her seat and then said, "Matter-of-fact, I have the perfect venue for your first event."

"I'm all ears." Carmella leaned forward, anxious to hear what Rose had to say.

"I already have a caterer for the party Steven is throwing for clients in a few weeks, but we still need the sweet stuff. So, I am officially hiring you as my pastry chef."

Carmella was excited, but apprehensive. "Can you do that? I mean, would Steven be okay with you hiring me? I'm not a professional or anything." Rose's husband was an investment banker. His clientele would be top notch.

"Are you kidding? I wouldn't be able to find pastries better than yours. And if you're worried about looking professional, just give your business a name and order some business cards."

"Thank you, Rose." Carmella reached her arms toward her. "You are the best friend anyone could ever have. I don't know what I would have done without you."

"Are you kidding, Carmella? You are doing this all on your own. I've been watching you, girl, and you're reinventing yourself." Rose leaned over and hugged her friend. "I'm so proud of you."

When they finished hugging, Carmella said, "I just hope you're still proud after I deliver the pastries to your event."

Before Rose could respond, the telephone rang. Carmella hopped up and grabbed it. The caller ID told her that the call was coming from Dontae's high school. As she answered, she prayed that Dontae hadn't hurt himself in football practice like he'd done two years ago.

After she said hello, a deep rich, voice on the other end said, "May I speak with Mrs. Marshall."

"This is she," Carmella said as her toes began to curl. Even after all these years, she still recognized that voice.

"Oh, hi Carmella, this is Ramsey. I need to speak with you for a moment."

Ramsey Thomas had been her high school sweetheart. Everyone had assumed that they would get married and live happily ever after. Even her yearbook had been filled with well wishes for her and Ramsey. But after high school they had attended separate colleges. Ramsey met Pam and she met Nelson.

Ramsey's wife had died five years ago. Carmella had gone to the funeral and taken several cakes over to his house for the children. Two years ago Ramsey had transferred to Dontae's high school as the principal.

"How've you been, Ramsey?"

"I'm doing well."

"And the kids?" Carmella asked. If she remembered correctly, Ramsey and Pam had five children.

"I dropped the last one off at college last month, so I'm experiencing that empty nest syndrome. But I'll get over it… the kids are all happy and healthy."

Carmella felt for Ramsey. He and Pam should be having the time of their lives, traveling and doing things that couples couldn't afford to do during the early stages of marriage. But instead, Ramsey had to experience the joy and heartache of the last child leaving the nest all by himself. Life just didn't seem fair sometimes.

"I'm actually calling about Dontae," Ramsey said.

Carmella turned to Rose, lifted the one minute sign and then asked, "Has something happened with Dontae?"

"That's what I wanted to ask you." Ramsey hesitated for a moment and then trudged on. "I don't mean to pry, but since I've been at this school, I've heard nothing but positive things about Dontae from his teacher. But something changed this year. He's moody, getting into scraps with his classmates and he hasn't been turning in his work. Interim reports will be going out next week, and I guarantee that you will not be happy with what you'll see."

"Thank you so much for giving me a call, Ramsey. I know Dontae skipped a few classes. I talked with him and he promised not to do it again. I didn't know that he was having any other problems."

"His teachers started complaining to me about two weeks ago. I tried to talk to Dontae last week. But since I'm now getting ready to suspend him, I don't think he's listening."

"Suspend him! Why? What happened?" This is just going from bad to worse, Carmella thought.

"He got into a shoving match with one of his teammates."

Carmella put her hand to her mouth. She wanted to scream, but she refused to fall apart. Dontae couldn't have a suspension on his record, not with him being so close to getting into the college of his choice. "Is there anything else that can be done, Ramsey? Dontae knows better than this... especially now with all of his college applications sent out."

"Maybe Dontae thinks he's above the rules here since he's a senior. It might do him well to suffer the consequences of a suspension," Ramsey said.

Carmella shook her head. "It's not that, Ramsey. Dontae has been going through a lot lately. We all have." She took a deep breath and blurted out the facts. "Nelson left me and we're in the middle of a divorce. Dontae is having trouble dealing with the whole sordid mess."

There was silence on the line and then Ramsey said, "I'm sorry to hear that, Carmella. I had prayed for a lifetime of happiness for you and your family."

"Same old Ramsey, huh? Always thinking of others, even when you don't have to. Like my mother used to say, 'You must have been raised right.'"

"Brenda Thomas wouldn't have had it any other way."

She smiled.

Rose whispered, "What'd he say?"

Carmella waved her friend away and turned her back, so Rose wouldn't be able to see any more of her facial expressions. She asked Ramsey, "Is there anything else that can be done? Like making him wash all the faculty members' cars or something?" She held her breath for the answer.

"Now that I understand a bit more clearly what he's been dealing with, I think I can assign him to detention instead of suspending him."

"Thank you. Thank you so much for that, Ramsey. And when he gets home, I'll be taking those car keys from him until he can get his act together."

"I think that's a good idea. And Carmella…"

"Yes?"

"I'm sorry about Nelson."

She thanked him again for his kindness and then hung up the phone. Turning back to Rose, Carmella said, "I've got to figure out how to help Dontae get over what Nelson did to us before he ruins his life trying to get back at his father."

"The last thing you want him doing is messing up when he's so close to finishing school. You've got to do something quick," Rose said.

A devious smile crept across Carmella's face.

"What?" Rose asked.

"I'd been putting off repairs around the house, because I didn't have the money. But if Dontae isn't studying and isn't motivated to go to college anymore, he might as well get some experience in becoming a jack of all trades, so that he can earn a living."

"Oh, that's good."

"It's going to be all bad for him. Just wait until he gets home."

10

"Mom, why is Dontae outside cleaning the gutters?" Joy asked as she came into the house.

"Is that boy still working on the gutters?" Carmella opened the kitchen window and hollered for Dontae to come into the house. He came running while taking off his gloves. Carmella asked, "Why haven't you finished the gutters yet?"

"I just finished. I was on my way in to get my keys," Dontae told his mother.

"Keys?" Carmella picked up the rake that she had leaning against the wall. "You're not getting ready to go anywhere. There's a lot more work to do around here." She handed him the rake and informed him, "I don't want to see a single leaf in the yard when you're done."

"I've got homework, Ma. I can't be doing all this yard work."

"You weren't thinking about your homework a minute ago. You came in here to get your keys so you could go hang out with your friends," Carmella corrected.

"I was going over to Marco's house so we could study for our science test."

"Boy stop lying, you know you haven't been studying or doing any homework. Now get back outside and rake those leaves." She wasn't dealing with his foolishness. But one thing was for sure, by the time this week was over, her son was going to beg for the opportunity to study—and he would mean it.

Dontae walked back out of the house, dragging the rake and mumbling under his breath.

"What is going on around here?" Joy asked.

Carmella watched Dontae walk out the door, she then turned to Joy and said, "My son is trying to sabotage his future and I'm not going to let him."

Joy put her Louis Vuitton on the counter and sat down. "What's he done?"

"Besides fighting and goofing off in school, nothing much." Carmella sat down next to her daughter. "I failed you and your brother by falling apart after your father left me. But I'm not falling apart anymore and I'm not letting Dontae get away with this."

"What's your plan?"

"I'm going to work him like a Hebrew slave. When he's done with all the manual labor I have lined up for him, studying and getting into college is going to seem like a trip to Disney World."

"Okay Pharaoh, so when are you going to let Dontae go?"

"I don't know." Carmella tapped her fingers on the counter. "I'm just praying for direction and a miracle."

"Wow, I wonder what you're going to pray for when I give you my news."

Since leaving her apartment and moving back home, Joy had been nothing but a comfort to her. "Please tell me you haven't done anything crazy?"

"I don't think so, but I'm not sure how you're going to feel about it." Joy sat in silence looking at her mother, gaining the courage to say what came next. Then she opened her mouth and let the words trickle out, "I dropped out of law school."

"Have you lost your mind?"

"No, I'm completely sane and finally thinking for myself," Joy said.

Carmella stood up and ran her hand down her face. She was so mad that she wanted to drive over to Nelson's love nest and swing at him again. He got to run off with a girl half his age, while she got to stay home and put their family back together. "Think about this, Joy, you only have one more semester and you'll be done. Leaving school now might just be the biggest mistake of your life."

"Going to law school was the biggest mistake of my life. I only did it because Daddy wanted it so bad. But I'm done trying to please that man."

"Well, what does Troy think about this?"

Joy lifted her left hand, to show her mother that she was no longer wearing her engagement ring. "I gave the ring back. I'm not ready to get married."

"You can't just drop out of law school and call off your engagement without giving yourself time to think and pray about it." Carmella wrapped her arms around her daughter and kissed her on the side of her forehead and softly said, "Oh Joy, I know you've had to deal with a lot in the last few months by coming to terms with the end of your parents' marriage, but don't let him win... don't let him steal your dreams."

Joy's eyes filled with tears. She closed her eyes and the tears spilled over onto her cheeks. "I just need time to figure out what I really want, Mom."

"I know you do, baby, we all do," Carmella sat back down across from Joy and allowed Joy to lean her head on her shoulder. The two women then cried together until they couldn't shed another tear.

"What's going on?" Dontae asked as he came into the house. "Why are you and Joy crying?"

Carmella looked up. Her son was staring at her with fear in his eyes. He and Joy were fragile right now. She needed to make the right moves so that they could heal properly. Carmella was going to show compassion to her children, but she wasn't going to coddle them. The world wouldn't, so neither would she. She wiped the tears from her face as she told Dontae, "We're okay, we just had a moment."

"Are you sure you're okay?"

"Perfect." Carmella nudged Joy. "Isn't that right?"

Wiping her face also, Joy nodded. "I just needed a good cry. But I'll be all right."

Carmella then put her hands on her hips as she asked Dontae, "What's going on with the yard?"

"I did everything you asked. I've cleaned the gutters and raked the leaves. So, can I please go hang out with my friends for a little while?"

"How are you planning to get to your hang out spot?" Carmella asked, preparing to drop the hammer.

"I'm going to drive over there," he told her as he walked to the key holder by the garage door and noticed that his keys weren't there. "Who moved my keys?"

"I moved them," Carmella declared. "You're not driving until you bring your grades back up."

"Mom, why are you tripping," he whined. "My grades are fine."

"That's not what your teachers say. So I suggest that you make it your business to figure out what assignments you're missing and get them turned in immediately."

Dontae huffed and puffed, then kicked the counter.

"You might as well unflare those nostrils, because I couldn't care less how angry you are right now. But what you need to worry about is how angry I was when I heard that you'd rather fight than do your school work."

"Mr. Thomas told you about my detention, didn't he?"

"Told me about it? I had to beg him for it. You were getting ready to get suspended." She almost asked him what he thought the colleges he'd applied to would think about a kid who liked to fight rather than study, but she knew that was the point. Dontae was trying to self-destruct.

"He told you that?"

Carmella nodded.

"So when I told you that I had to stay late for football practice, you knew I was lying?"

"Don't you know by now not to lie to Mom? It's spooky how she figures stuff out. But I've learned to just 'fess up," Joy told her brother.

With a smirk on her face, Carmella picked up a can of white exterior paint and the paint brush that she'd placed on the kitchen table earlier in the day. "Enough chit-chat, I need you to paint the trim on the shed out back."

"What!" Dontae exploded. "Haven't I slaved around here enough today?"

"Don't complain, Dontae. I'm just trying to provide you with a skill."

"Why do I need a skill? I'm not trying to get a job; I'm still in high school."

"Look at it this way, Dontae, if you don't do your school work, you might not receive an acceptance letter from any of the colleges you applied to, so you'll need to figure out how to earn a living without a degree." She shoved the paint can toward him. "So here you go."

Rolling his eyes, Dontae took the paint and stomped his feet as he went back outside.

Joy started laughing. "I bet he won't do this again."

"I don't know what you're laughing about. I've got something for you to do also."

"Me... why?"

Carmella put a yellow notepad and pen in front of Joy. "Let's see... you quit your job a few weeks ago, you just dropped out of law school and you even broke up with your fiancé." Carmella ticked each item off with her fingers as she spoke. "You might be grown and can do what you want, but you are not sitting around this house, doing nothing."

"Okay, so what do you want me to do?" Joy asked, resigning herself to whatever task her mother might assign.

"I want you to help me plan my new business," Carmella announced.

Joy's eyes lit up. "What new business?"

"I'm going to be a pastry chef. I've decided to call my company Hallelujah Cakes & Such."

"Huh? I don't get it. Why would you add the word 'hallelujah' to a pastry business?"

"Think about it, Joy, the word hallelujah is the highest form of praise. And I have decided, come what may, I will live the rest of my life praising God for all He has done for me. So what better way to remind myself to praise the Lord, than to name my business something that indicates praise?"

Joy nodded. "All right then, Hallelujah Cakes and Such it is. So tell me, do you have a location for this business?"

"Not yet. I plan to operate right out of my own wonderful kitchen until I have enough cash flow to lease a location."

They talked for hours about the business, coming up with ideas and making plans for her first event. Carmella even let Dontae come in the house and get to his homework. But she wasn't finished with him.

Late that night, when Carmella finally made it to her bedroom, she fell on her knees and began praying. Her heart was full of so much animosity towards Nelson. The man was so selfish that he hadn't even taken a moment to worry about how his actions would affect his family.

"Lord Jesus, I'm putting Joy and Dontae in Your hands. You see the heartache and the trials they are dealing with. See them through this storm, Lord… they didn't ask for any of what is going on in our lives. Both Joy and Dontae adored their father, and I believe they are having such a hard time with our divorce because they have had to take their father off the pedestal they had placed him on. Help them to see that Nelson is just a man… a man who happens to be their father, and who still needs their love.

"But most of all, Lord Jesus, I am asking that You give them peace to ride through this storm. Give them direction for their lives and help them to come to know and love You as much as I do."

When Carmella was done praying, she began singing, "You are great… You do miracles so great"… and she believed every word she uttered. For God had truly been great in her life. He'd given her peace of mind and was even mending her heart. She'd never expected that she and Nelson would get a divorce, but with God by her side, she was determined to get through it. And even if she had to drag Dontae and Joy kicking and screaming, they would get through this horrible time in their lives also. In Jesus Name, she made that declaration.

She climbed in bed, turned on the radio that was next to her bed and drifted as a praise song lullaby her to sleep.

11

Over the weekend Carmella did everything but beat Dontae like Toby and say, "grits dummy" to her son. By Monday morning Dontae told her that his body was aching from all the physical labor he'd endured, but that he wanted to go to school anyway. Carmella knew that Dontae thought the torture would end if he went to school, but she wasn't done with him yet.

Since Dontae wasn't allowed to drive until he pulled his grades back up, Carmella drove him to school. "This is lame, Mom. I have a reputation to uphold. How do you think it looks for people to see my Mom dropping me off at school?"

Carmella parked the car, turned the engine off and said as innocently as possible, "I hope the fact that I'll be auditing a few of your classes and helping out in the office this week won't drop your cool points with your friends."

Dontae inhaled and then exhaled slowly, making signs with his hands as if he was trying to get in a Zen kind of mood. "Please tell me this is a joke."

"No joke," Carmella said as she got out of the car. She began walking towards the front doors of the high school, but noticed that Dontae wasn't walking with her. She turned and saw him still sitting in the car looking about as miserable as a teenager could before being prescribed anti-depressants. Good, Carmella thought. He'll think twice before goofing off at school again. Carmella strutted back to the car, knocked on the passenger side window and yelled, "Come on, boy. We don't want to be late to your first class." Okay, she didn't have to keep rubbing it in, but she was determined to drive her point home.

"This ain't right," Dontae said as he got out of the car and stalked off toward the school building.

She closed her passenger door since her son left it wide open as if by magic, the door would close itself. Her Lexus SRX could do a lot of things, but closing its own doors wasn't one of them. She let Dontae rush ahead, because she needed to sign in before going into any of the classrooms.

The school secretary was at her desk when Carmella walked in. "Good morning, Mrs. Bell, how are you doing today?"

"Oh, Mrs. Marshall, how nice to see you. How've you been?"

"Things are going well," was Carmella's statement of faith. "I was hoping that I could audit a few of Dontae's classes today."

"I don't think that would be a problem. Just sign in right here." She pointed to the sign-in sheet. "And I'll get an approval for your day pass."

"I might want to come back a few more days this week if that would be possible."

Mrs. Bell smirked, getting the message. "Turning the screws on him, huh?"

"I'm throwing everything I've got at him, while still praying for a miracle."

"Okay, let's see if we can rustle one up for you."

Carmella sat down in the administrative office, waiting to receive her pass so she could stalk her son all day long. She only prayed that he would forgive her for what she was about to do. Maybe years from now when he became a huge success at whatever he decided to do with his life, he'd call and thank her for this—or maybe not.

Instead of the school secretary bringing her the day pass, Carmella looked up and saw Ramsey headed her way. She stood and gave him a hug, "Hey Ramsey, I didn't mean to bother you."

"No bother at all. You can have the pass and audit all of Dontae's classes, but I was hoping that we could maybe go about this another way."

"Like what?" Carmella asked, trying her best to concentrate. Ramsey was regal and gorgeous all at the same time. He was captain of the basketball team when they were in high school and she was on the cheerleading squad. That was many years ago, but she wanted to grab her pom-poms and give this brother a "Rah! Rah! Sis-Boom-Bah!"

"I can call Dontae down here and let him know that you've been okayed to attend all of his classes anytime you want."

Carmella was catching on. She added, "And then we can give him the opportunity to beg me not to do him like this and let him promise to do his work, right?"

"Right."

"Let's do it," Carmella said. She hadn't really wanted to humiliate her son, but she couldn't think of any other way to get her point across. Ramsey escorted her to his office and she sat down and waited for Dontae.

Ramsey sat down behind his desk and stared at her in a way that made Carmella squirm. "What?" she asked when he kept on staring.

"Nothing, I was just thinking that you're still the prettiest girl this high school has ever seen."

Was she blushing? Carmella hadn't blushed in years. Probably because Nelson hadn't said anything to make her blush in years.

Ramsey leaned back in his seat and kept going. "Looking at you, I feel like we're back in high school."

"Now you might as well stop lying, Ramsey Thomas. It's been twenty-nine years since we were in high school and I know I don't still look the same."

"You're right," he said with a gleam in his eye. "You look better."

Before she could respond, there was a knock at his door. Ramsey jumped up and opened the door. Dontae walked in.

"Mom, what are you still doing here?"

"I told you that I was going to audit your classes this week."

Ramsey held up a piece of paper. "I've signed off on her request and Mrs. Bell is about to print off a list of all your classes and the room number for each."

"Come on, Mr. Ramsey, help me out here. You know this isn't right," Dontae would plead for help from God Himself, if that was what it would take to get his mom to stop the torture.

Ramsey turned to Carmella and said, "I think what Dontae is trying to say is that he's kind of a big deal around here and having his mother checking up on him will make him look bad."

"I seem to remember someone else who was kind of a big deal around this school. When his mother visited this school, it caused him to straighten up and get his work done."

Ramsey's mouth hung slack and then he asked, "You remember that?"

"I sure do. And Mrs. Thomas was right in what she did…straightened you up."

"Yeah, but I was humiliated, Melly."

"The way you ran around this school acting like the king of the hill, you needed to be brought down a notch or two," Carmella told Ramsey with a hint of laughter in her eyes.

"Excuse me," Dontae said, trying to draw some attention back to him. "Did he just call you Melly? Am I missing something?"

Blushing again, Carmella told Dontae, "Ramsey and I went to school together."

"Oh okay." Dontae glanced at Ramsey and then back at his mother. He then got back to the discussion at hand. "Can you just please go home?"

"I don't think I'm ready to go home yet."

"Look Dontae, your mom has a day pass, so she can go anywhere in this school she wants. But if you want her to leave rather than follow you around today, then I suggest you ask why she's here and what she wants from you."

Dontae turned back to his mother. "Why are you here?" he asked while rolling his eyes.

She ignored his insolence. "Because I want you to win."

Dontae sat down in the chair next to his mother. "I don't understand what you're talking about, Mom. I don't get this at all."

She put her hand on her son's shoulder and gently said, "I know you're having a hard time with the divorce," her voice turned sharper as she added, "but that doesn't concern you as much as your school work does. I don't want you to mess up your last year of high school and then end up hurting your chances of getting into college."

"I'm not going to sit here and cry the way you and Joy cried the other night," Dontae told his mom as his lip slightly quivered.

"I don't want you to cry. I've done enough of that for the whole family. What I want you to do is strive to enjoy your life and keep getting the good grades you've always gotten." She put her forehead against his. "Can you do that for me?"

"If I promise to do my work, will you please leave?" A tear dropped from Dontae's eyes as the two continued to lean on each other.

Carmella pretended not to see the tear. "I'll leave now. Just do your work, okay?"

"Okay." Dontae stood up and turned his back on them as he wiped his eyes. "I gotta get back to class. I'll see you at home, Mom."

"Don't you need me to pick you up after school?" Carmella quickly asked.

"I'll catch the bus home." With that Dontae escaped.

Carmella turned back to Ramsey and said, "Thank you for that. Dontae might not have ever forgiven me for embarrassing him the way I had planned."

"I don't know about that," Ramsey had a grin on his face as he admitted, "I forgave my mom after my third year in college."

As she laughed, Carmella reminded him, "Remember how she busted up in our English class and was supposed to be sitting quietly. That lasted about ten minutes, until the teacher upset her by not calling on you to read any of the passages that we were going over that day."

Ramsey mimicked his mother as he said, "My son ain't no dumb jock. He can read, too. Show him, Ramsey... stand up and read something."

They both burst out laughing, then Carmella shook her head. "I can't believe that I was getting ready to do that to Dontae. But desperate times, call for desperate measures."

"But I have to admit that my head was pretty big when we were in high school. I just knew I was going to the NBA. If my mother hadn't convinced me that my education was important because nobody could ever take that away from me, I don't know where I would be now."

"You did play overseas for a few years, though," Carmella reminded him.

"I enjoyed playing overseas, but I couldn't stay there forever. So, when I got homesick, I was thankful that I had finished college and only needed a few certifications to become a teacher."

Carmella was silent, but the sadness that crossed her eyes was unmistakable.

"Did I say something wrong?" Ramsey asked.

"Oh no, not at all. It's just that I had intended to become a teacher also, but it just didn't work out that way." She felt as if she was starting to bring down the mood with her woulda-coulda-shouldas, so she stood up. "I'm sure you need to get back to work, so I'll get out of your way."

"Actually, I was just getting ready to invite you to breakfast. There's an IHOP one block over."

12

Carmella felt as if she were walking on clouds. Breakfast with Ramsey had been just what she needed. He made her feel young again, and reminded her of what it felt like to be cherished. Because one thing was for certain, she and Ramsey had loved each other. She had allowed herself to move on when she and Ramsey chose different colleges, because she had believed that teenage love wouldn't last. But now she was questioning that decision.

She'd given Ramsey her cell phone number and had boldly told him that the divorce papers would be signed soon, so he should feel free to call her. Carmella had been feeling so good that she even gave Dontae back his car keys when he arrived home that evening.

Then things started going wrong. Carmella received a call from her attorney. She smiled as she noted the name on her caller ID. Deidre was probably calling to tell her that Nelson had signed the papers and she was free. It amazed her that she could smile about something that, only a few months ago, had seemed like being left behind after the rapture. But maybe she was doing some healing herself.

"Hey Deidre, how are you doing today?"

"Not so good, Carmella. I have some news that I really don't like delivering."

"What's wrong? Is Nelson still balking at the amount of alimony he'll have to pay?"

"He's refused to sign the papers, Deidre. He doesn't want the divorce."

Carmella sat down as she tried to wrap her mind around what she was hearing. Did Nelson really think that he could just call off their divorce as if it had just been a bad joke? "What do you mean? Does he think he can just come back home after all that's happened?"

"I don't think he's interested in coming home," Deidre said.

Now she was really confused. "If he doesn't want to come back home, why won't he just sign the divorce papers and get on with it?"

"They won't say. But Clark did let me know that Nelson is prepared to give in to all your demands as long as you let him postpone the divorce until December."

"But that's not fair. Why should he get to put my life on hold without even giving us a reason?" Carmella was outraged, pacing back and forth, wishing she had something to throw. She had already given Ramsey her number… had already started dreaming of a life without Nelson and now he had the nerve to put her life on hold again. No, she wasn't going to stand for it.

"I think I know how we can get him to sign the papers."

"How?"

"I can tell his attorney that if he doesn't have those papers signed and in my office by the end of the week, we will go public with our story."

She was ready to be rid of Nelson, but she didn't want to do anything to cause him any problems. "I don't think I could do that, Deidre. I may not want to be his wife anymore, but I don't want to do anything to hurt him either."

"You are truly a woman after God's heart, Carmella Marshall. But I don't want you to worry about this. I said that I would threaten to go to the press on him—we don't actually have to do it. I'll call Clark back and let you know if I make progress with them."

After that call from her attorney, Carmella felt depression trying to set in again, especially after she'd received a call from Ramsey. He'd called to tell her how much he had enjoyed having breakfast with her and had asked if she would like to have dinner with him. Carmella wanted to scream yes from the rooftop, but she was still a married woman. She didn't want to play games with Ramsey and make him believe that she was just a signature away from divorce when Nelson was throwing her for all kinds of loops. She also didn't feel like letting him in on her melodrama, so she simply said, "Can I think about it and give you a call back?"

"Sure. I don't want to rush you. I know you're dealing with a lot right now."

Ramsey was so understanding and pleasant to talk to. How could she have ever thought her life would have been better without this man? It hurt so bad to say goodbye to Ramsey, because she felt as if Nelson was holding all the cards and she was once again powerless against him.

***

The next morning before getting out of bed, Carmella turned her praise music on while reading a few chapters in the book Joshua. When she reached the twenty-fourth chapter and fifteenth verse, Carmella felt convicted by her attitude as she read, as for me and my house, we will serve the Lord. She realized that Joshua had made a definitive statement that didn't take into account what might happen tomorrow or the next day.

Come what may, Joshua and his household would serve the Lord. And if serving the Lord for her meant staying married to Nelson and saying goodbye to Ramsey, then that was what she would do. However, she didn't feel as powerless the next morning as she had the night before. Because that morning after reading from the book of Joshua, Carmella knew that God would carry her through that time of uncertainty. Hadn't He helped Joshua fight the battle of Jericho by causing the walls to come tumbling down?

So, maybe God was at that very moment working to tear down Nelson's hard-hearted walls. Maybe God wanted her to give her marriage a chance by allowing Nelson a few more months come to his senses. The ironic thing was that since Nelson was delaying the process, she was the one who wanted it to move faster. Her heart had been changed and she no longer lived, slept and ate Nelson Marshall.

What scared Carmella, though, was that maybe it wasn't God that had brought about that change in her attitude towards her husband. Maybe seeing Ramsey and having him flirt with her and take her out to breakfast had moved her heart away from her husband. That wasn't right. Too many people lose their marriages because of wandering eyes. Carmella had too much respect for the institution of marriage to allow that to happen to her.

With her mind made up, Carmella had two calls to make before she started her workday. The first call was to Ramsey. She hadn't been truthful with him last night and Carmella felt that she owed him that.

He picked up on the first ring, and Carmella quickly said, "I know you're at work, so I won't keep you."

"Don't worry about it. This is my planning time, so I can talk for a while."

She cleared her throat as she gathered the strength to do what she believed was right. "I wanted to thank you for calling to check on me last night and for taking me to breakfast yesterday. That was the most fun I've had in a long time."

"Just imagine how much fun we'll have when I take you to dinner," Ramsey said.

He sounded as if he was grinning, and Carmella sure hated to take the smile off his face. "That's why I'm calling, Ramsey. I won't be able to go to dinner with you."

"Would you rather do breakfast again?"

"No Ramsey, that's not it. Nelson hasn't signed the divorce papers and has decided that he can't do it until December."

"What's going on, Melly? Didn't you tell me that the divorce was his idea?"

"I did and it is. I don't understand Nelson anymore, so I won't be able to explain the way his mind works. But I can't see you until I am actually divorced. You do understand that, don't you?"

Ramsey puffed out a longsuffering breath as he said, "I understand. I don't like it, but I understand."

They hung up and Carmella made her next phone call. When her attorney got on the line, Carmella said, "Tell Nelson that the only way I will agree to postpone the divorce is if he agrees to attend marriage counseling with me."

"If that's what you want, I'll pass your demand along to them."

Carmella could hear the disappointment in Deidre's voice. But to her credit, Deidre held her tongue and handled her business.

Carmella then got dressed and walked out of her bedroom and went to her kitchen, her new workstation. Joy was already in the kitchen, pulling spices out of the cabinet.

"What are you doing up so early this morning?" Carmella asked her late-to-bed, late-to-rise daughter.

"Mom, it's nine-thirty. I could ask what you're doing getting up so late, but I could tell that you were in a bad mood when you went to bed last night."

Her children were still worried about her. Nothing Carmella said would convince them that they could stop worrying; she would just have to show them one day at a time. "I was upset, but I prayed about it and I'm just going to let the Lord handle it."

Joy left her spot by the cabinets and sat down at the counter. "I was doing inventory on all your spices, so we'd know what to pick up at the store for these cakes you want to bake."

"Thanks for getting on that, Joy. I can't believe my first event is only a week away."

Joy grabbed her mom's hand and gave her a serious stare down as she asked, "Do you want to talk about what upset you last night?" When Carmella seemed to hesitate, Joy added, "You'll feel better if you just get it off your chest... no more letting stuff fester, okay?"

"Okay Joy, no more letting stuff fester." Carmella sat down next to her daughter, she breathed in deeply and then said, "I was upset last night because your father has all of a sudden decided that he doesn't want to sign the divorce papers until sometime in December. But after praying about it this morning, I called my attorney and told her that I would agree to it if he would agree to go to marriage counseling with me."

Joy shook her head. "Mom, don't take this wrong, but for a smart lady, you are very naïve."

"I'm not being naïve, Joy. I'm just trying to do what I think God would want."

Joy closed her eyes, leaned her head back and as she reopened her eyes, she said, "Has it slipped your mind that the election is next month?"

"What does that have to do with anything?"

"Think, Mom. Daddy has probably had some advance polling done and he now realizes that he would most likely lose the election if he divorced you right now. My guess is, he'll be ready to sign the papers the moment he is re-elected to his judgeship."

"I don't think that your father is as cold and calculating as you seem to believe. And neither you nor I know what the Lord has to say about this matter, so I choose to wait to find out."

"Suit yourself, Mom. I hope it turns out the way you want it to."

"Me too," Carmella said, without indicating which way she wanted things to turn out.

13

Feeling like a fool, she sat in her pastor's office waiting for Nelson who was an hour late. She glanced at her watch one more time and then said, "I'm really sorry about this, Pastor Mitchell. Nelson told my lawyer that he would come to this counseling session. He must have changed his mind and just didn't bother to let me know."

"These things happen sometimes, daughter."

She had been a member of this wonderful church for twenty years. Pastor Mitchell was twenty-five years older than she, and he always called her daughter whenever they spoke. Being that her father was long gone, it made Carmella feel all warm inside every time she heard him address her as daughter. She wanted to put her head on his shoulder and cry her eyes out as she told him about all the problems she'd been having with Nelson and the kids.

Instead of doing that, she put her purse on her shoulder and stood. "Sorry to have wasted your time, Pastor. I think I'll just head on home now."

Pastor Mitchell came around his desk and took Carmella in his arms, giving her a warm, caring hug and asked, "How are you holding up?"

His shoulder was there, so she leaned her head on it and let a few tears seep out. "It's been hard, Pastor. I was caught off guard by this divorce, because I thought Nelson and I would be together until one of us buried the other."

As they moved apart, Pastor Mitchell patted her on the back while shaking his head. "I hate divorce. But if you've done all you can do, then rest in God, daughter. Let's see what He says the end of this matter will be."

Carmella was upset when she left church, but by the time she drove home, she had almost convinced herself that God was working this thing out for her, so she didn't need to stress over anything. But then she went inside her home and had to face her children.

Joy was the first to pounce. "So how was the counseling session?" She looked at her watch and then commented, "With all of Daddy's issues, I would have expected ya'll to be there all night."

"Shut up, Joy," Dontae said as he rose with hope in his eyes. "Just let Mom tell us what happened."

Carmella wondered if Nelson knew just how much Dontae needed him to do the right thing. If for no other reason, she would hold on as long as she could so that Dontae could get his hero back. But now she would have to tell them the truth. She put her purse and keys down and then said, "Your father didn't show up."

"What do you mean? He agreed to the counseling session, right?" Dontae asked.

"He did agree," Carmella answered her son, while looking at Joy. And if she wasn't mistaken, Carmella saw disappointment on Joy's face. It was as if she had lost all faith in her Dad, but was still secretly hoping that he would restore her faith. She tried to sound bright and cheery as she said, "Look, I don't want you two worrying about this. I'm sure Pastor Mitchell will allow us to reschedule the meeting. I'll just call Nelson and get a time that works for him."

"Stop it! Stop it!" Joy screamed at Carmella.

"I don't know why you're so upset with me, Joy. I haven't done anything. I'm just trying to make this right for all of us."

"Don't worry about us, Mom. You need to make this right for yourself." Joy was still yelling as she added. "Daddy is playing you for a fool. He's just stringing you along until the election. Don't you get it? He's never coming back home."

Carmella was getting a headache. Why had Nelson thought it was okay to leave her to handle the fall out of the mess he created. She couldn't take much more. Lord Jesus, I am weak, so I need You to be strong for me, she silently called out to her God as she sunk down onto the sofa in the living room and began rubbing her temple.

"Mom, don't stress," Dontae admonished. "We know you've tried to work with Daddy. It's his loss, though."

If it was Nelson's loss, Carmella wondered why she felt so lost and alone. Help me, Jesus!

"That's it. I'm going to handle this myself," Joy said as she stormed out of the house.

***

The next few days sped by as Carmella and Joy worked on the final preparations for her first paid event at Rose's dinner party and Dontae busied himself with homework and football practice.

It was the day of her event. Carmella had her business cards and she was putting the final touches on her cakes, pies, pudding and two different kinds of brownies. Her radio was on and Carmella was praising the Lord as she decorated her cakes. Joy had her checklist out and was busily counting the items and checking things off of her list. The praise music stopped as the radio station went to breaking news.

The newscaster said, "With the election coming up, here are some things we thought you ought to know…"

Carmella was stuffing frosting into a Ziploc bag. She cut a hole in the bag and frosted her pastries as the radio announcer talked about one issue after the next that affected North Carolina residents. The announcer then said, "And we have it on good authority that Judge Nelson Marshall, the same man who is running for re-election as a judge who will fight for family, has evidently stopped fighting for his own. Because he has left his wife and is now living with his pregnant girlfriend."

The frosting bag in Carmella's hand dropped, as her hands went to her mouth. She had no idea that she would be this devastated to hear that Nelson had gotten another woman pregnant. "Oh my God," she said as she started backing away from the table. She wanted to run to her bedroom and lock the world out as she digested this news.

"Mom, wait," Joy said, as she grabbed hold of her mother.

"I just need a moment, Joy. I'll be back, okay?"

"No, I don't want you to go." Joy hugged her mother. "It's not true, anyway. Jasmine isn't pregnant, so don't get upset for nothing."

Carmella pulled away from her daughter and then glanced over at the radio. "But they just said—"

"I gave that information to the media. I never told them that she was pregnant, but I insinuated it."

Carmella sat down. She lowered her head as she inhaled and exhaled. As she calmed herself, she turned back to her daughter. "Why would you do something like this, Joy?"

"Instead of asking me why I would do what I did, why don't you ask him how he could have done all this to you?"

"You had no right to put our business out there for everyone to hear. How do you think this makes me feel? Now I have to go to this party tonight and face all of these people while trying to get business from them." At this point Carmella wanted to call Rose and cancel. If this event had been for anyone but Rose, she would have done just that. She took a deep breath, decided to put one foot in front of the other and move forward.

Carmella got back to putting the frosting on her items. She tried her best to ignore Joy as she floated around the kitchen. But alas, Joy would not be ignored.

"I'm sorry, Mom. Don't be mad at me."

Carmella shook her head, still steaming at what Joy had done.

"I did it for you, Mom."

Carmella gripped the edge of her prep table as she told Joy, "I never asked you to humiliate me. Nor did I ask you to lampoon your father's chances of getting re-elected."

"He doesn't deserve that job. He's a hypocrite."

Carmella blew out an exhausted breath. "Joy, one day you are going to have to find a way to forgive your father. I don't want you going through life bitter and unyielding."

"I'm not bitter and unyielding," she declared.

Carmella held up a hand. "I don't have time for this right now. Let's just finish getting everything together and get through this event." Before turning back to her pastries, Carmella pointed a stern finger in Joy's face, "But I'll tell you right now, Joy Lynn Marshall, I'm going to make sure that you are the one passing out the pastries tonight. I'm going to stay at my station and let you handle all of the people who want to tell you how sorry they are about your dad."

"It's the least I can do for you, Mom. And again, I'm sorry that I embarrassed you. I hadn't thought about the other side of this story when I was passing it on to the media."

***

Rose's party was fabulous. And even though Carmella worried about receiving pity comments from the guests at the party, no one bothered them. She passed out her business cards and received orders from five of the guests. As they were driving home, Carmella's phone rang.

It was Deidre. Carmella pushed the phone button on her steering wheel and said "Hello?"

Deidre's voice traveled through the car as she said, "I have good news. Nelson signed the divorce papers."

Joy rolled her eyes.

"Are you kidding?" Carmella said, "I thought he didn't want to sign until after the election?"

"Apparently, having everyone know that he's living with his girlfriend without the benefit of a divorce from his wife is a big problem for his career goals," Deidre said.

"Okay, well thanks for letting me know."

"You don't seem happy," Joy said with a worried expression on her face.

"I doubt if anyone is happy when their marriage comes to an end. And I had been married to your father for twenty-five years." A tear flowed down her face as they pulled into the driveway. "I'll be all right," she told Joy as they got out of the car.

Carmella went to her bedroom, took a shower, threw on a pair of pajamas and then climbed into bed. She turned on the radio next to her bed. Let the Church Say Amen by Marvin Winans was playing and Carmella thought the sound was fitting for that evening. God had indeed spoken, her marriage was over and all she could do was say, "Amen".

Joy ran into her room. "Mom, turn on the news."

She turned the television on. Joy hurriedly put it on the news channel and Carmella saw Nelson being interviewed by a reporter, and he had the nerve to say, "Look, what could I do? My wife hired a lawyer and made all types of demands for a divorce. We'd been married for twenty-five years, but since she seemed ready to divorce me, I had no choice but to move on... and just for the record, I do not have a pregnant girlfriend."

"Can you believe him? He's putting the divorce on you, as if it was your idea."

"He's trying to save face. But it doesn't bother me. Now let me make a quick call and then get some sleep, okay?"

"Are you sure you're all right?"

Carmella nodded.

Joy left the room.

Carmella picked up the phone and dialed the number she'd wanted to dial from the moment she heard that she was a free woman. Life had thrown her for a loop, but thank God she was confident that she would be landing on her feet.

Ramsey answered the phone and said, "I'm so glad you called. My fingers were itching to call you, but I wasn't sure if that was the right thing to do or not."

"Well, did you pray about it?" she asked, holding her breath, waiting for the answer.

"I've been praying about us for a few weeks now. I've already gotten my answer; I'm just waiting on you to get on board."

"Nelson signed the divorce papers, Ramsey." She was a bit breathless as she made this declaration. Carmella could hardly believe the excitement growing in her at the thought of beginning again... with Ramsey.

"So, how about dinner," Ramsey said.

She could hear the smile in his voice again. This time she wasn't about to do anything to remove that smile. "I'd love to go to dinner with you."

"Okay, let me make the reservation and I'll let you know where we'll be eating. Is tomorrow night okay with you?"

"Tomorrow is perfect."

Carmella put the telephone back on the receiver and turned up her radio. They were playing Take Me to the King by Tamela Mann. Carmella pulled the cover over her body, exhaled as she laid everything at the feet of her King and then went to sleep, excited to see what tomorrow would bring.

Epilogue

After only three dates, Ramsey asked Carmella to marry him. But she said no. Perplexed by the matter, Ramsey took Carmella's hands in his and said, "But we love each other. I can see it in your eyes, Carmella. You never stopped loving me."

"I do love you so very dearly, Ramsey. You are the man of my dreams, but I'm on a journey with God right now, and I don't want to stop until it's finished."

"You and I have so much in common, especially our love for God… Let me go on this journey with you."

She pulled her hands away from Ramsey's, and lightly touched his beautiful face. Carmella wanted to marry this man like she wanted to get up every morning and sing praises to the Lord. But she loved Ramsey too much to accept his offer at this moment in her life. "I can't ask you to fix what another man has broken. I need to spend this time with God to heal myself and my children; can you understand that?"

Reluctantly, he nodded, leaned his forehead against hers and asked, "So what do we do now?"

She was tired of crying, but tears formed in her eyes anyway. "I have no right to ask you to stick around, or to wait on me to resolve my issues, but I sure wish you would."

He kissed her, and then held her in his arms, not wanting to let her go. "I'm not going anywhere," he told her.

Carmella was comforted by Ramsey's words, but there was another man on her mind who she very much wanted to go somewhere, but it appeared as if his life had stalled on him. Dontae had received his acceptance letter from Princeton. Then a rejection letter came from Yale, but most importantly he then received an acceptance from Harvard, his father's alma mater. But neither the acceptance nor the rejection moved him. Dontae seemed stuck. Carmella kept praying, but she was at her wits' end as to how to get him to move forward with his life.

But one day while she and Joy were working on a pastry order at her prep table, Dontae came running into the kitchen, full of smiles and all bubbly as if he'd just been put in the running for the Heisman trophy. "Mom, you won't believe," he told Carmella as he grabbed her arms and swung her around.

Carmella grabbed a towel and wiped her hands off. "Boy, what in the world has you in such a state?"

He had to catch his breath, but when he did, he said, "A scout for the University of Alabama came to my football practice today. They want me to play, Mom. They're going to give me a scholarship!"

Joy started jumping around the kitchen now. "Oh my God, Dontae, I'm so happy for you."

But Carmella was puzzled. "We never discussed Alabama. I thought you were going to pick between Harvard and Princeton. Both those schools want you. Even if you don't want to go to your daddy's old school, why not go to Princeton? Do you know how many kids spend their lives wishing and praying for this opportunity?"

A little bit of light went out of Dontae's eyes as he turned back to his mother. He shook his head. "I don't want either of those opportunities, Mom—at least not for my undergrad. I want to play for the Crimson Tide, and they want me. This is the best news I've received all year long. Can't you just be happy for me?"

What was she doing? Hadn't she asked God for a miracle for her son? How had she been so boneheaded as to think that the miracle had been when Dontae received acceptance letters to two colleges that he didn't want to go to in the first place? The miracle was standing right before her, his excitement about being able to play football for his favorite college team. Carmella would not be a foolish woman and continue arguing her point. She was just going to say Amen and get out of the way. "Well, I guess I'll have to sell a ton of cakes and pies so I can fly to all of these Alabama games."

At hearing those words, Dontae and Joy began jumping around the kitchen, again, giving each other high fives and doing dances that

Carmella didn't recognize. She stepped back and watched her children. Nelson had left them, but God would never leave. This was why happy moments like the one they were having now were still possible.

"One down and one more to go," Carmella silently said to God as she lovingly glanced at her beautiful, big hearted, but bitter daughter.

Later that night as Carmella and Joy sat in front of the television watching the Cooking Channel, Carmella noticed that Joy wasn't as interested as she in what the chefs were doing and she made a decision. Carmella turned to her daughter and said, "I want to thank you for helping me get my business started."

"It's been fun; don't worry about it."

"You're fired," was all Carmella said next.

Joy had been slouching on the sofa. She shot up. "I'm what? How can you fire your own daughter? And on what grounds? I have been a model employee... and if I haven't been, you never told me anything was wrong."

"Listen at you... arguing your case. Don't you see, Joy? You weren't meant to follow my dreams. You have to follow your own, and I know that you love the law. You'd be an excellent lawyer."

Joy shook her head. "That was Daddy's dream for me."

"No, baby. Your father might be good at a lot of things, but he can't put something in your heart that's not already there."

Joy's fists curled as she punched the sofa, bitterness ruling her life. "I can't do it. Daddy gets everything he wants. He won the election, even after I told the media how horrible he has been to you. If I finish law school, he's won, and I don't want that."

Carmella wagged a finger in her daughter's face. "Now you listen to me, Joy Lynn, you let the good Lord handle your daddy, because you can't live with all this bitterness pumping through your veins."

Joy shrugged, not caring how childish she appeared.

"And contrary to what you believe, your not finishing law school does not make you the winner... you're the one losing out, because it's the thing you want more than anything."

They sat in silence for a while, Joy rolled her eyes and harrumphed a few times, but in the midst of it she must have been mulling things over, because when she finally spoke to Carmella again she said, "If I did go back to law school, maybe I could practice family law and help women like you when men like my father try to do them wrong, the same way Deidre helped you."

Carmella nodded. "You could do that, if that is truly where your heart is." She stood up and handed her daughter the remote. "I'm going to bed."

"You mean, you're going to call Ramsey," Joy said as if her mother was a teenager and she was the parent.

"I'm going to mind my own business and I suggest you do the same," Carmella told her as she headed upstairs to do exactly what Joy had said. She missed hearing Ramsey's voice and had to know that he was still there for her. As she picked up the phone, Carmella realized that she had had three love affairs in her lifetime.

She'd loved Nelson for over twenty years, but now that love affair had come to an end. Ramsey had been her first love, and he was back in her life to stay this time, she hoped. But the third love affair had turned out to be the most important of all; it would be an enduring one, forever after. She didn't have to wonder or guess about this love, because it was the love she shared with her Lord and Savior, Jesus Christ... all else would be secondary from here on out in the Marshall household.

Joy Comes in the Morning

THE PRAISE HIM ANYHOW SERIES

1

Psalm 137: 1-4

By the rivers of Babylon, there we sat down, yea, we wept, when we remembered Zion. We hanged our harps upon the willows in the midst thereof.

For there they that carried us away captive required of us a song; and they that wasted us required of us mirth, saying, "Sing us one of the songs of Zion."

How shall we sing the Lord's song in a strange land?

Joy Marshall strutted into the Municipal Courthouse at 8:55 am, just minutes before the judge would be seated. She was wearing the Michelle Obama sleeveless dress look. And since she was a P90X workout girl—with the t-shirt to prove it—Joy had the arms to carry off such a look. Her hair was pulled up on top of her head, giving her face an exotic look that caused the law breakers and the law makers in the courthouse to stop and stare. But Joy didn't even notice. She had one thing on her mind that morning… revenge. As far as Joy was concerned, revenge was best when served cold and she was about to serve up a heaping pile of it.

She hadn't spoken to her father in five years. He'd shown up at her law school graduation four years before, and Joy had turned her back to him when he tried to congratulate her. Her father had sent roses to her office when she had accepted an Assistant District Attorney position a year and a half ago, but Joy had sent the roses back. She'd also sent him a very unflattering picture of herself hugging a toilet and puking up her guts. She'd told her father that the picture represented the girl he had created... but he could never lay claim on the woman she would become.

Ramsey, her stepfather had taken that picture of Joy after one of her famous nights of drinking. The next morning he took her to breakfast at the same IHOP he'd taken her mother on their first, unofficial date. While Joy struggled to hold her head up, Ramsey slid the picture over to her. After taking a quick look at the picture, Joy's head started pounding. She ran her hands down her face, as a look of embarrassment crept up. "Where'd you get this?"

"I took it when you came home last night. I wanted you to see what a fine and upstanding woman you turned out to be."

She heard the sarcasm in his voice and didn't like it one bit. "Marrying my mother doesn't give you the right to get in my business. I'm a grown woman and prefer to be treated as one."

The waitress placed scrambled eggs and bacon in front of Ramsey and pancakes in front of Joy. When the waitress left their table, Ramsey said, "I'm not in the habit of treating people who live in my house like grown folk when they don't pay bills, and do nothing with their lives."

"I finished law school. Isn't that what my mother wanted? Okay, I did it, so stop harassing me."

Ramsey leaned back in his seat. He studied her for a moment and then let her have it, no holds barred. "Look Joy, I know that this adjustment has been hard on you... probably harder on you than anyone else, but you can't self-destruct over it."

What did he know about the pain she was dealing with? As far as Joy was concerned, her father hadn't just betrayed her mother when he cheated with Jasmine. He'd betrayed her as well, because she had looked up to her father and believed he could do no wrong. And then one day she discovered that he wasn't just doing wrong, but he was doing it with Joy's best friend. So in one crazy and heart-wrenching day, she'd lost not just her father and best friend... she'd lost her trust in mankind. And no matter how hard she tried, Joy just couldn't figure out how to get it back.

"Joy, I know that you're angry with your father, and you're trying to punish him for what he did to you. But you're going about this the wrong way."

Her stomach was not in the mood for food, so she pushed her plate away. But she was finally ready to listen to Ramsey. "What do you mean?"

"Success is the best revenge, Joy. Drinking yourself into an early grave is not going to hurt Nelson Marshall. You know what will stick in his gut, though? Show your father that you succeeded even though he chose to walk away."

Ramsey's words had so encouraged her, that Joy stopped drinking and put an honest effort towards finding a job. Now she was an Assistant District Attorney and today was the day that she would finally exact her revenge on her father.

The so-called Honorable Judge Nelson Marshall had been assigned to preside over her most recent case. When he saw her name, he should have recused himself on the spot, but since he chose not to do the right thing, as usual, Joy was about to do it for him.

"Good morning, Ms. Marshall. You're looking good today," a big bellied security guard, who obviously needed Ramsey to give him a good talking to so he could lay off the beers, said to her as she walked over to the security area.

"Thanks, Malcolm, how are you doing this morning?" Joy handed her Michael Kors handbag and briefcase to the security guard and prepared to go through the metal detectors.

"I'm doing good. Getting married next week," Malcolm told her as she walked through the metal detector.

Joy almost offered her condolences. But she reminded herself that not everyone viewed marriage as an apocalyptic occurrence. But they knew just as well as she did that over half of all marriages end in divorce. That includes the ones that claim to be Christian marriages, like the one her mother and father had, until the day he decided to leave her for his girlfriend. After her father had done his dirt and divorced her mother, Joy hadn't been able to look at marriage the same way. She'd even called off her own engagement to Troy Daniels and she'd been living happily single and not interested in mingling at all ever since. She didn't have time to go over all of her woes with Malcolm, so she simply said, "Congratulations. I wish you the best." Joy took her belongings and walked away from him as fast as she could.

Joy got on the elevator heading to the third floor. She walked into courtroom A, where Lance Bryant and his repeat offender were already seated and waiting on Judge Do-Wrong to make his royal appearance.

She caught Lance staring at her as she made her way to the prosecuting table. He was a fine brother with wavy hair and a beautiful smile, but she wasn't interested. Joy put her briefcase down as Lance leaned her way and said, "Long time no see… how've you been?"

Joy gave him a close lipped smile and then turned back to her paperwork. She had tried two other cases against Lance in the short time that she had been an Assistant DA. Lance seemed like a good guy, but he sure picked some loser clients. He handled everything from assault to robbery, and always seemed to believe that his clients were as innocent as new born babes.

"Oh, so it's like that, huh? You not speaking today? Guess you're still upset about that whuppin' you took the last time."

She'd won the first case, but Lance had, indeed, won the second case. Joy was actually thankful that Lance won that case, because as it turned out, his client had been falsely accused. But he wasn't about to win this case, not even close, nor was she about to deal with her father the entire week that it would take to wrap this case up.

"All rise," the bailiff said as Judge Nelson took his seat behind the bench.

Joy's fists instantly clenched as she watch her father sit in a chair he didn't deserve to be in. She had tried her best to get him out of that seat during the last two elections, but the people of North Carolina just kept voting the adulterer back in. A few years back, Joy had delighted in telling her father that she had been the one to provide the media with information about his girlfriend and his divorce. He'd tried to apologize to her for what he had done to their family, but she wasn't interested in hearing it.

Judge Nelson shuffled a few papers around as he avoided looking in Joy's direction. He then said, "All we are doing today is setting bail, so let's get to it."

Joy said, "I am not prepared to have a bail hearing yet."

Nelson took his glasses off and glanced in his daughter's direction. "What's the problem, Counselor?"

Joy smirked. Using the court in this manner could seriously damage her career, but she didn't care. Every chance she got, she was going to let her father know what an awful human being he was, and if anyone had a problem with it, she would simply start her own law firm. "You are the problem, Your Honor." As she said the words *Your Honor*, her eyes rolled and it was obvious to all present that she thought he was anything *but* honorable.

Nelson Marshall seemed to shrink in his seat for a moment. He closed his eyes and rubbed his temples. "This is not the time or place for this, Joy. You have a job to do and so do I. Let's just get on with it, all right?"

"No," Joy said flippantly. "You should have recused yourself from this case the moment you saw that I was the attorney of record, but since you didn't, I am now publicly asking that you recuse yourself."

"Am I missing something?" Lance asked as he looked from Judge Marshall to Joy. His client nudged him, and then whispered something in his ear.

"I see no reason why I should recuse myself. I am more than able to be an impartial judge in the matter that is before the court."

"It is well known that I informed the media about your marital misconduct, so if you do not recuse yourself, I will request a judicial review."

Lance lifted his hand in order to get the judge's attention. When Judge Marshall turned to him, Lance said, "If there is some sort of problem between you and the assistant DA, then I respectfully request that Attorney Joy Marshall recuse herself so that we can move forward with the case. My client is entitled to his day in court and he does not want to delay the process waiting for another judge to be assigned to the case."

Joy hadn't seen that coming. The defendant was entitled to a speedy trial, so his wishes might outweigh hers. She turned to Lance and said, "If the defendant is concerned about being able to post bond today, I am more than willing to work out bail with this judge."

Lance took her up on the offer. Bail was set for ten thousand and then Joy got back to her mission. "Now that we've handled that bit of business, I would like to reiterate the fact that I would like you to recuse yourself," she said to her father, the judge.

The defendant nudged Lance again. Lance spoke up again, "Your honor, if one of you has to go, my client would prefer that it be the prosecutor. He does not like the idea that his case would be delayed while he waits to be put on another judge's docket."

"What's his problem?" Joy asked indignantly. "If he makes bail, he'll be at home with his family and friends while he awaits a new trial date."

Lance turned back to Judge Marshall. "My client has a right to a speedy trial. His rights shouldn't be tossed aside at the whim of the prosecution."

Nelson turned to his daughter and said, "Well, Counselor?"

"Well what?" she snapped at her father, confused by the entire incident. Why on earth wouldn't a criminal be happy to have his court appearance moved back? He'd have more time to spend with his family and fellow criminal buddies before he is proven guilty and spends the next ten years behind bars.

"It looks like you're the one who needs to recuse," Nelson said to his daughter.

Joy threw up her hands, grabbed her briefcase and shouted, "Fine. You win. You always win!" She grabbed her purse and rushed out of the courtroom before she made a bigger spectacle of herself.

It just wasn't right. Her father was an awful human being, but things kept coming up roses for him. She wanted Nelson Marshall to pay for leaving her mother and ruining the family unit that she,

106

her mother and brother had held dear. She had been a Daddy's girl, wanting to be just like Judge Nelson Marshall, for she had imagined that there was no greater human on earth than her dad. But that was before her father left her mother for Jasmine, her ex-friend, the skank. As a matter of fact, Jasmine had been Joy's roommate and her father had met Jasmine when Joy brought her over to the house for Sunday dinner.

As Joy reached the exit door, her head swiveled to the left as she spotted Jasmine seated in the last row of the courtroom. The woman had the audacity to roll her eyes at Joy as she looked her way. Joy wanted to reach across that aisle and go upside her head, the same way her mother had done to Jasmine years ago. But she reminded herself that she was in a courthouse and could get arrested for doing something like that.

Joy pushed open the door and walked out of the courtroom, and had almost made it out of the building when she heard Lance hollering behind her.

"Hey Joy, wait up."

She turned and waited for him to catch up. When he was standing in front of her she said, "Make it quick, Lance. I have a ton on my plate today."

"What happened in there? I've never seen you so frazzled."

Feeling foolish, she looked down at her feet and then glanced towards the wall behind Lance. She didn't owe him an explanation for her behavior. He wanted her to recuse herself and she did. That's it, end of story.

When Joy didn't respond he asked, "Is there anything I can do to help?"

"Yeah," she said, regaining her voice. "You can stay out of my business." With that she turned and left the building.

2

Jeremiah 29:11

> For I know the thoughts that I think toward you, saith the Lord, thoughts of peace, and not of evil, to give you an expected end.

"I just can't believe that I made a fool of myself like that today." Joy was seated at a table inside of the Hallelujah Cakes and Such Bakery that her mother, Carmella Marshall opened a year ago.

The bakery sold decadent cakes, donuts, brownies and any other sweet treat that Carmella could think of, all freshly baked and served within hours of coming out of the oven. Since firing Joy and sending her back to law school, Carmella had gained ten other employees. Each of her employees loved baking just as much as Carmella did. They had all worked hard to make her growing business a big hit in the neighborhood.

Carmella handed her daughter a warm wheat donut with a cold glass of milk as she sat back down at the table with her. "You always let bitterness get the best of you where your father is concerned."

Joy dunked her donut in her milk and then took a bite. "It just makes me so mad that he gets away with everything."

"You let God deal with your father. You need to concern yourself with finding a husband and getting me a few grandchildren."

Coughing loudly, Joy almost hacked her delicious donut back up. She was finished with college, had been working in her field for almost two years now, and making strides as a prosecutor, but her mother's favorite question was still, 'when are you going to get married so you can give me some grandchildren?' But Joy wasn't even entertaining the thought of dating. Men simply weren't on her radar… they had been at one time. Joy had been engaged to be married five years ago. But after her father showed his true colors, Joy didn't know how she could ever trust another man. So she'd called off her wedding and hadn't so much as been on another date since. "Not interested, Mom."

"If you say so," Carmella said while giving her daughter the look of a doubting Thomas.

"What's that look supposed to mean?"

"I'm not saying anything." Carmella held her lips together and locked them with an imaginary key.

Joy could play that game, too. She put her hand up to her mother's mouth and unlocked her lips. "Spill it."

"Well, if I was going to say something, I'd probably mention that defense lawyer you mention every time you have a case against him. And if I had to guess, I'd say you're probably more upset about not being able to spar with that Lance Bryant, than you are about what happened with your dad."

"Mom." Joy's mouth hung open. "Why would you even say something like that? I have no interest in Lance or any other man, for that matter."

Carmella held her hands up. "Hey, I'm just saying."

"Mom, you have to stop this. Just because you found love again with Ramsey, doesn't mean that everyone wants to get married."

Just as Carmella opened her mouth to respond to her daughter, the door swung open. Carmella looked toward the checkout counter to make sure that Sylvia, her part-time afternoon clerk was standing behind the counter, prepared to serve the new arrival.

"What is she doing here?"

At the venom in her daughter's voice, Carmella swung her head back towards the door. "Dear Lord, and all the disciples except Judas,

109

give me strength," was all Carmella could say as Jasmine Walker strutted over to their table like she had stock in the place, and was about ready to demand that they get back to work, so they could make her money grow. Five years ago, Carmella had beat this woman like she'd stolen something, because she had... she'd stolen Carmella's husband. Most days, Carmella was over it, and had no desire to fight over her ex-husband, especially since she had now been married to her wonderful new husband for the past two years. But Jasmine might not want to test her.

"I knew you'd be here," Jasmine said as she walked over to the table, glaring and waving her finger at Joy. "I need to talk to you."

"And people in Hell need ice water, but from what I hear, they're still thirsty." Joy wasn't about to waste another second of her life on a scallywag like Jasmine. The woman had befriended her, just so she could get her hooks into her father. Joy now questioned the motives of anyone who tried to befriend her. She had become closed off and unapproachable and Joy blamed the woman standing in front of her for that.

"Who do you think you are?" Jasmine demanded. "I'm tired of you treating Nelson like he's some sort of pariah. He is your father and he deserves respect."

When Joy didn't respond, but rather sat there staring at Jasmine as if she was two seconds away from going to jail for assault, Jasmine ignored the warning signs and continued on. "Fine, if you want to continue disrespecting your father like a two year old, that's your problem. But what you won't ever do again is disrespect him in his own courtroom. Because if you try to get him kicked off of one of his cases again, I'll file so many complaints against you that you'll be begging for traffic court cases by the time I'm done with you."

"Don't you come in here threatening my daughter. Haven't you already done enough to this family?" Carmella's blood was boiling as she popped out of her seat and got in Jasmine's face.

Jasmine backed up a bit. "If you touch me, I'll have you arrested."

Joy stood and grabbed her mother's arm, pulling her back into her seat. "I got this, Mama... wouldn't want you to break a nail on this unworthy piece of trash."

"Call me all the names you want, Joy. But I'm not playing with you. Nelson has lost a lot of money behind the outrageous alimony and child support your mother demanded of him, so I'm not going to stand by and let you cause him to lose another dime. Not now that he is finally through with alimony and child support."

The alimony had stopped three years ago, when Carmella married Ramsey, the love of her life. But she had received child support for Dontae until six months ago, when Dontae graduated college and got drafted into the NFL.

"I know you don't want another beat down, so what on earth could have possessed you to come to my mother's place of business and bother us?" Joy asked as she stepped in front of Carmella. Her mother had rededicated her life to Christ since she'd given Jasmine the beat down she deserved, but by the look on her mother's face, Joy wasn't so sure that Carmella Marshall-Thomas wouldn't be willing to go a few more rounds.

Jasmine swung her Gucci bag onto her shoulder, and put her hand on her hip as she told Joy. "I just don't like the way you've been treating your father."

"What were you doing in the courtroom, anyway? Did he call you for moral support or something?"

"Nelson and I had lunch plans until you ruined his day with your pettiness. You really need to grow up."

"Get out of here, Jasmine. How I treat Nelson Marshall," she refused to call him her father, "is none of your business."

"I beg to differ. As Nelson's wife, everything that affects him, affects me."

"Well, since you're not his wife, then it's like I said before... none of your business."

Jasmine lifted her ring finger and declared. "We're engaged, and we will soon be married, you can bet on that."

Joy waved a hand in the air, dismissing Jasmine. "Get real. It's been five years. If he hasn't married you by now, I can guarantee you that Mr. Marshall has figured out that he made the biggest mistake of his life when he left his wife for you."

"That's not true," Jasmine yelled and started wagging her bony finger in Carmella's direction. "Nelson has been afraid to get married since your mother stole his money in the divorce. But things are getting back on track for us, so you'll be receiving our wedding invitation soon enough."

"Don't bother, I already have enough trash to throw away," Joy said with a smirk on her face.

Another customer walked into the bakery, glanced over at the three women and then hesitated for a moment, as if she was unsure if she'd entered a safe environment.

Carmella waved the woman in. "Come on in, Betty, Sylvia has your order packed and waiting for you at the register."

"Oh, okay," the woman said, but still appeared nervous as she headed towards the checkout counter.

Jasmine opened her mouth to say something else, but Carmella shushed her. Betty paid for her baked goods and then rushed out the door as fast as she could. Once her customer had left, Carmella went to the door, opened it and pointed toward the cool outside air. "Get out. And please refrain from bringing your drama to my place of business in the future."

Jasmine rocked her hips as she strutted towards the door. "Do you think I keep a figure like this by hanging out in donut shops?"

Carmella wanted to yell at her to get it right. She didn't own a donut shop. Her bakery was high-end and supplied its customers with all sorts of tasty treats. But she didn't want to waste any more lung activity on her. She was too busy silently praying for the Lord to stop her from acting on her fleshly desires—hitting Jasmine until blood gushed out of her head.

"Leave my man alone," was Jasmine's finally parting shot as she left the building.

Carmella closed the door behind her and exhaled. "Whew, I barely passed that test. I need to turn on my praise music and get my mind right after dealing with that woman." Carmella walked behind the counter, and switched on her CD player. Kirk Franklin's *Smile* was playing. Carmella popped her fingers and danced back to the table where she had been sitting with her daughter.

Joy looked despondent as she said, "See that's the difference between you and me. I've been so angry about the whole situation that I couldn't praise God if I wanted to."

Carmella gently put her hand on her daughter's shoulder. "Honey, I know that things didn't turn out the way you dreamed they would. But God didn't do this to us. Nelson chose to leave of his own free will. And you know what?"

"What?" Joy reluctantly asked.

"I spent a lot of time in prayer asking God to give me the kind of heart that forgives. And one day, as I was praising the Lord, I realized that I wasn't angry with Nelson anymore."

"How long did it take you to get to that point?"

Carmella answered honestly. "About two and a half years. Once I freed myself from the bondage of unforgiveness the situation with your father had put me in, I was then free to marry Ramsey."

"But Ramsey would have married you much sooner than that, Mom. I talked to him... he was ready from day one."

"Yeah, but I didn't want to bring bitterness into our marriage. That wouldn't have been fair to him. I love Ramsey too much for that."

Joy nodded as she put her hand to her heart. "I'm happy for you and Ramsey, Mom. I really am. But I don't think I'll ever find love again. I know you think that I'm just bitter, and I can admit that I am. I don't know how to get past this barrier that has me so full of hate."

"Can you take some advice from your old mom?"

Joy grinned. "Of course I can. You know I value your opinion."

"Start praying again. Talk to God about how you're feeling and what's troubling you. And in the midst of all of that, you'll begin to sing a new song of praise... I guarantee it."

Joy shook her head. "If I tried talking to God it would probably come out as a bunch of angry questions."

"And that would be a good start," Carmella told her daughter.

"Mom, come on. All I heard since I was a child was how God was sovereign. He could do what he wanted to do, and we couldn't question Him about any of it."

"Oh really," Carmella said as she leaned back and studied her child. "So do you think that Daniel never had a question for God when he was thrown into the lion's den, or the three Hebrew boys when they were thrown into the fiery furnace? What about King David, when he and his men came back from battle and discovered that their families had been captured and taken from them? How about Apostles Peter and Paul… all that time they spent in service to God and what was the thanks they got for it? Prison and death. Do you think they never questioned God?"

Joy raised a hand. "Okay Mom, I get your point. Bad things have happened to a great deal of people who have gone on to serve God anyhow."

"That is correct. But what I'm really trying to get you to understand is that we are all human. Sometimes we question the wisdom of God for allowing certain things to occur, because we can't see the future and we don't always understand that better days are ahead. So, if your prayers start off as questions to God, go ahead. Asking those questions might just be the loudest praise song you'll ever sing. As far as I'm concerned, it's just praise in disguise."

"How can my questioning God be considered praise?" Joy was confused about the concept.

"Going to God in the first place, is your acknowledgment of who He is in your life. So go on and ask your questions… praise Him in disguise, and see if you won't get your answers."

Joy kissed her mother on the cheek and stood. "I've got to get back to work. Next time I stop in for lunch, at least have a turkey sandwich or something in this place."

"This is a bakery, Joy. You'll have to bring your own sandwiches and bring one for your mother, also."

As Joy headed towards the door *Are You Listening* began playing. Joy put her hand on the doorknob, but didn't move. Carmella could tell the words of that song were affecting her. Numerous big name gospel singers were involved in the album that Kirk Franklin had produced for Haiti. None of the singers mattered at that moment, only the words.

Paraphrasing the words, Carmella told her daughter, "Yes, Joy, God is listening, talk to Him, because He feels your pain."

3

Psalm 13: 1-2

How long wilt thou forget me, O Lord? For ever? How long wilt thou hide thy face from me? How long shall I take counsel in my soul, having sorrow in my heart daily? How long shall mine enemy be exalted over me?

When Carmella arrived home that night, Ramsey was on the phone with Dontae. Carmella felt a twinge of jealousy as she listened to her husband talk with her son as if they were the best of friends. Oh, she was thrilled that both her kids were over the moon about Ramsey; that made her decision to remarry a whole lot easier. She wanted her son to feel like he could come to her with anything. But she realized his need for a father figure and tried to calm her jealous heart. She sat down on the sofa, picked up the remote and turned the television to the evening news.

"I got you, man, don't even worry about it," Ramsey said as he and Dontae ended the call.

"What did Dontae want?" Carmella muted the television as Ramsey joined her on the sofa.

"Do you normally greet your man with questions or a kiss after a long day of work?"

She smiled. Ramsey was a wonderful husband… and the fact that he was so into her, didn't hurt matters one bit. Carmella threw her arms around him and lovingly kissed him. But as soon as they parted, she asked again, "What did Dontae want?"

Ramsey placed a kiss on her forehead. "He got us a box for his game against the Panthers and he made me promise that all of us would be there."

"But how can you make that promise? Only Joy, Renee and Ronny still live in North Carolina."

"Raven and Ramsey Jr. are only a plane ride away, but you are right about RaShan, he's still on his mission trip to Africa, so he won't be able to attend," Ramsey conceded.

All of Ramsey's children's names began with an 'R'. If that didn't signify just how much love was going on between him and his first wife, Carmella didn't know what would. Even though Carmella wished she had never let Ramsey go in the first place after having been high school sweethearts, she was still thankful that Ramsey's first wife had adored him. And she understood that a small part of Ramsey would always belong to his deceased wife.

Carmella didn't mind. Ramsey was able to love her and give his heart without worrying about what Carmella might do to him, because of the love relationship he had already experienced. Carmella, on the other hand, still dealt with insecurity issues because of the way Nelson had discarded her and she suspected that she would have those issues for some time to come. But Ramsey was patient with her. He recognized the baggage that Carmella brought into the marriage, so he was careful not to do things that stoked her insecurities like sneaking around or keeping secrets and Carmella was grateful for that. The Lord knew just what she needed in a forever partner since her first marriage had ended so horribly.

"It's important to Dontae that we all come to his game. He plans to treat us like royalty with our own box where we can watch the game and eat to our hearts' content."

"You did tell that boy not to order alcohol for us, right?" Carmella knew her son. He was in his partying stage and she wasn't about to put up with his shenanigans.

"He knows." Ramsey lifted Carmella's hands and held onto them as he added, "But hon, we need to talk, because there's something else you need to know."

His comment worried her, but it wasn't the kind of I'm-leaving-you-for-my-twenty-three-year-old-girlfriend worry that she had when Nelson wanted to talk. Her worry was that Dontae might have gotten himself into some other trouble, like the time he'd gotten arrested for busting out Jasmine's car windows or the time he'd been arrested for drunk driving two years ago, when he and his fellow college football players were out celebrating a win.

"He's not in any trouble, is he?"

Ramsey shook his head. "No, Carmella. It's nothing like that. This is good news. Dontae wants to introduce us to a lady friend of his."

Carmella's eyes got big. "My baby is serious about someone?"

Nodding, Ramsey said, "I think he is. And he's not your baby anymore. Dontae is a grown man and you're going to have to accept that."

"Grown man?" She rolled her eyes at that comment. "He's twenty-two, Ramsey. What boy do you know that is fully grown at twenty-two and able to make a decision about getting serious with a woman?"

"I was," Ramsey said with a hint of sadness in his eyes.

"Aw honey," Carmella said as she gently put her hand on Ramsey's face. "I'm sorry that things ended the way they did with your first marriage."

"Before you came along, I didn't think I would ever be happy again. I'm thankful that God reconnected us."

"So am I." They kissed again.

Then Ramsey said, "One more thing. And I need you to take a deep breath."

She did.

"Dontae wants Nelson to come to the game that night, also. And he really needs you to be okay with that."

Carmella took another deep breath. "Whew," she said as she fanned her face. "I didn't expect that. But then again, I guess I should have." She took another deep breath, calming herself. "Okay, if that's what Dontae wants, then I'll find a way to be all right with it."

"I'm anxious to meet this girl who has Dontae all tied up in knots," Ramsey said, trying to get the conversation away from Nelson.

"She better treat him right, that's all I have to say."

Ramsey shook a finger at her. "Carmella, be nice to this girl. It's important to Dontae."

Carmella lifted her hands. "Hey, as long as she knows how special Dontae is, she'll have no problems with me... what's her name?" Carmella asked, but then something on the television caught her eye. She picked up the remote and turned up the volume. Nelson was on the news, but he was in handcuffs.

"What's this about?" Ramsey asked as he turned his face toward the television.

They sat there listening as a newscaster reported that Nelson had just been arrested on charges of accepting bribes on some of the court cases he handled.

"What the devil?" Carmella said as her mouth hung open. Joy and Dontae had a hard enough time dealing with the demise of their parents' twenty-five-year marriage. How on earth would they deal with having a father in prison?

***

Joy was rubbing her hands together and inwardly dancing like no one was watching. Oh how the mighty have fallen, were the words that kept repeating themselves in her head as she rushed into the courtroom for her father's arraignment. Since her father was an elected official, the district attorney's office was bringing out the big guns, but she had begged for the second chair spot, and now she was running into the courtroom, anxious to see her father squirm.

But once again Joy's day was ruined by Lance Bryant. Evidently her father had hired Lance. The moment she walked into the courtroom, Lance and her father started whispering. When the judge took his seat and the arraignment began, Lance had the doggone nerve to say, "Judge Blake, I think we need to do a little house cleaning before we can begin this morning."

"What type of house cleaning?" Judge Blake asked.

Lance pointed towards the prosecution table. "Ms. Marshall is my client's daughter and we believe that she needs to recuse herself from this case."

"Recuse myself?" Joy said as if she'd never heard of the concept.

Lance wasn't above reminding her, however. He looked her way and said, "You do understand why you would need to do that, don't you? For the same reason you wanted my client to recuse himself... the relationship the two of you share as father and daughter presents a problem for the court."

"I am more than capable of doing my job. It doesn't matter who the defendant is. I can prosecute him just as well as I could any other criminal," Joy said emphatically.

Lance turned back to Judge Blake. "Assistant DA Joy Marshall has very strong feelings against her father since he divorced her mother. Therefore, we do not believe that she will be able to handle this case objectively. As a matter-of-fact, we don't understand why the DA's office would even allow a daughter to prosecute her own father."

I begged them for the second chair, that's why, Joy wanted to shout at Lance.

Assistant District Attorney Markus Gavin spoke up. "I am the first chair on this case, and I can get another attorney for my second chair, if that will solve the problem."

"No, Markus." Joy shook her head.

Markus turned to Joy. The look on his face was not sympathetic. "They're right, Joy. I never should have given you the second chair on this case. Let's just make this go away so we can get on with the case, okay?"

Joy wanted to object, throw herself on the mercy of the court... something... anything. But in the end, she knew she wasn't going to win the argument. So she yielded to the court. She caught the smirk on Lance's face, as if he thought he'd won against her again. She wanted to jump across the prosecution table and wipe that smirk off of his face.

After bail was set, Joy was still fuming, so before leaving the courtroom, she pulled up beside Lance, touched his arm to get his attention. When he turned toward her, she said, "I need to speak with you for a moment."

Lance turned to his client for approval. Nelson said, "Go ahead, I'll meet you in your office in about an hour." Then Nelson looked toward Joy and nodded. "Good to see you this morning, Joy."

"It wouldn't have been good for you if your lawyer hadn't had me thrown off the case. Are you afraid of your own daughter? Is that what this is about?" Joy fired back.

"I just didn't want you mixed up in this mess. I've damaged our relationship enough. I don't want one more thing to come between us."

"That's real sweet of you, Daddy dearest. But you can save it. I don't have any bail money for you."

"He already has his bail covered, but thanks for thinking about my client," Lance said as the guards took Nelson away.

"Don't try to be cute." Joy turned and stalked off. But when she noticed Lance wasn't following, she swung back around and said, "Are you coming?"

He pointed at his chest as if to ask, "Who, me?"

"Who else?" The man infuriated her. He acted all innocent, when he knew exactly what he was doing to her. Well, Joy wasn't putting up with his games anymore and she was going to let him have it. They made their way to an empty office on the same floor as the courtroom. The moment they walked in and Joy shut the door behind them, she got in his face. "Just what is your problem?"

"Wait a minute." Lance waved his hands as if waving a white flag. "Where's all this hostility coming from?"

"You know exactly where it's coming from. You keep getting me thrown off my cases. What's that about, huh?"

"Hey, you're the one who came into the courtroom the other day with guns blazing, trying to get your father thrown off a case. It just so happens that my client preferred your dad."

Joy wasn't listening to him. "And then you and my dad get me thrown off of a case I had to beg just to be allowed to sit second chair on."

"You had no business asking for this case in the first place. You know good and well that there is a conflict of interest here." Lance was not backing down.

"I also know that this is going to be a big deal case, and I could have used it as an opportunity for advancement, but you've ruined that for me now."

Lance stepped back and leaned against the door as he studied Joy without saying anything.

"What?" Joy said when Lance kept staring at her.

"I'm just wondering if the beautiful woman I spend my free time fantasizing about is truly as cold hearted as she seems."

Did he just say that he's been fantasizing about me? What was she supposed to say to that? Joy had no idea, so she chose to focus on the 'cold hearted' part of his statement. She folded her arms across her chest and said, "You stand by and watch your father try to destroy your mother, after he leaves her for your best friend and then come back and see me if your heart hasn't turned a little cold. I'd love to know how you do it."

He was staring at her without saying anything again.

"What's wrong with you? Say something, already."

"If you want to know what I'm thinking, I'll tell you." He pushed off from the door and sauntered toward her, prompting her to back further into the room. But he kept moving closer. "I'm glad that you've been recused from this case. Matter-of-fact, I'm going to ask that you be recused from all of my cases going forward."

He was standing so close to her that she could feel the heat pulsating off of him. Her voice got caught in her throat as she lifted her head, stared straight at those baby brown eyes of his and said, "I see no reason why I shouldn't go up against you on another case."

He lowered his head, and with their lips just inches apart he said, "I've got a reason for you." And then Lance dipped down, their lips met and he got acquainted with the taste of her mouth.

When the kiss was over, the fire lingered, and Lance told her, "I wouldn't be able to do that if we were going up against each other on another case."

Joy couldn't think. Words were swimming around her head, but they weren't making sense. Her feelings were jumbled. She wanted to stepped away from Lance and give him a good dressing down for putting his soft, luscious lips on hers. But before she could make up her mind what she needed to do, the door to the small room opened and her boss, the district attorney peeked his head in. "I'd like to speak to you when you get a moment, Joy," he said without acknowledging the fact that she had practically been caught with lips locked with the enemy.

But Joy saw it in his eyes, and knew that the meeting she was about to have with the District Attorney would be nothing like the day he shook her hand, telling her she had a bright future with the department and welcomed her aboard.

4

Psalm 13:3-4

Consider and hear me, O Lord my God: lighten mine eyes, lest I sleep the sleep of death; Lest mine enemy say, I have prevailed against him; and those that trouble me rejoice when I am moved.

"I am so sick of this, Mom. I'm not just whining either. Some days I feel like I can't win for losing so I might as well just give up," Joy declared.

"It's not that bad, Joy. Please calm down," Carmella said as she sat in her kitchen with Joy.

"Not that bad? Mom, my boss just wrote me up. He said that my vendetta against Dad is clouding my judgment and making the office look bad."

Carmella handed her daughter a cup of hot chocolate. "So you just need to do your job and stop worrying about Nelson."

Joy rolled her eyes and then ran her hands down her face. "You act as if I want to feel this way. I can't help it, Mom. Just thinking of Dad and everything he did to us makes me see red. And now I'm going to lose my job."

"Stop being so dramatic, Joy. You are a good lawyer, so I doubt you'll lose your job over this. Just be careful and stop this vendetta you have against your father."

"I just get so angry every time I think about what he did to us."

Carmella put her hand over Joy's hand. "The divorce was hard for all of us. But I truly think you fared the worst in all of it. You were so busy taking care of me after I fell apart that you didn't have time to grieve or to deal with the loss of your hero."

Joy scoffed at that. "Some hero... the man is a felon."

"Your dad has done a lot of things, but I don't know if I believe he would take bribes. Nelson has too much respect for the law to do something like that."

Joy shook her head. "I don't understand you, Mom. The man left you for another woman and you are still defending him."

"After being married to someone as long as I was married to your father, I kind of think I know him a little bit."

"You didn't know that he was a cheater." When Joy saw the pained expression on her mother's face, she quickly said, "I shouldn't have said that. I'm sorry, Mom."

Carmella waved Joy's concern away. "Your father lost his way. I know that. But I once knew a man who was gentle and kind, and he loved God as much as I do. Now I don't know what happened to turn Nelson away from God, but I don't believe that he's gone so far that God can't snatch him back. That's why I'm still praying for his soul. So, I don't want you to give up on your father. Okay?"

Her mother was right. Her dad had been her hero. She had been a daddy's girl from the minute she was pushed out of the womb. Everything she did was about making her father proud. But he'd crushed her heart and spirit, and now Joy was still trying to put the pieces back together again. "I don't know if I can promise that, Mom. I think I've pretty much written him off. I'm even anxious to attend his sentencing."

"I hope you don't mean that, Joy. Nelson may have done a lot of wrong, but he loves you."

Unyielding, Joy said, "I don't trust him… and I think he's as guilty as sin."

"Have you done what I asked you to do yet?"

Joy wracked her brain, but couldn't come up with anything that her mom had asked her to do. When Carmella first started her business, Joy had been assigned as the go-get-it girl. Her mother would need flour or cream cheese or baking pans and Joy would run to the store and go get the stuff. But she hadn't been called on to do any of that in a long while. "I don't recall that you asked me to do anything."

"Joy, don't you remember that I asked you to start talking to God about some of the things that have been bothering you?"

"Oh... yeah, I remember you saying that asking questions of God might be the loudest praise song I've ever sung. And believe me, Mom, your words touched me. But I still don't see what good talking to God is going to do at this point in my life."

"Hold that thought," Carmella said as she got down from her kitchen stool and ran upstairs toward her bedroom. When she returned she was carrying a multi-colored journal. She handed the journal to Joy.

Joy looked at it. Three dancing women paraded about at the bottom of the front cover. The words, *When the Praises go up, the Blessings rain down*! were plastered at the top of the cover. "I just told you that I didn't want to talk to God. And now you want me to write to Him? I don't get it."

"You'll get it if you give it a try. I just simply want you to jot down how you're feeling. Tell God what hurts and why you are still so angry with your dad and with Him, for that matter. But then I also want you to take the time to tell God when something happens that makes you smile." Carmella stopped talking, took a deep breath and then continued. "What I'm hoping you'll discover from your self-examination, is that life really isn't that bad. And that God has given you plenty of good days."

"My life is going just fine, Mom. You act as if I need to be placed on suicide watch or something." Joy didn't understand why her mother was always harping on her about this. She had done pretty well for herself... hadn't she gone back to law school and finished, just as her mother had asked her to do? She had even been moving up the ladder in the DA's office—that is, until she managed to get her first verbal warning.

"Your professional life is fine, for now. But the God-centered life you used to have is dead, and I'm just trying to help you resurrect it." Carmella pointed at the journal. "Will you do this for me? I promise you, if you give it a try, God will show up for you. And your eyes will begin to open to other possibilities as well... like the possibility of a loving relationship, maybe even with Lance Bryant. I mean, the man did kiss you today, right?"

Joy blushed. She couldn't believe that she had opened her mouth and told her mother about kissing a man while she was supposed to be working. "Why do I tell you all of my business?" There was a joking tone to Joy's voice.

But there was no laughter in Carmella's voice as she answered, "I know exactly why you tell me everything... I'm the only one you trust."

Joy opened her mouth to deny that, but she couldn't think of anyone else that she had willingly let into her world. So she closed her mouth and let her mother finish the indictment.

"You refuse to make friends because of the way Jasmine betrayed you. You refuse to date or give love a try, because of the way your father treated me." Carmella put her arms around Joy, hugged her real tight as she added, "You're a grown woman, living on your own these days, but when I look at you I am reminded of that seven-year-old-girl who ran in the house after school one day and declared that she was never leaving the house again because the kids at school were too mean."

"Those kids were mean," Joy declared.

"Yeah, but you got over it. You kept going back to school and day by day, things got better for you. This is the same thing, Joy. And if you need to dig deep to find some strength from that seven year old you used to be, then that's what I need you to do."

That incident at school occurred a little over twenty years ago, but Joy still remembered how she'd run into the house and tried to hide under the covers on her bed. Her mother had come into the room, sat down on her bed and listened as Joy had cried and confessed to having a hard time in her new school. Carmella's ready answer had been prayer. Joy had gotten down on her knees that afternoon and prayed for all the mean girls. When she went back to school and the girls were still mean to her, Joy told her mother that prayer didn't work. But Carmella told her that she needed to keep on praying. Within a couple of weeks, the meanest girl, Sally something-or-other had gotten sick and was out of school for two weeks. Joy had asked her mom to take her to Sally's house so she could pray with the girl. They did that and when Sally came back to school, she told everyone how nice Joy had been to her... problem solved.

"I just don't know if a seven year old's answers will work for my current problems."

"You'll never know, unless you give it a try. Just consider it your own little praise journal," Carmella told her.

Joy looked down at the journal in her hand and read the words on the cover again, *When the Praises go up, the Blessings rain down*! She didn't know about that, but maybe she did need a new outlet for telling all her business. Since she didn't have any friends outside of her mother, maybe this journal thing would work for her. "Okay, I'll do it."

***

When Joy arrived at work the next day, she went straight to Markus Gavin's office. Since Markus was the senior ADA, he had the ear of the District Attorney and she was quite sure that Markus was upset after she'd been thrown off her father's case. Markus probably felt that she'd made him look bad, so he'd ratted her out to the DA. When her boss first approached her about his concerns, Joy had been angry with Markus, but after hearing Lance, the DA and her mother tell her that she had no business on the case in the first place, she realized that she owed Markus an apology.

She knocked on his office door. Joy didn't have an office, just a cubicle, but she had no doubt that she would one day move up to her own office also... if she could get her act together as the DA told her to do.

"Come in," Markus said from inside the office.

Joy opened the door and stepped inside.

Markus immediately lifted a hand, halting her. "I don't want to hear it. You deserve whatever you got from the DA."

"Hey, I came in here to apologize to you, but if you don't want to hear it, fine. I'll just go back to my cubicle and get to work."

Markus leaned back in his seat, studying Joy. "You must have gotten chewed out pretty bad to be in here begging my pardon."

Markus was a good ADA, but he was a real jerk. "Nobody chewed me out." *Okay, she was lying about that.* "But after careful consideration, I realized that I shouldn't have been so anxious to be a part of a case against my father in the first place."

"Didn't you used to work in his office?"

Joy nodded. "While I was in law school."

"Did you notice any improprieties?"

"Everything was handled above board when I worked there. Never once heard anyone claim that their case had been fixed."

"Then why do you believe he's guilty?" Markus asked, still studying her.

Even as she said, "I have my reasons," Joy heard her mother declaring that her father wasn't guilty of the crime. And for one brief moment she felt ashamed that she wasn't even willing to give her own father the benefit of the doubt.

"Anyway, I just wanted to apologize." Joy rushed out of Markus' office and made her way back to her cubicle. She had been so sure that her father was guilty the day before, so why was she letting her mother's words get into her head and cause her to second guess herself? And why was Lance Bryant leaning against her cubicle, staring at her as if she was a strawberry that had been double dipped in chocolate. "What are you doing here?" she asked as she strode past him into her cubicle.

Lance followed her and sat down in the chair on the side of her desk. "I wanted to make sure you were all right."

Joy leaned over and lowered her voice as she said, "It wasn't good enough to get me thrown off of my father's case. I guess now you want to get me fired as well, huh?"

"Are you kidding? If I got you fired, your father would fire me. And plus, I doubt if you'd ever agree to have dinner with me if I got you fired," Lance said with a sheepish look on his face.

Joy wasn't in a playing mood. "What do you want, Lance?"

"Okay well, we can talk about the date later."

"I'm not going out on a date with you. You're defending my father and this office is prosecuting him." Lance was fine… she didn't know too many women who wouldn't be drooling over him, and some would ask him out themselves. But Joy wasn't about to get caught up in some man who would probably be cheating on her two seconds after she said, 'I do'.

"As I said, we can save the date for later," Lance persisted. "But I do need help with your father's case."

Joy forgot to whisper as she exploded. "Is this a joke? Are you and my father trying to play a little game of entrapment?"

Lance started waving his hands. "No Joy, you've got it all wrong. I wouldn't do that to you. I just think the DA's office is making a big mistake by prosecuting this case and I thought you'd like to do something about it."

"What would ever make you think a thing like that?" Lance had called her cold-hearted, but he didn't know the half of it. Her heart had iced over where her father was concerned.

"Nelson is your father, Joy," Lance said, as if reminding her of a neglected fact. "I would think that fact alone would at least earn him the benefit of the doubt."

"Well you thought wrong. This office didn't bring a frivolous case against your client. But if you believe so much in my father, then I suggest you prove us wrong, rather than asking me to do your job for you."

"You're wrong, Joy. And you owe your father more loyalty than this." Lance stood and walked out of her cubicle without so much as a glance backward.

Guess he no longer wants that date. Joy tried to pretend that Lance's dismissal didn't bother her, but in truth, it bothered her that anyone would try to act as if it was somehow her fault that her father might be a criminal. It was that *might* word that lingered in her brain. Joy was ready to pronounce her father guilty, but something kept nagging at her. She couldn't figure out what it was, but knew that she had missed something. When Joy turned her attention to her desk, she found herself staring at the journal her mother had given her. She was conflicted, so she decided to take the advice of the only person she trusted.

She opened the journal. At the top of the page a scripture from Proverbs 3:5, *Trust in the Lord with all thine heart; and lean not unto thine own understanding.* After reading those words, Joy wasn't just conflicted, she was angry. She wrote:

I used to trust that You could do anything. But how can I trust You anymore when You allowed my father to cheat on my mother and desert his family? And now I'm supposed to feel bad about thinking my father is guilty when he's the one who should be ashamed of himself.

And why, oh why did you send Lance Bryant my way? That man is hot. He's too fine to resist.

Did she really just say that while writing in her journal to God? And why was she writing to God in the first place? It wasn't as if He was listening to her anyway. Her mother was the only one who still believed in fairy tales these days. Joy closed the journal and got back to the real world.

5

Three days had passed since Joy's first praise journal entry. In that time another person had come forward, claiming that he had paid her father for a not-guilty verdict. The only problem with this guy's claim was that he was behind bars while making it. The DA's office was trying to figure out if Nelson took the money and just didn't return the favor, or if the claim was false altogether. Since she'd worked for her father several years back, everyone was looking to her to provide answers. But what could she tell them? She never noticed any illegal activity going on when she worked in her father's office, but she didn't know the Nelson Marshall who'd recently been arrested.

At home that night, Joy opened the journal and began to write about how hurt she had been to find out that her father was no longer her hero. She no longer believed in fairy tales and happily ever after and Joy not only blamed her dad for that—she blamed God, also. And every word she wrote in that journal let the Lord know just how she felt. After she had written five letting-God-know-just-what-she-thought pages, Joy closed her journal and went to bed.

After putting all of her hurts and pains on paper the night before, Joy was feeling pretty stress free as she drove into work the next morning. But when she parked her car, got out and saw Jasmine walking towards her, her stress level crept back up. "What are you doing here? Do I need to get a restraining order against you or what?"

Swinging her red lamb skin Chanel handbag, Jasmine strutted closer. "Why would you want to get a restraining order against your stepmom?"

"You are not my stepmother, my friend or anything else, just stay away from me." Joy tightened her grip on her briefcase and walked past Jasmine.

"Don't walk away from me, Joy. I wouldn't be here if I didn't need to talk to you." Jasmine caught up with Joy. "Your dad needs you to be a character witness for him."

Joy stopped in her tracks, and just about spit the words, "My dad has no character," in Jasmine's face.

"Why are you so ungrateful? You never wanted for anything, because Nelson did everything for you. Now that he needs you, you're M. I. A."

"Why don't you be a character witness for him, Jasmine? You can go to court and tell the jury just how upstanding and honorable your boyfriend is. Then you can tell them how you pretended to be my friend so you could sleep with my father and steal him away from his family." Joy put her hands on the door to go into the building. She turned back to Jasmine and said, "If you continue to follow me, I'm going to have the security guards arrest you."

As Joy walked into the building, Jasmine held the door open and yelled, "We're going to have you subpoenaed, so you're going to have to testify one way or the other."

It infuriated Joy that Jasmine even had the nerve to come and ask her for anything after all that she had done to her. It had all happened a little over five years ago, but Joy still thought about it as though it had happened only yesterday... she couldn't make herself forget and she certainly couldn't forgive...

"You better be glad we're friends, Jasmine. Because I would have to charge you for making me carry this heavy headboard if we weren't," Joy put the headboard down and massaged her arm.

Jasmine Walker grinned. "You know I appreciate you, girl."

"Well, I would appreciate this mystery man of yours, if he showed up to do the heavy lifting."

Jasmine poked her bottom lip out. "He's at work, Joy. Come on, help me load this stuff on the truck, and I promise I'll make him take everything off the truck."

They picked up the headboard and made their way to the truck. "So, I'm finally going to meet this mystery man who swept you off your feet, but never bothered to pick you up for dates." Joy rolled her eyes.

"I truly don't understand why you've kept on seeing him. For as long as I've known you, you've never let a guy treat you so cavalierly."

They placed the headboard in the truck, and then Jasmine said, "Well, he's made up for it now, hasn't he?"

"I don't know, Jasmine... renting is temporary. If he were really serious, he would have bought the house and bought a ring."

Jasmine put her arm around Joy's shoulder as they walked back into the house to get the rest of her things. "You'll see, Joy Marshall, my man loves me, and he's going to prove it to the world."

They packed all of Jasmine's bedroom furniture in the U-Haul truck, Jasmine jumped behind the wheel and Joy got in on the passenger's side. As they drove down the highway toward Jasmine's new home.

"We're here." Jasmine pulled the U-Haul truck into the driveway of a spacious two-story home.

Joy's eyes widened as she looked at the house. From the looks of the outer structure, Joy figured the house had to be at least four thousand square feet. "Are you sharing this place with another couple or something?"

Jasmine laughed. She then shook her head. "No, he likes to entertain, so we needed enough room to be able to host parties."

"You sound like my mother. She's always hosting one party or another for my dad. You need to go take some cooking lessons from her so you can really do your parties up right," Joy suggested.

"Girl, please, I don't plan to do any cooking. That's what caterers are for," Jasmine opened the truck door and got out. Joy opened her door and followed Jasmine into the house.

Standing in the foyer, Joy was once again struck by the expansiveness of the house. The white marble floors, spiral staircase and the upstairs balcony that overlooked the foyer—all gave the house a feel of importance, as if someone with stature and influence lived there. "How can your guy afford to rent a house like this?" She knew it was rude to ask, but the question was out of her mouth before she could stop herself.

"Girl, just help me get those boxes out of the truck and stop being so nosey," Jasmine said with a good-natured grin on her face.

"I just can't believe this place, Jasmine. Troy and I sure can't afford anything like this."

They headed back out to the truck. "Once the two of you put your money together," Jasmine said, "I'm sure you'll be able to afford something nice, so don't sweat it, Joy."

"Please. After we get married, we'll probably spend the next five to ten years paying off our student loans. After that, we'll be able to start saving for a house like this."

Jasmine pulled a box out of the back of the truck. "I'm trying not to think about my student loans. At least your parents paid most of your tuition. But what I didn't get in financial aid, I had to cover in student loans."

Joy grabbed a box, and as they walked back to the house, she said, "Yeah, just when I started feeling grateful about not having so much debt to pay back after college, I met Troy and it seems like his middle name is debt."

"See, if you would have listened to me, you would have hooked up with an older guy who'd already paid off his debt. That way he would be able to take care of you in style."

They set the boxes down in the foyer and as they turned to go get more, Joy said, "I'm happy with Troy. Besides, my father had a lot of school debt when he married my mom, but they worked together and paid everything off. They're living pretty well now."

Jasmine didn't respond. She grabbed the next box and took it into the house. They followed that same process until all the boxes were unloaded.

Exhausted, they sat down on the floor next to the boxes. Joy said, "I don't think I want to be your friend anymore."

"I understand. I'm so tired; I don't want to move from this spot."

"I'm thirsty," Joy said.

"We have lemonade and iced tea in the fridge."

"I'll take the lemonade."

Jasmine stood. "I'll be right back. Do you need anything else?"

"A pillow. I'm about to crash." Joy pulled out her cell phone. "I'm going to have Troy come pick me up. Your man is taking too long."

"Suit yourself, but he should be here any minute." As if on cue, the doorbell rang. "Can you get that for me, Joy? I'm going to go get our drinks."

"Sure," Joy said. She got up and headed toward the front door. Before she could get to it, the doorbell rang again, and then the person on the outside started pounding on the door. Joy was walking as fast as she could, so whoever was so anxious would have to wait. She was too tired to move any faster.

By the time she got to the door, the doorbell rang for the third time. Joy was tempted to stand there a little longer and let the person on the other side of the door suffer a while longer. But when she looked through the peephole and saw her father, she immediately swung the door open.

As Nelson Marshall stepped into the house, he said, "I lost my key again."

Joy didn't hear him because as he was talking, she asked, "What are you doing here, Dad? Did Mom send you after me or something?"

Nelson swung around to face his daughter. His eyes widened. He stuttered, "Wh-what are y-you doing h-here?"

"I'm helping Jasmine move into her new house," Joy told her father. Then with a look of confusion on her face, she asked, "If you didn't know I was here, why did you come to Jasmine's house?"

Before Nelson could respond, Jasmine walked into the room carrying two glasses of lemonade. She handed one to Joy and then walked over to Nelson, kissed him, and then handed him the other glass. "You're late. What took you so long to get home?"

Nelson stepped back and turned toward his daughter. "I-I can explain."

But Joy was figuring things out all on her own. Jasmine's mystery man was her father, and the two of them had been sneaking around for over a year. "The person you need to explain something to is my mother," Joy declared, storming into the family room and grabbing her purse.

This was too much for Joy. Her father wasn't a cheater. He was a good man who went to work every day and attended church on Sundays with his family. But as she walked back into the entryway and saw the smirk on Jasmine's face, Joy began to believe what her eyes were telling her.

"You did this on purpose," Joy accused Jasmine. "You wanted me to know that my father was cheating on my mother."

Jasmine put her arm around Nelson and said, "It's time you knew the truth."

Nelson stepped away from Jasmine again. "This isn't how I wanted to tell her, Jasmine. You had no right bringing Joy here without letting me know."

Tearfully, Joy said, "What are you doing, Dad? This is going to break Mother's heart."

Nelson tried to put his arm around Joy. She pulled away. "Your mother already knows that I want a divorce. I'm surprised she didn't tell you."

Joy asked, "Why didn't you tell me? I spoke to you last night, but I don't recall you saying anything about divorcing my mother, so you could move in with someone young enough to be your daughter."

"I'm a grown woman," Jasmine said, "and Nelson and I are happy, despite our age difference."

Joy turned her back to Jasmine and held up her hand. "Don't speak to me ever again. I am not interested in anything you have to say." With that, Joy headed for the door.

"Don't go like this, baby-girl," her father said. "I really want to help you understand why I decided to leave your mother."

Joy opened the door and then shot back at her father, "Oh, I know exactly what was on your mind." She walked through the door and slammed it behind her. Joy was so angry that she wanted to hit something. She had looked up to her father almost to the point of worship for as long as she could remember. Nelson Marshall had been a man of integrity... someone she, her brother and her mother could count on.

Tears rolled down Joy's face as she walked away from her father's new home. She heard the door open behind her, but didn't stop or turn around to see who was coming after her. She wanted nothing to do with her so-called best friend or her dishonorable father.

What Jasmine and her father did, just about destroyed her. She'd lost faith and trust in everyone but her mom, and she'd eventually called off her wedding to Troy; a man who'd done nothing but love her. It hadn't been Troy's fault that Joy's father was a cheater. But he and Joy had paid the price for it just the same. Now he wanted a character witness, she'd sooner see him rot in prison.

6

Psalm 30:9-10
What profit is there in my blood, when I go down to the pit? Shall the dust praise thee? Shall it declare thy truth?
Hear, O Lord, and have mercy upon me; Lord, be thou my helper.

Joy tried to go on about her day and ignore Jasmine's comment. But the more she thought about it, the angrier she became. She'd told Lance that she would do nothing to help her father, and now Jasmine had the audacity to come to her office and threaten to have her subpoenaed. By lunch time, Joy decided that she'd had enough. Fuming, she jumped in her car and drove to Lance Bryant's law office.

Stepping out of the car, she checked her appearance in the side view mirror. She loved the way her indigo blue and tan wrap dress with the sash at the waist not only looked professional, but felt feminine on her. He'd always seemed to turn whenever she strutted into court with this number on. She figured Lance would most likely drool all over himself when he saw her, but she couldn't care less. Joy was there to give him a piece of her mind and nothing more.

She'd never been to his law office before, but as she walked in, she found that she was impressed by how spacious and well decorated the waiting area was. Abstract art decorated the walls and dark, comfortably cushioned furniture greeted guests that entered the Bryant and Associates office building.

"May I help you?" A petite, older woman behind the receptionist desk asked.

"I'm here to see Lance Bryant."

"Do you have an appointment?"

"He wanted to talk with me about setting a date," Joy said without feeling the least bit troubled by stretching the truth.

"And your name?" the woman asked as she took off her glasses and picked up the phone.

"Tell him that Joy Marshall is here to see him."

The receptionist turned away from Joy and called Lance. All Joy could hear was the one sided conversation of, "yes", "that's fine", and "will do." She hung up the phone and then told Joy, "Mr. Bryant will be with you momentarily."

Joy sat down on the comfy looking sofa and proceeded to wait about fifteen minutes for Lance Bryant. She was just about to get up and leave his office, when he finally showed his face. Standing up, Joy told him, "I didn't make you wait this long when you brought yourself unannounced to my office."

"That's only because you didn't have a door to hide behind."

"So you admit that you kept me waiting on purpose?" Right hand was on her hip and she was getting ready to let her neck roll.

"I admit no such thing. I've been extremely busy putting out fires lately."

"As long as there are criminals, I'm sure you'll have no shortage of fires to put out."

Lance bowed before her. "I do try to do a good job for my clients who are always innocent until proven guilty."

Joy was enjoying her back and forth spar with Lance. But she was about to bring him down. "I'm sure you know that my father is guilty as sin, especially since another defendant who appeared in his court has come forward and admitted that he also bribed your client."

Glancing around the waiting room, Lance asked, "Would you like to step into my office so we can talk privately?"

Giving him an, I-got-your-number stare down, she said, "Oh, I thought you wanted to hold this little chit-chat in your waiting area. You certainly didn't make any mention of your office until your client's felonious activity came up."

Lance had been enjoying the light banter with Joy, too, but he didn't play when it came to his clients. With a look of seriousness on his face, he said, "If you'd like to discuss my client, I would prefer to do that in my office." He turned and headed towards his office.

Joy followed, but she was a bit taken aback by the fact that Lance had not looked at her with the same hungry eyes... the way he'd been caught looking at her on numerous occasions. He hadn't even noticed her dress—a dress that never failed to rein in compliments.

Lance seemed different towards her... uninterested was the word that came to mind. From the moment she'd gone up against Lance the first time, he had always given her that look. Joy had brushed off all of his advances, because she didn't want to date anyone. But now she wondered why she was so bothered by Lance's apparent lack of interest in her. Wasn't that what she wanted... to be left alone?

"Have a seat," Lance said as he closed the door behind them.

Glancing around his office, Joy was struck by some of the things she saw. He had the normal stuff: desk, chairs, sofa and work table, but on his credenza, there was also a statue of a man on bended knee with his hands steepled.

Noting where Joy was looking, Lance picked up his pint size statue and said, "This is just my little reminder that my clients need more than my skill as an attorney." He set the statue back down and added, "They also need my prayers."

Caught off guard by that comment, Joy couldn't help but say, "I wouldn't have pictured you as a church boy."

"I bet you wouldn't say that to my mama." There was laughter in Lance's voice as he added, "When I was a kid she bullied me unmercifully about going to church—said if I laid my head on her pillows every night, I could at least get up and go to church on Sunday."

Joy and her brother, Dontae had grown up in church, also. Her mother and father encouraged them to get involved at church, but she didn't recall any bullying. "Didn't that make you mad?"

Lance nodded. "I did get upset a time or two when I was a teenager. But I thank God that my parents followed the words in Proverbs where it admonishes parents to *Train up your child in the way he should go, and when he is old he will not depart from it.*"

Joy didn't believe a word he said, and just about accused him of being a liar with the way she asked, "So you're telling me that you never strayed away from God... not even while you were in college?"

Leaning against the credenza with his arms folded across his chest, he smiled at her. "I'd be lying if I told you that."

Joy didn't know how he did it. But standing there smiling, with those dimples dipping into his caramel cheeks, he transformed from a person she wanted to hate, to a man she could see herself loving.

"I strayed away from everything God and my Mama taught me when I was in college," Lance continued, "but after a few hard knocks, I got my head together and went running back to the good Lord."

Joy wasn't planning to run back anytime soon. Her family had fallen apart and God hadn't done anything to stop it from happening. Since she was a little girl, Joy had always believed that God could do anything... change people, make them better. But her father had only gotten worse. How was she ever supposed to trust God with anything after that?

"Joy, are you okay?"

"Huh? Yeah sure, I'm fine."

"Where did you go? You got this faraway look on your face."

Joy rubbed her hand down her face and plastered on a smile. "Your comment caused me to think about something." And then to change the subject, she pointed toward the same credenza, which also held a replica of a boxing ring with two boxing figures who looked beat down, worn out and ready to throw in the towel. "I suppose you're a boxing fan?"

"Not really. I'm more of a football fan."

"Then why do you have this replica of a boxing match in your office? Does this depict any particular boxer?" Joy couldn't help herself, she had gone there to give Lance a piece of her mind, but she had to admit, she was curious about the man.

Lance nodded. "Mohammad Ali is one of the boxers in the ring."

She pointed at the boxing replica and began jumping up and down as if she was on Family Feud and had the twenty thousand dollar answer. "Is it the Rumble in the Jungle?"

With an impressed look on his face, Lance asked, "What you know about the Ali and George Foreman fight?"

"Unlike you, my father is actually a boxing fanatic. When I was a kid, we'd spend Saturday afternoons watching old boxing matches."

"My father is a boxing fan, too. Matter of fact, when I opened my law office, he came to my office and put that boxing ring on my credenza, and then he sat down and reminded me of something that I think about every time I'm about ready to throw in the towel and give up on a case."

"I'm all ears," Joy told him as she waited for him to continue.

Smiling ruefully, Lance said, "I can't let you in on all my secrets."

She turned back towards the boxing match, trying to pull the message out of it. At that moment she realized that if it wasn't the Rumble in the Jungle, then it had to be, "Thrilla-in-Manila, the match between Ali and Joe Frazier." Lance acknowledged that she was right, and then Joy said, "I know what your father told you, because mine told me the same thing years ago."

"I'm all ears," Lance said, mimicking her earlier statement.

"He reminded you about the last seconds in that fight. Joe Frazier's trainer told him to quit, but Frazier said no. Meanwhile Mohammad Ali was on the other side of the ring telling his trainer that he wanted to quit. His trainer hesitated and then Frazier's trainer called off the match, because he was afraid that Frazier might die if he continued. A lot of people think Frazier would have won if his trainer had just waited another second."

"So, what's the moral of the story?" Lance asked, wondering if he was standing in front of a kindred spirit.

"Pay attention to your opponent and never be the first one to blink."

Lance smiled, and then he snuck in a right hook. "I take it that you and your father spent a lot of time together? I was told that the two of you were once very close."

That caught her off guard. Joy hadn't meant to reveal anything of the relationship she once had with her father, but the boxing ring had taken her back... had reminded her of a father who once cared about putting smiles on his children's faces. She was tired of thinking about her father... tired of being reminded of things that no longer mattered.

Joy pulled her purse strap up on her shoulder and said, "Look, I have to get back to work. I just came here to tell you that I am not interested in being a character witness for my father. You see, I don't believe he has any character. So, if you subpoena me, it will be to your client's detriment."

"Your father is very proud of you, Joy. He really wants to make amends for hurting you. I wish you would give him a chance."

Lance looked so sincere that Joy almost thought her decision mattered to him. But he would be disappointed. "That won't be happening any time soon, so I suggest you tell your client and his girlfriend to leave me alone."

Lance reached out and touched Joy's arm. His eyes were full of compassion as he said, "I'm sorry that your father's infidelity hurt you."

At that moment, Joy wanted to lay her head on Lance's shoulder and let the tears fall. During her parents' divorce, her mother had been such a basket case, that Joy had to be strong for her. As the years went by, she became angrier and angrier about the situation, but she had never taken the time to just be sad. Maybe if she would just let a few tears fall, she would be able to move past all the pain.

"Have you ever thought about forgiving your father for his shortcomings?"

He almost had her singing Kumbayah with him. But Joy wasn't falling for it. Lance wanted her on the stand, being a character witness for her father. And there was no way that would ever happen. "Nice try, but I'm no amateur. I've gotten in the heads of my share of witnesses, also. Throw in the towel already, Counselor. You're going to lose this one." With that said, Joy turned and walked out of his office.

***

Lance couldn't throw in the towel. It wasn't in his nature. And he couldn't help but stand there and watch as Joy strutted out of his office. He'd played it cool when he greeted her when she first arrived, but he'd noticed that dress she was wearing and wondered if it was legal for a dress to cling to a woman's body like that. Her curves were in all the right places and if it wasn't for the fact that Lance had been trying to get Joy out of his mind, he probably would have asked her out again.

Joy was one of the finest women he'd seen in a long time, but she was also very damaged. Lance glanced over at the statue on his credenza and he did the only thing he knew to do… he prayed.

7

Psalm 13:5-6

But I have trusted in thy mercy; my heart shall rejoice in thy salvation.

I will sing unto the Lord, because He hath dealt bountifully with me.

They traveled from Raleigh to Charlotte for the football game. Joy arrived at the stadium with Renee and Raven, her stepsisters. The two women were twenty-four and twenty-five, respectively. Joy always enjoyed herself whenever they hung out, but she'd never been able to relax and be comfortable in their presence. When her mother had mentioned Dontae's football game, she made Joy promise to have fun, and that's exactly what she planned to do.

"Renee, girl, you must be trying to catch yourself a baller with that short skirt you're styling tonight," Joy said as she watched her young sister strut her stuff in four-inch heels and a three-inch skirt.

"You better know it," Renee said as she swiveled around so her sisters could check her out. "Dontae better not play me today. We're at the game in style sitting up in these box seats, so he better bring some of his teammates up here after the game."

"And if he does, what are you planning to do with Dontae's friends?" Ramsey asked as he and Carmella appeared in the open doorway.

"Daddy, leave Renee alone. If she wants to snag a rich husband, I say go for it," Raven said. She wasn't as scantily dressed as her sister, but her style was showing through with the cute little silk sundress she sported. No high heels, just flip flops... the two sisters couldn't have been more different in their style of dress.

"That's my baby-girl; I'll never leave her alone. Not even when she's been married for twenty-five years," Ramsey declared.

"Thank God I'm not the baby-girl," Raven said.

"Oh, the same goes for you," Carmella told her jokingly. "I've seen how protective Ramsey is over you girls. So, just make sure you're on your best behavior tonight."

"That includes you, too, Joy." Ramsey hugged her and then added, "I know you don't get out much because you work so hard, so I want you to have fun tonight." He then squinted his eyes and leaned forward until their foreheads were almost touching. "But I'm watching out for you, too."

"Leave these girls alone, Ramsey." Carmella grabbed his arm. "Come with me over to the food table. I want to see how the caterer set up everything. I might be able to get a few pointers from them."

"That's my wife, always thinking about business," Ramsey said as he allowed himself to be pulled away from the girls.

"Hey, I'm just trying to make us millionaires by the time you retire."

"Carmella, it will be another decade before I retire, so I'm going to need you to become a multi-millionaire in that timeframe. After being a principal for all these years, I'm going to need to rest my mind in Hawaii, Germany, France, and London."

"Don't forget about Italy and Paris… that's where I want to go," Carmella reminded him.

"Baby, I would take you around the world and back," Ramsey said just before kissing Carmella.

"Get a room already," Ramsey Jr. said as he and his younger brother, Ronny entered the box.

Ramsey, senior would not be deterred; he held onto Carmella, planted a kiss on her forehead and told the group. "I can kiss my woman anywhere and anytime I feel like it. I keep telling you, boy… that's the privilege of marriage. Get some of that in your life and then come talk to me."

Junior waved away that comment. "Go head on somewhere with that. I'm only twenty-seven," he said while popping his collar. "I'm too young to settle down."

The boys went over to where Joy and their two sisters were seated. "Hey, who invited our parents to the game?" Ronny asked.

"Tell me about it," Joy said. "I'll have to have a talk with Dontae. The next time he wants to hook us up with some box seats… no parents allowed.

The game had begun, but Joy wasn't paying it any attention, because the moment she said, 'no parents allowed' her father and his concubine stepped into the box.

Nelson walked over to Carmella and Ramsey, Jasmine was two steps behind him. There was sadness in Nelson's eyes at he looked at the way Ramsey held onto Carmella. Playing it off, he held out a hand to Ramsey and said, "Thanks for inviting us. I'm thrilled to be able to watch Dontae play ball with all of you."

"We are happy to have you. And more importantly, Dontae will be very happy that you're here," Ramsey told him as he stood about a foot taller than Nelson, in spirit and body.

"Yes, I'm thankful for that," Nelson said.

There was a bit of humbleness to Nelson that Carmella hadn't seen in a long time. She prayed that the Lord was working on his heart. "I'm glad you could join us tonight, Nelson." She looked to Jasmine who was standing behind him, looking everywhere but at them. "I hope you enjoy the game, Jasmine," was all Carmella said to her. She wasn't interested in lying, so she said as little as possible to the woman.

"I'm sure I will," Jasmine said as she grabbed hold of Nelson's hand. "Come on, Nelson. Let's take a seat so we can watch the game."

Nelson let her hand go. As he turned and walked away, he looked like a man who was already in prison, rather than one awaiting trial.

Joy stood up and stomped over to Carmella. "What are they doing here?" She demanded of her mother as she stood in front of her and Ramsey, with her back to her father.

Calmly, Carmella said, "I told you that your brother wanted all the family here tonight."

Crossing her arms over her chest in protest, Joy said, "You didn't tell me that Daddy was included."

"He is part of the family, Joy. And it's important to Dontae to have him here."

Joy couldn't care less how loud she was as she said, "I don't understand you, Mother. Doesn't it bother you that this man—" she swung around to point at her father, when out of the side of her eye she saw Lance entering the box. He was holding the arm of a beautiful Nia Long look alike with the same stylish short cut and voluptuous body that Nia Long is famous for. The fashionista had on a pair of thirteen-hundred dollar Bianca Spikes with the red outer sole by Christian Louboutin. Joy knew how much the shoes cost, because she had been stalking them online, waiting for a pair to show up on eBay so that she would be able to afford them on her Assistant DA salary.

"Thank you for showing me to our box," the fashionista said to Lance as she let go of his arm and strutted into the box and down to the front where she promptly took the front row seat as if this was her world and everyone else was blessed to have her in it. "Who does she think she is?" Joy mumbled, but inwardly she was also asking herself who the woman was to Lance.

"I think that's her," Carmella whispered to Ramsey.

Joy turned back toward them and asked, "You know her?"

"I think she's the woman Dontae has been dating. He wanted all of us to meet her tonight," Carmella said.

"Well, she doesn't seem all that interested in meeting us. The only person she even looked at was Lance Bryant and he isn't even a member of our family."

Carmella's head swiveled toward the handsome Boris Kodjoe-looking man who was standing in the entryway. "Is that the young man you work with?"

"I don't work with him, Mother. He is the defense attorney who is handling Dad's case, remember?"

"I think he's looking over here at you," Carmella said, "Let's go over there so you can introduce me to him."

"I'll pass. I'd rather go talk to the movie star who just walked in." Joy walked over to the mystery lady, curious to discover if she was Dontae's girlfriend or someone Lance was dating.

149

Joy sat down next to the woman and stuck out her hand. "Hi, I'm Joy. So, are you hanging with the family tonight?"

Instead of taking her hand, the woman reached out and hugged Joy. "Oh my goodness, you're just as beautiful as Dontae said."

Taken aback by the affectionate way in which this woman greeted her, Joy leaned away from her a bit as she said, "I'm sorry, but Dontae hasn't told me your name." *Or anything else about you*, Joy wanted to add but didn't. What was her brother up to?

"It's my fault," the woman said, "I should have introduced myself, but I was so anxious to get to my seat and watch Dontae play that I forgot my manners." Now she held out a hand to Joy, "My name is Tory Michaels. Dontae and I are dating."

"So you're the big surprise that Dontae had planned for all of us tonight?" Joy was starting to feel bad about the way she had approached Tory. She obviously was very important to Dontae for him to arrange a party of sorts, just so his family could meet her. Deep down Joy knew that she had been less than charitable towards Tory because Tory walked into the room with her hand on Lance. *But why did that bother her? Was she really falling for Lance Bryant?* No... Lance was the enemy, and he would stay that way if she had anything to say about it.

Dontae had the ball and he was running for a touchdown. So Joy turned her thoughts away from Lance and toward the field. Tory was on her feet, shouting, "Go Dontae, go... show 'em what you're made of."

"He can't hear you all the way up here, Tory," Joy told her.

"Touchdown!" Tory screamed her excitement, then as she tried to calm it down, she sat back down next to Joy. "I just get so excited when I watch him play. My Daddy used to play the game. Actually, the reason Dontae and I met in the first place is because I was loudly cheering his team during one of his first games with the Saints."

"Do you live in Louisiana?"

"Born and raised."

Joy was beginning to like this woman. She seemed interested in Dontae's career and was being supportive. Joy could roll with this...

150

Her brother had someone to share his life with, and she was happy for him. "Come on Tory, let me introduce you to everyone."

The two women stood and Joy began taking Tory around the room, introducing her to everyone. Carmella and Ramsey hugged Tory, Raven asked if she could borrow her shoes, Ronny asked if he could have her number. They all laughed at that, because everyone knew Ronny was just joking. He and Dontae didn't grow up as brothers, but they had quickly formed a bond once Carmella and Ramsey married.

Ramsey Junior was laid back as usual with his one handed salute. But Renee took the cake. She pulled Tory to the side and asked, "I like athletes, too. Can you give me some pointers on how to land one of these players?"

"Girl, pay my little sister no mind," Joy said, without even giving a thought to the fact that she had just acknowledged Renee as her sister.

"Don't worry, Dontae already explained to me how colorful his family is," Tory said. She then pointed in Lance's direction and asked, "The man sitting with Lance, is that your dad?"

Joy had been avoiding that side of the room ever since her father and Jasmine walked in. She wasn't prepared to go over there and make nice, so she stalled by asking Tory, "How is it that you know Lance?"

Tory put her hand against her mouth as a low giggle escaped. "These shoes may look great, but I almost broke my neck trying to walk here in them. Lance caught me before I fell, and then allowed me to hold onto his arm once we realized we were headed in the same direction."

Joy glanced in Lance's direction. He was engrossed in conversation with her father. Nelson said something to him and then Lance leaned his head back and burst out laughing. They were a few feet away, but Joy could still see his dimples.

"He said that he works for your father," Tory continued.

"What, huh?" Joy hoped that she hadn't been caught staring at Lance. What was the matter with her? She needed to get her head back in the game. "Oh, yeah, he's dad's attorney. Come on, let me take you over there so you can meet Dontae's father."

"Oh, I didn't know that you and Dontae didn't have the same father." The look on Tory's face was one of confusion.

Joy said, "It's complicated." They walked over to her father and Joy made the introductions.

After the introductions, Lance stood up and said, "Can I speak to you for a moment, Joy?"

She wanted to say 'no' and then ask him not to bother her anymore. But Lance had been bringing out feelings that she had long ago suppressed. Joy needed to discover what kind of hold the man had on her. "Let's step into the hall." Joy walked away from everyone without looking back. She waited in the hall for Lance to join her.

When he came out into the hall, Lance took one look at Joy and asked, "Do you ever feel ashamed of the way you act?"

"Excuse me?" Joy thought Lance had wanted to talk to her about his feelings for her. She never imagined that she was going out there for a lecture.

"Well, your name is Joy, but I've never seen so much as a smile on your face since I met you."

"That's not fair. It's not my fault that my father makes me angry."

Lance wasn't letting her get around her issues. "What your father did to make you angry may not be your fault, but the way you've dealt with it certainly is. You won't even give your father a chance and all he wants is to be a part of your life."

Joy was simply tired of trying to make right what had gone so terribly wrong. She put her hands on her hips and came back with, "He has the woman he wanted in his life. She's always around... we can't have a family event without her showing up. He can't even go to work without her sitting in the courtroom stalking him."

"What are you talking about? Nelson didn't tell me that Jasmine sits in the courtroom while he's working."

"Didn't you see her that day I tried to get him recused from my case?"

Lance shook his head.

"Well she was there and she even came looking for me after court... she didn't appreciate that I was making her man look bad or some other nonsense like that."

"Go, Dontae, go," they heard Tory scream.

152

Joy imagined the look on Tory's face as she cheered Dontae on. Suddenly, she wished she had someone in her corner... someone to cheer her on. "If you're done telling me how awful I am, I think I'd like to go back in and watch my brother play."

Lance appeared to be a million miles away, thinking about something else. He looked back at her and said, "Okay, but can I ask you something first?"

Tory was still yelling, rooting Dontae towards another touchdown. Joy put her hands on her hips. "What?"

Before he could get a word out, Carmella scream, "Oh Lord Jesus, NO!"

From the sound of her mother's voice, Joy knew that whatever had just happened was all bad. She took her hands off her hips and stepped back into the box. Tory was holding her hands over her eyes and Carmella was on her knees with hands steepled. There were looks of shock all around the room as the announcer's voice streamed through the room. "Aw, folks. That had to hurt. I'm not sure if he's getting up from that."

Joy turned toward the field. Two big burly football players were getting up off the ground. Another player was still lying on the ground, holding the ball, but he wasn't moving. "Is that Dontae?" Joy asked.

Everyone just kept looking at the field. A stretcher arrived on the field.

Nelson jumped up and ran over to Carmella. He grabbed hold of her hand, pulling her off of her knees. "Come on, Carmella. We need to get down there and see about our son."

Carmella got up and followed behind Nelson as they made their way to the field.

Joy turned toward her stepfather and asked, "What is he talking about, Ramsey? What happened to Dontae?" Her voice was louder now... demanding an answer.

Ramsey walked over to Joy, putting his arm on her shoulder. "Calm down, Joy. He is going to be all right."

She backed away from Ramsey, shaking her head. "Don't tell me to calm down. What happened to my brother?" Joy's heart was beating fast. Dontae was being placed on a stretcher, but he still wasn't moving. She had experienced so many losses in her life that she just couldn't deal with one more sorrow... one more pain. If her brother didn't recover from the blow he'd just received, then Joy didn't know if she would recover.

Tory got out of her seat, an anxious look on her face. "I can't just sit here. I'm going down to the field to see what's going on with Dontae."

"That's a good idea," Ramsey said, trying to be the calming force in the room. "Why don't we all head on down, so we can figure out what's going on."

Everyone began filing out of the room. Joy took two deep breaths and followed behind Ramsey as they walked out of the room.

As Joy attempted to walk past him, Lance pulled her into his arms and held on tight. "I'm sorry this is happening, Joy. I will be praying for you and your brother."

Prayer... It sounded good, but when does it ever work? Joy was at her wits' end and trusting God just wasn't on her agenda.

8

Psalm 66:18-20

If I regard iniquity in my heart, the Lord will not hear me:
But verily God hath heard me; he hath attended to the voice of my prayer.
Blessed be God, which hath not turned away my prayer, nor his mercy from me.

Joy was beside herself as she sat in the hospital waiting for the doctor to come out and tell them how Dontae's surgery went. This was supposed to be a night filled with family and fun. But Dontae's concussion had ruined all of that. The doctors said the hit shook his brain and knocked him out cold for several minutes. But that hadn't been the worst of it. When Dontae finally came to and tried to stand up, the scream he let out as he grabbed hold of his knee and fell to the ground, told them that something was terribly wrong.

Her brother had gotten through high school and college with no injuries, but his first year playing pro ball had just landed him on an operating table. Joy was so worried that this knee injury was about to end her brother's career just as it was beginning, that she wasn't even thinking about the concussion he had suffered—that is, until the doctor came out after Dontae's surgery and put them on notice.

Carmella and Nelson stood in front of the surgeon, Joy and Tory were directly behind them with Ramsey in between, holding their hands. "I feel pretty good about the knee. He'll need rehabilitation, but I'm confident that Dontae should be walking on his own in about six to eight weeks."

The room erupted in cheers. Then Carmella said, "Oh thank God… thank God. So, everything is okay, then?"

"I didn't say that," the doctor began again.

"I thought you said that his knee would heal fine. What else is wrong?" Nelson demanded.

"The Cat scan we did shows that the hit Dontae took on the field today shook his brain in such a way that I doubt he'd be able to sustain another hit."

"So what are you saying?" Nelson asked with an edge to his voice.

"It means that Dontae has a decision to make," the doctor answered.

Carmella wanted to know, "When can we see him?"

"He's in the recovery room right now, but you should be able to see him in about an hour. However, because of the concussion I would advise that you make it a quick visit and then come back in the morning. He really needs his rest." After saying that, the doctor excused himself.

"I don't like the way he tried to insinuate that Dontae needs to quit football," Tory said with an exasperated look on her face.

"Well hon, tackling is part of the game of football and if one more tackle might bring irreparable harm to my son, then I seriously think he might need to find another career," Carmella said.

"What other kind of career do you expect him to get? Dontae is a football player and I can tell you right now that I am not marrying no pencil pusher," Tory declared with hands on hips for all to hear.

"Who said anything about marriage? The two of you are just dating… slow down," Joy said as she decided that she didn't like little Miss Fabulous after all.

Tory snapped open her purse and pulled out a ring that had a diamond on it that was so big, it appeared more gaudy than elegant. She put the diamond on her ring finger and declared. "I'm Dontae's fiancée. He wanted to wait and tell everyone tonight. But since he didn't get the chance, I'm serving notice that I will not allow anyone to go in Dontae's room and talk him out of being what he was created to be."

"Don't you care about my son's life at all?" Nelson spoke up.

"Of course she doesn't care," Joy interjected. "She's just like the skank you left Mama for. Don't you see the similarities?"

"Who you calling a skank?" Tory swung around to face Joy.

Jasmine popped up from her spot in the back. "Nelson, you need to tell your daughter to respect me."

"Just let it go, Jasmine. We have other things to deal with tonight," Nelson told her.

"I'm not going to let it go. I'm sick of your family thinking they can treat me any kind of way, and you just let them do it." She angrily swung her purse onto her shoulder. "I'm going back to the hotel. Are you coming or not?"

Nelson looked as if he was finally getting angry about what life had put him through and he wasn't about to take one more thing. He stalked over to Jasmine, grabbed hold of her arm and turned her to face him. "My son is facing the most trauma he's ever had to deal with. I need to be here to support him and I need you to support me. Can you do it or not?"

Joy turned to her mother and said, "I guess he's finally seeing her true colors."

"Stop it, Joy. Your father is worried about your brother. This is not the time or the place to act foolish."

"You are always taking up for him. Why do you do that, when you know as well as I do that he deserves everything he gets," Joy said to her mother.

Ramsey stepped in front of Carmella and took his turn trying to talk some sense into Joy. "Stop acting like a child, Joy. We need to find a way to help Dontae deal with the news the doctor just gave us. We don't have time for all the nastiness."

"Yeah, I need my mind together so I can uplift my man. I can't be spending time focusing on his evil sister," Tory said with as much venom in her voice as Joy had displayed earlier.

Jasmine apologized to Nelson and sat back down.

But Joy wasn't in the mood to apologize to nobody. Matter-of-fact, she didn't even want to be bothered with any of them for the rest of the night. "I'm out of here. Tell my brother I'll talk to him in the morning."

Carmella grabbed her daughter's arm. "No one said that you had to leave."

"You want me to be respectful to someone that I have lost all respect for. So the best thing for me to do is to just get out of here and let all y'all become one big happy family." Joy grabbed up her belongings and left the hospital in a huff.

Carmella was about to follow her, but Ramsey stopped her by saying, "Let her go, Carmella."

Carmella leaned her head against her husband's chest as a tear fell from her eyes. "She still hurting so much and I don't know how to help her."

"I know you don't want to hear this, baby, but we can't help Joy. We are just going to have to pray and trust God."

"Looks like we have a laundry list of things to pray for," Carmella told him.

Ramsey wasn't moved by the circumstances. He shrugged and said, "Then let's get started right now."

Getting herself on one accord with her husband, Carmella smiled up at him. This was the man of her dreams… her soulmate. She could get through anything with Ramsey by her side. Her children would be okay, Carmella was sure of it, because she wasn't going to stop bombarding heaven on their behalves until it was so.

So much anger and bitterness filled Joy's heart as she left the hospital, that when she arrived at the hotel her family was staying at, she did something she hadn't done in over two years. She went to the hotel bar and ordered a drink. And then she ordered another and another.

On her third drink, Joy received a tap on her shoulder. She thought someone in her family had found her, so her eyes were rolling as she swiveled around in her chair. "What is it?"

"Dang," Lance said, "you're even a mean drunk. What in the world am I going to do with you?"

"Not now, Lance. I'm not in the mood."

"And you think I'm in the mood to watch you drink yourself under the table?"

Joy signaled the bartender and then turned back to Lance. "I hope you came over here to drink with me, because I'm in no mood to spar with you over anything tonight."

When the bartender approached, Lance lifted a hand. "The lady is finished drinking for the night."

The bartender nodded. Then Lance pulled his billfold out. "How much do we owe you?"

"I don't need you taking care of my bar tab. I'm a grown woman with a j.o.b." She opened her handbag, attempting to pull out her billfold, but the first thing she pulled out was her praise journal. Time stopped for a moment as Joy looked at the journal that her Mom gave her so that she could communicate with God. The very thought made her laugh. And the more she thought about what a joke the journal turned out to be, the more she laughed.

"What's so funny?" Lance asked as he handed the bartender two twenties.

Joy pointed at the journal and kept laughing. Nothing had gone right for her or her family since she'd started this little journal writing journey. It was a useless waste of time and she was going to tell her mother exactly that.

Lance picked up the journal and opened it to the first page. He read the words and then gawked at Joy.

"What?" she demanded, not even noticing that he had her journal in his hands.

"You think I'm hot… and way too fine." He was pointing at the words in the journal as he spoke.

"Give me that." Joy snatched her journal away from Lance and slammed it back on the bar. "You had no right to read my personal business."

"Looks like that journal is your and God's business. I've never tried writing my thoughts to God like that. How's that working for you?"

In answer, she lifted her glass. It had less than an ounce of her drink left in it. She turned the glass up and drank it down.

Lance took her purse out of her lap and picked up her journal. "Let's go. You've had enough."

"As I said before, I'm grown. I don't need you coming down here telling me what I've had enough of. I stopped listening to my daddy a long time ago, and I don't need no too-fine-for-his-own-good man to try to take his place." She was swaying in her seat with each word. At one point she almost fell off the seat, but caught herself and kept on talking.

"You're drunk, Joy. I'm taking you to your room so you can sleep it off. We'll talk in the morning." Lance put a hand on her arm and helped her get out of the chair.

"What do we need to talk about?" Joy asked as she allowed Lance to lead her away from the bar.

"I came to tell you something. But you're in no condition to discuss it tonight."

"What did you want to tell me?"

"It can wait." They got into the elevator. "What floor are you on?"

"Eight." Joy leaned against the back wall of the elevator and held out her hand. "Give me my purse so I can find my room key."

Lance handed it over, then pushed the number eight and stood back while the elevator doors closed.

As she searched through her purse, Joy began mumbling and angrily shifting things around. By the time they reached the eighth floor, Joy had found her key and stepped out of the elevator, but she was still mumbling.

"What are you over there mumbling about?" Lance asked as he helped her to her room.

"I'm just tired. I'm mad and I'm tired," she said as she stumbled around. "God just keeps letting all these things happen to me and my family and I'm tired of pretending it's okay."

They arrived at her door and Lance said, "I don't believe that God is letting things happen to you. Dontae's accident on the field today didn't occur because God has some secret vendetta against the Marshall family."

"Whatever," Joy said, and then struggled to get the key card in the slot. Lance took the card away from her and opened the door.

Lance handed Joy her journal. "Get some sleep, Joy. We'll talk about all of this tomorrow. Okay?"

She didn't respond to Lance. Joy stumbled into her room and closed the door behind her. Walking from the living room to the bedroom, Joy threw her journal and purse onto the sofa, lost her balance and then stubbed her toe on the coffee table. She then proceeded to blame God for hurting her toe.

"Why are You so against me? Why don't You ever help me with anything? I'm so tired of dealing with all the hurt and pain that I go through." Joy entered the bedroom and kicked off her shoes. "Everybody wants me to trust You, but trust You for what? You don't care... You don't ever do anything."

In her drunken state, Joy even told the Lord, "All You do is listen to prayers and then ignore them. I could do that job." As she thought about her father's betrayal and the injuries that could end her brother's career just as it was getting started, she got angry and then swung at the air as if trying to box with God. She lost her balance. Her legs left the ground, her butt landed on the bed, but she was in a free fall that she couldn't stop, so her head hit the headboard. It felt to her as if her brain had shifted and her body was spiraling down a vortex of some sort. Joy wondered if God had just won the fight, by giving her a concussion, just like her brother. Then she heard a voice speaking to her as if out of a whirlwind.

Who is this that questions me without knowledge? I have let you have your say, now prepare yourself while I ask a few questions of you.

Joy became frightened at the voice she was hearing. Somewhere within herself, she knew that the voice she was hearing was God's. Now she was wondering if she had gone too far, and if it was too late to take her words back?

Where were you when I laid the foundations of the earth? Declare, if you have understanding?

When Joy didn't respond, the Lord continued His questioning...

Where are the foundations fastened? Who laid the corner stone there of? Who caused the morning stars to sing together or all the sons of God to shout for joy? Have you ever commanded the morning or caused the dayspring to know its place?

She lifted her hands to her ears, trying to drown out the sounds of God letting her know just who He is, and who she was not. Hands over ears could not block out the booming voice of God.

__Who do you think provides the raven his food when his young ones cry unto God? Who wakes you up in the morning? Who put the breath of life in your body? If you can do it all for yourself, then declare it.__

__Shall you that contend with the Almighty instruct Him? You that reprove God, can you give an answer for yourself?__

What had she done? Who did she think she was to tell God that she could do His job? She was now terrified that because of her arrogance, she would die in this whirlwind and never see her family again. Suddenly, with the thought of losing her life, Joy realized that things weren't as awful as she kept telling herself they were.

She wanted to live and she wanted God to forgive her, so she said, "I cannot declare anything. I had no right to speak to You that way. I will put my hand over my mouth, because You are God all by yourself."

But the Lord wasn't finished and the whirlwind persisted. *__Get yourself together and stand before Me, for I will demand answers of you. Do you cancel My judgments and condemn Me so that you can be righteous? Do you have an arm like God? Can you thunder with a voice like Mine? Deck yourself now with majesty and excellence; and array yourself with glory and beauty if you can."__*

"I cannot do anything unless You allow it, Lord. Please forgive my foolish words and allow me to live with the knowledge of your greatness."

After humbling herself, Joy was released from the whirlwind and felt herself drifting downward. She opened her eyes and discovered that she was, once again, on the bed in her hotel room and her eyes were wide open. She had been so wrong to be angry with God, who provided for her every single day of her life. These last few years, she'd felt as if she had been placed in a barren land with no hope of finding the promised land. But at that time, in that moment, it didn't matter to Joy. She had found God in the midst of a whirlwind and she now knew that He was worthy of her praise.

With tears streaming down her face, she opened her mouth and began to sing a song that the choir used to sing at her mother's church when she was a child:

"I will sing a fruitful song, in a barren land. Although everything seems wrong, I will still sing a fruitful song…"

She kept singing those words over and over, trying to get them down in her spirit. She wasn't feeling the effects of alcohol anymore. She was feeling grateful that God had kept her alive all these years so she could come to terms with the fact that God deserved her praise… even when things in life weren't going the way she wanted them to go… praise Him anyhow. Just because He is God all by Himself.

She got off the bed and down on her knees. As she steepled her hands to pray, she was reminded of the figurine of a person praying in Lance's office, and wondered if Lance was praying for her at that same moment. It didn't matter, because she needed to go to God for herself. So, she began her prayer by thanking Him for who He was. And then she said, "I know I'm not a pleasant person to be around. I know that I have let bitterness get in my way, but I don't know how to let it go. Prove to me that I've been wrong about You… help me."

9

Psalm 137:5-6
If I forget thee, O Jerusalem, let my right hand forget her cunning.
If I do not remember thee, let my tongue cleave to the roof of my mouth; if I prefer not Jerusalem above my chief joy.

The events of the night before had tired Joy out. So it was 9:00 a.m. by the time she opened her eyes and her telephone was ringing. Joy reached up and grabbed the phone. "Hello," she said, her voice was groggy.

"Hey, I was just calling to check on you."

She recognized the deep, smooth voice immediately. It was Lance. "I'm much better. Thanks for calling."

"Actually, that's not the only reason I'm calling," Lance told her.

She wasn't thinking about sparring with Lance anymore, she was just happy that he even had her own his mind. "What can I do for you?"

"One of my college buddies invited me to attend his church this morning and I wanted to know if you'd like to go with me?"

Joy laughed. "If this is your way of trying to get me on a date, I've got to say that you're losing all cool points by taking me to a place that doesn't even charge admission."

Lance laughed also, then said, "Believe me, I'm not trying to weasel out of paying for a date. I just figured that since we are both in Charlotte, and away from our home churches, you might be in need of a place to worship this morning."

"To tell you the truth, I don't go to church when I'm home… haven't for a few years now. But I think I'd like to go this morning, thanks for thinking of me."

"Okay, be ready in thirty minutes. I'll drive."

"I'll meet you in the lobby," she said before they hung up and then Joy flipped the covers back and jumped out of bed. She jumped in the shower, threw on a sundress and then called her mother.

"Good morning, Joy. How are you doing?"

"Mom, I have a lot to tell you. But we can talk later. How is Dontae doing?"

"When we left last night, he was alert and just happy to be alive."

"He has a good attitude… at least you raised one of us right."

"Hey, I don't know where you got that idea, but I raised both of my children right," Carmella informed her oldest child.

"I just wanted to let you know that I'm going to church with Lance this morning and then I'll meet you over at the hospital."

"Well… well. Okay then, I'll see you at the hospital this afternoon."

Joy heard the surprise in her mother's voice, but chose not to comment on it. She wanted to wait until she could tell her mother the entire story of how God had finally answered some of her questions and how she'd willingly praised God.

She met Lance in the lobby and then they headed out. "What church are we going to?" she asked once they were seated in the car.

"Turning Points Ministries, it's right off of South Tryon."

"Okay." Joy leaned back in her seat and got comfortable for the ride.

Lance gave Joy a questioning glance, then asked, "You didn't have anything else to drink this morning, did you?"

Her eyebrows furrowed. Then she told him, "I almost forgot that I had been drinking last night. No, I didn't drink anything this morning. I am completely sober."

"Then what's got you so chill?"

"I can't tell you all my secrets," she said, because the last thing she wanted to do was tell Lance that she'd had an encounter with God the night before. Her mother would believe her— that was the kind of relationship they had—but she didn't want Lance to think that she'd lost her mind.

"I don't even want to know. I'm just glad to see that you're in a much better mood. You even smiled at me when you came downstairs."

Joy didn't say anything, but her lips formed a smile again.

As Lance continued driving, he said, "I better strike while the iron is hot. Do you remember when I told you that I wanted to talk to you about something?"

"Mmmhmm."

"Well, it's about your dad."

Her smile evaporated. "Come on, Lance. I was enjoying hanging out with you. Please don't ruin my day."

"This is important, Joy. Just hear me out, okay?"

She waved a hand in the air. "Go on."

"You got me to thinking when you said that Jasmine was always around and that she sits in on some of your father's cases. And that she was present for the case when my client asked for you to recuse yourself."

"You must really hate the fact that I'm in a good mood, because you're trying to bring me down by rehashing this stuff."

"No, no, no... Listen to me," Lance demanded. "It always bothered me that my client didn't want to delay his trial while another judge was located. I mean, he would be out on bail, so why would he care, right?"

Now Joy was listening. "That's the same thing I thought. But once my father got arrested for accepting bribes, I figured your client had probably paid him off, just like the others."

"I don't think so. Your father assured me that he's never spoken to any of the defendants outside of court and I believe him. But what if Jasmine has been talking to these defendants and getting them to give her money so that she can talk your dad into letting them off easy?"

"If he did what Jasmine wanted, he's still just as guilty," Joy said.

"But I don't think he knew that he was doing what she wanted. Let's look at the facts. Your father has a total of six accusers, but two of them are behind bars, so they obviously didn't get the outcome they paid for."

"So you're saying that Jasmine has been playing my father for a fool all these years, and he doesn't even know it?"

"That's exactly what I think," Lance said as he turned in to the office park area where Turning Points Ministries held service.

"Even if it's true, I don't know what you want me to do about it." She also didn't know if she wanted to do anything about it, but she didn't want Lance to think of her as cold hearted again, so she kept those thoughts to herself. "I'm off the case, remember?"

"Come on, Joy. This is your father we're talking about. When you go back to work, just talk with the DA, ask him to interview those witnesses again to see if you all missed anything."

Her eyes did a half roll and then she said, "I'll think about it." Then she pointed in Lance's face and sternly told him, "But I don't want you running to tell my father that I'm considering doing anything on his behalf."

Lance lifted his hands in surrender. "Okay, but I'm telling you, your father is innocent. I just need a little bit of help to prove it."

Joy did a full eye roll as she got out of the car. She didn't want to hear anything more about her father. It was the first time in years that she had gotten dressed for church on Sunday and she didn't want thoughts of Nelson Marshall to ruin that bit of progress.

As they entered the small church, they were greeted by smiling faces and warm hearted people. Joy was immediately drawn to the place. Turning Points Ministries was not in a traditional church building. It was located in a business district. A realty company was next door and other businesses were all around it. But Joy felt the spirit of God the moment she walked in the building and she had a feeling that all the surrounding businesses were being blessed of God, simply because of the presence of Turning Points Ministries.

The praise and worship team was small and mighty. Joy was immediately put at ease by the sound of worship coming out of the mouths of the three women at the front of the church. Sometimes tears would flow down their faces as they worshipped, and she could see the pain of longsuffering on the face of one of the worshippers, but she praised Him anyhow... just like her mother had done. And just as Joy was doing right then and there as she lifted her hands in praise to God and gave Him all the praise she had, even as tears streamed down her face, because she, too, had longsuffering issues.

Fred Lott, Jr. was the presiding pastor of Turning Points Ministries. He was a tall fair-skinned man with a heart of gold. He reminded her of Ramsey as he spoke lovingly about his wife and about members of his congregation.

He then told the congregation, "You were meant to be free, and today I'm going to show you how to get your freedom." He opened his Bible and flipped a few pages. "Turn with me to Luke, chapter thirteen. I'm going to begin reading at verse ten.

"And Jesus was teaching in one of the synagogues on the Sabbath. And behold, there was a woman which had a spirit of infirmity eighteen years, and was bowed together, and could in no wise lift up herself. And when Jesus saw her, he called her to him and said unto her, Woman thou art loosed from thine infirmity. And he laid his hands on her: and immediately she was made straight, and glorified God."

"And the ruler of the synagogue answered with indignation, because that Jesus had healed on the Sabbath day... The Lord then answered him and said, thou hypocrite, doth not each one of you on the Sabbath loose his ox from the stall, and lead him away to watering? And ought not this woman, being a daughter of Abraham, whom Satan hath bound lo, these eighteen years be loosed from this bond on the Sabbath day?"

Pastor Lott finished his Bible reading and then looked up at the congregation and said, "I want you all to understand that there are some things that have us bound and we can't get free from them of our own accord, because this thing is a work of the devil.

"The woman with the infirmity stayed bent over, unable to fix her situation for eighteen years because she kept trying to do it herself."

Joy tried to imagine what it must have felt like to have to walk everywhere bent over for eighteen years. It must have been awful for that woman.

Then Pastor Lott said, "You can easily see people's physical disabilities, but what about the spiritual ones... what has you bent over? Is it financial... marriage... family?"

Joy's hand pressed against her mouth as she tried to stifle an involuntary scream. Her mom had told her that bitterness was eating her alive and now it felt as if this pastor was preaching directly to her.

She had been carrying the spirit of bitterness for five long years and it had her bowed so low that she couldn't raise herself up.

"I came here today to tell you to straighten up!" Pastor Lott's voice roared throughout the building. "You might have been dealing with things all your life, but you can let it go today. Some of you have been dealing with bitterness that you refuse to let go of, but I guarantee you, the minute you let it go, that's when your deliverance will come."

It was as if God had allowed this pastor to read the very thoughts and intent of her heart. By the end of the sermon, Joy was an emotional wreck, but she didn't know what to do about it. Pastor Lott's words sounded good in theory, but she had been carrying her bitterness for so long that she honestly didn't know what she would do without it. She'd finished law school, stopped drinking herself into a stupor, gotten herself hired on at the District Attorney's office... all to show her father that she didn't need him and could be successful even without him in her life. If she let her bitterness go, what would be her driving force?

As he closed the Bible and ended his message, Pastor Lott said, I'm feeling very strongly, that God wants me to pray for a few of you. You know what... we're a close-knit group. Why don't you all just come on up here and let's form a circle of prayer."

Joy had kept to herself for so long, that even though she knew that she was probably one of the people God wanted Pastor Lott to pray for, she never would have singled herself out and gone up to the altar. But now that Pastor Lott had asked for everyone to come, if she stayed in her seat, she would be singled out for that. So Joy grabbed hold of Lance's hand and joined the rest of the congregation as they formed their circle of prayer.

Pastor Lott said a general prayer for the group and then he began anointing the forehead of each person in the circle. As he touched them he said a quick prayer that seemed tailored to that person. The closer he got to Joy, the more worried she became, because if this man read her mail and looked into her innermost thoughts, he would know how truly wicked she had allowed herself to become.

Tears began to flow again and Joy couldn't stop them. She had allowed her father's sins to turn her into someone she never intended to become. She felt as if she'd been given a life sentence with no chance for parole. But then Pastor Lott touched her. And from the moment he placed his hand on her forehead, Joy felt a consuming fire ignite her from within.

Pastor Lott stepped back and looked at her for a moment. He closed his eyes as if listening to the voice of the Lord and then said, "God has loosed you, daughter. Walk in your freedom and never turn back to that thing that tried to bind you for a lifetime."

Joy felt every bit of the freedom that Pastor Lott had just declared God had given her. She lifted her hands and began praising God like never before. Her mom had been right all along. For it was through her questions and bitterness that she had found God and learned how to praise Him while waiting on her breakthrough. Her brother was still in the hospital, her father had left the family, but Joy could now see that even Nelson Marshall's actions couldn't destroy them. As long as they had God, she and her family could get through any storm.

10

Psalm 51:7-8

Purge me with hyssop, and I shall be clean: wash me, and I shall be whiter than snow.

Make me to hear joy and gladness; that the bones which thou hast broken may rejoice.

After church, Lance took her back to the hotel. They said a long goodbye, as the hug he gave her lingered so long that the smell of his cologne stayed with her even as they parted. "I've got to head back to Raleigh. I want to get a jump on my investigation, so I can get your father out of this mess."

"My father should be grateful that you're on his case, because I know for a fact that you're not going to throw in the towel. You'll fight to the end on his behalf."

"True that."

She smiled at him, then said, "Thanks for inviting me to church today, Lance. I can't tell you how much that meant to me."

"You don't have to tell me. I can see it in your eyes." Lance lowered his head and lightly kissed Joy then backed away with his hands in the air. As if he needed to keep them in the air or he'd do something else with them. "I'll see you when you get back to Raleigh."

Joy nodded. She then got in a cab and headed for the hospital. Carmella was waiting for her when she arrived. She and Ramsey had just come out of Dontae's room and now her mother wanted answers.

"How was church?"

"Wonderful." Joy grabbed her mother's arms and swung around with her. "Pastor Lott preached just what I needed to hear. But Mom, you'll never believe what else happened… Last night, I had an encounter with God. You told me to question God, and He showed up when I needed Him most and let me know just who He is, and that encounter made all the difference."

"I'm so proud of you, hon. You look so happy and I'm thrilled to see that look on your face again."

"I feel…" Joy hesitated as she tried to put words to her feelings, "like that seven-year- old child that I used to be. The one who used to believe that God could do anything, but fail. That's how I feel."

Carmella lifted her hands and gave praise to God. Although her son had a traumatic brain injury, he was alive, and now she also knew that her daughter was not only alive, but born again. She was truly amazed by God. He was a wonder worker.

Joy gave Ramsey, Raven and Ronny a hug, they were all in the waiting room, taking turns going into Dontae's room. The doctor didn't want all of them crowding Dontae at one time and the family was trying to be respectful of that. Ramsey Jr. and Renee both had to fly back home to get ready for Monday morning meetings, but they'd both come back to the hospital early that morning before flying out.

Joy and her mom went into Dontae's room. His fiancée was already in the room along with her father. Joy was thankful that her brother wasn't going through the ordeal alone. It was good to have a supportive family. Especially now with Dontae's head and knee aching so badly that he kept moaning and alternately rubbing either his head or knee. Joy didn't know what else to do, so she started praying for him.

Dontae smiled at his sister. "What's gotten into you? I haven't heard you pray in years."

"I finally came back to my senses," she told her brother.

"I'm just happy that she's smiling again," Carmella said.

"I got my joy back, thank you very much. The only thing I'm worried about right now is my brother."

"No need to worry about Dontae, he's going to be just fine. Isn't that right, baby?" Tory interjected.

Dontae winced and then said, "That's right. I'm Superman."

"Well those big linebackers must be your kryptonite." Joy walked over to Dontae's bed and put her hands on the bedrail. "Please tell me that you're not thinking about going back on that field. I know that you love the game, but we love you more."

Tory rolled her eyes and folded her arms over her chest. She was acting ugly, but Joy ignored it. There were many days that she had acted just as ugly and her family put up with her behavior; so instead of telling her off, she was going to pray for Tory and also pray that Dontae opened his eyes. *Good Lord, what was her brother doing with a woman like that?*

Dontae put his hand over hers. "It's hard, Sis. This is all I've ever dreamed of doing. If I'm not a football player, then what am I?"

"Exactly!" Tory shouted as if someone had been talking to her.

"Let it go, Tory. This is my family. They have a right to be concerned about me."

"I know, baby," she said as she came to stand by his side. "I just don't want them talking you out of a career that you love so much, just because of a little bump on the head."

"He was out cold for several minutes," Carmella corrected.

"You and I already talked about this, Mom. I listened to everything the doctor said. So, my goal right now is to go through with the rehab on my knee and then I'll make my decision on whether or not to return to the NFL." He looked around the room, from Tory, to Joy, to his mother and father and then asked, "Can everybody live with that?"

Tory pursed her lips and then strutted back to her seat.

The others nodded their agreement and Nelson said, "We just want you happy and safe, Son. That's all."

"I know, Dad. And to tell you the truth, if this had to happen to me, I'm just glad that my family was here. I probably would have gone into a deep depression if I had to face this alone."

"You are never alone, Dontae. And don't you forget it," Carmella told her son. "We're not just here for the football player, we're here for you."

They visited for a little while longer, then Joy went to the waiting area and asked Raven to walk down to the cafeteria with her to get something to eat.

Ramsey popped up. "If you're going to be out of the room for a while, we're going in." Ronny stood up and joined his father.

"Y'all can have it. I don't think I can take much more of Miss Hollywood-Tory right now. I need a long break."

"Was she that bad?" Raven asked as they headed to the cafeteria.

Shaking her head, Joy told her stepsister, "I honestly don't understand how both my brother and my father, two very intelligent men, could be so easily duped by these blood-sucking women."

"Tell me about it," Raven agreed. "And meanwhile, women like us, who want to be a support to a good man… we sit on the shelf just waiting to be noticed."

Joy couldn't imagine that as beautiful as Raven was, that she had spent much time on any shelf. But life was strange, and anything could happen, because Joy had put her own self on the shelf to avoid the hurt and pain loving a man could bring. She'd seen firsthand how her mother had dissolved into almost nothing after her father had walked out on her. She didn't want to ever feel like that. But did that mean that she would never give love a try?

"I don't know," Joy said with a look of hope in her eyes. "Lately, I've been thinking about taking myself off the shelf and giving love another chance."

"Oh my goodness… you've met someone." Raven was so elated, that she hugged her stepsister.

Joy could hardly believe that she was telling her business to anyone other than her mother and her praise journal, but she also felt like letting her guard down and learning to trust people again. "You remember Lance Bryant? He was at the football game with my dad."

In the cafeteria, they picked up trays and began grabbing salads and sandwiches. Raven responded to Joy's comment about Lance, "How could I miss him? The man is hot."

"I hope Renee didn't notice," Joy joked.

"Girl please, my sister was too busy trying to get hooked up with a pro-baller."

Joy and Raven ate their food and sat in the cafeteria laughing and joking with each other. As they got up to put their trays over the trash can and head back up to be with the group, Nelson appeared.

He stood to the side of the room, looking Joy's way as if unsure of how to approach her. It was in that moment that her father seemed most vulnerable to her. Despite what he'd done to her mother, Joy knew that her father loved her, but she had denied him her love in order to make him pay for his decisions. Joy was thankful that God hadn't denied her His love because of all the bad decisions she had made.

Joy turned to Raven. "I'll meet you back upstairs in a little while. I need to talk to my dad."

Raven put her hand on Joy's shoulder. "Okay girl, I'll see you in a bit."

Joy silently prayed as she slow walked over to her Dad. She hadn't had a normal conversation with him in so long, that she honestly didn't know how to talk to him anymore. *Lord, be my guide.* "Hey," was her great conversation starter once she was standing in front of the man responsible for her being born and being a Marshall.

He pointed to one of the tables. "Would you like to have a seat with me for a moment?"

His voice was shaky as he asked, as if he wasn't so sure if she would agree to give her own father a few minutes of her time. And since she had denied him on other occasions, she understood his trepidation. "I think it's way past time for us to sit down and talk, don't you?"

Nelson nodded and then guided her over to a table in the back of the room. When they were seated, Nelson said, "First let me tell you how sorry I am for everything that I did. When I saw that picture of you with your face in the commode, throwing up, I just wanted to run to you... to save you."

"You wouldn't have been able to save me from any of the things I had to go through, Daddy. I couldn't even save myself. But I don't blame you for any of the things that I did to myself anymore."

When Joy said those words, her father exhaled like a weight too heavy to carry had just been removed from his shoulders. She was overcome with compassion for her father. Joy put her hand over his. "I'm so sorry for the way I've treated you."

Humbled and with his head low, Nelson said, "I deserved it."

Joy shook her head. "No, you didn't deserve what I did to you. I am your daughter and I should have been able to treat you respectfully. It took me a while but I finally figured out why I couldn't."

"Was it because I cheated with Jasmine? Someone who was supposed to be your best friend?"

"That's what I kept telling myself, but the truth of the matter is, I had made you my hero. When you fell down from the pedestal I'd put you on, it devastated me. But I found a new hero, and his name is Jesus Christ. So, now I can just let you be my dad and love you no matter what comes."

As Joy finished her statement, tears were brimming in Nelson's eyes. He reached over and grabbed hold of his daughter. After hugging her tightly, he said, "I've missed you so much."

She hadn't hugged her father in over five years. Joy had to admit that she had missed his touch... missed knowing that her father cared about what concerned her. Things would probably never be the same between them, but at least they would be better. "I've missed you, too, Daddy."

Nelson wiped his eyes and tried to get himself together. He cleared his throat and then told Joy. "I wanted to talk to you about what Lance told you this morning."

Joy cringed inwardly. She prayed that her father wasn't going to ask her to do anything illegal to help him out of the mess he'd gotten into by getting involved with Jasmine in the first place.

"Lance's theory might be right, but I don't want to get you involved."

She breathed a little easier and then asked, "Were *you* involved? I really need to know, Dad."

Nelson shook his head. "I wasn't. If Jasmine is the one who took those bribes on some of my cases, she never told me that she was doing it. I do recall that she began taking an interest in my cases a few years back."

"Jasmine is poison, Dad. I just don't know how you could have left Mom for someone like her."

Sadness shaded Nelson's eyes as he admitted, "I have a lot of regrets. But there are some decisions that you have to live with, no matter how much you wish you could turn back time and get a redo."

11

Psalm 30:4-5
Sing unto the Lord, O ye saints of His,
and give thanks at the remembrance of his holiness.
For his anger endureth but for a moment; in his favour is life; weeping may endure for a night, but JOY cometh in the morning.

Three months later...

"All rise. The case of Nelson Marshall and the state of North Carolina will come to order," said the bailiff.

The case against her father had begun and Joy had come full circle. She'd once declared that she would never be a character witness for her dad because he had no character. But there she was seated in the courtroom as she waited to be called on to testify about what she knew about her father's business practices. She could only testify about events that took place five years ago when she clerked for him. But Joy now counted it a privilege to be able to tell others about the good man her father had once been. She only wished that she had the opportunity to tell the court about the good man her father had become in the last few months.

Forgiveness goes along way, and when Joy opened her heart to forgive her father, Nelson found the strength to repent of his sins and return to the God he had once served. He was in court, prepared to deal with whatever judgment he received.

As promised, Lance went to work tearing apart the testimonies like a prize fighter. Each person who accused her father of taking a bribe from them, left the stand looking as if they were either confused or the biggest liars on God's green earth.

Then it was her turn. Joy put her right hand on the Bible and swore to tell the truth and nothing but the truth and then she sat down on the witness stand.

Lance looked down at his notes as Joy situated herself in her seat. He put his notepad down and sauntered over to the box where Joy sat watching him move toward her. Joy prayed that she would be able to concentrate with Lance standing in front of her. She could hardly believe that she'd told this man that she wasn't interested in dating him. What was she thinking?

"Ms. Nelson. Is it okay if I call you Joy?"

Call me anything you want, just as long as you call me tomorrow, was what Joy wanted to say, but this was no joking matter. Her father's life and career were at stake, so she needed to quit drooling over Lance and get serious. "Yes, you can call me Joy."

"Thank you," Lance said as he hesitated for a moment, looked toward the jury and then back at Joy. "Joy, can you please tell the jury who Nelson Marshall is to you?"

Joy glanced in Nelson's direction. He smiled at her and it warmed her heart. "He's my father."

"You work for the district attorney's office, right?"

She leaned forward, speaking into the microphone. "Yes I do."

"And when your father was arrested, you asked to sit second chair in order to help convict him, correct?"

Joy glanced at Markus. He looked as if he was about ready to pounce out of his chair and object to Lance's line of questioning. But he kept his seat, so Joy said, "Yes, I did."

"And why did you do such a thing, Ms. Nelson?"

She wanted to remind Lance that he had just asked for permission to call her Joy. But she knew exactly why he had decided to use her last name at that moment...to remind the jury that this was Nelson's daughter speaking. She refused to lie for her father or anyone else, so she answered truthfully. "I wanted the case because I believed that he was guilty."

Sounds of disbelief escaped the mouths of members of the jury and others in the courtroom.

Joy didn't know why Lance would ask her a question like that. If a man's own child believed he was guilty, then why shouldn't they.

But Lance didn't seem bothered by the reactions in the courtroom. He trodded on. "Do you still believe that your father is guilty of the crime he has been charged with?"

"No," was her simple answer while she prayed that he'd have some serious follow-up questions.

"No, huh," Lance repeated, and then took his time looking at each jury member, making sure they were paying attention. "And let me ask you something else, if I may. You used to work for your father. Can you tell the court how long ago you worked for him?"

"Five years ago."

"During the time that you worked in his office, had you ever seen anything that would cause you to believe that Judge Marshall was taking bribes?"

"Objection." Markus pointed towards Joy. "She was a law student at the time, so she only worked part-time as a clerk for her father. She couldn't possibly know everything that went on in that office."

"Your Honor, I'm only asking the defendant to testify to what she saw with her own two eyes. I have other witnesses that will also testify concerning the work environment in Judge Nelson's office," Lance said.

"Very well, the objection is overruled. Carry on."

Lance thanked the judge and then turned back to Joy. "You may answer the question."

Joy answered the question. Nothing out of the ordinary went on in her father's office during the time she clerked there. When prompted she also admitted that the reason she decided to become a lawyer was because at one time in her life, she hadn't known a more honorable man that Nelson Marshall and she desired to follow in his footsteps.

Joy didn't know if her testimony was helping or hurting her father, but saying nice things about Nelson Marshall felt *mmm good* to her soul.

True to his word, Lance called on numerous current and ex-employees who all verified that Nelson ran a good and honest office. Lance also introduced the theory that Jasmine had been the one who tried to profit from the cases that came through Nelson's courtroom.

When she took the stand, Jasmine tried to be as aloof as possible, but when Lance said, "It burned you up that Nelson's ex-wife was taking half of his money, didn't it?"

Jasmine couldn't hold her tongue any longer. She shot angry darts at Lance as she said, "How would you feel? One day you're living in a half-million dollar house and able to shop and purchase anything you want. Then the next day you're told that the ex-wife is entitled to retain her standard of living, so somebody's standard of living is about to go down. And guess whose that was?" Jasmine angrily pointed at her chest. "My standard of living what cut in half all because," she pointed at Nelson, "his wife was being so greedy. I had to move into a condo and be put on a strict allowance, like I was a child or something." She swung her long curly weave around and then just sat there, waiting for the next question.

Joy couldn't believe that Jasmine was that clueless. That she had no understanding or even care for the family that Nelson left behind. But her arrogance helped the jury to see her motive for going behind Nelson's back and arranging those bribes. Jasmine didn't admit to any wrong doing while on the stand, but no one was deceived.

On the last day of the case, Dontae and Carmella came to court to be with Nelson and Joy when the verdict was read. Dontae was walking with the aid of a cane. His knee was getting better, but it hadn't totally healed as of yet.

Carmella hugged and kissed her daughter. "Ramsey sends his love."

Joy would always be grateful to Ramsey for coming into their lives just when they needed him most. He'd been a father to her and Dontae when their own father had deserted them. As far as Joy was concerned, she now had two fathers.

The court came to order as the jury filed back in. Joy noticed that the members of the jury weren't trying to make eye contact with her father, which was always a bad sign.

The judge turned to the jury and asked, "Has the jury reached a decision?"

"We have, Your Honor," the head juror said.

The decision was handed to the judge; Nelson and Lance stood. Nelson had been charged with five counts of bribery and one count of accessory to commit bribery. The judge informed them that Nelson had been cleared on all five counts of bribery, then everyone held their breath as the judge read the verdict on the last count. "On the count of accessory to commit, the jury finds the defendant... guilty."

Carmella put an arm around both her children and squeezed them tightly. "He'll survive this, so you all need to be strong for your daddy."

"What just happened, Mama?" Joy was shaking her head. She could hardly believe that her father had eluded the bribery charges, but then had been snared by a conspiracy charge. She concluded that, in the final analysis, the jury just couldn't believe that Nelson could live with a woman like Jasmine and not have a clue as to what she had been up to. The time he would get for the accessory charge would be minimal, but Nelson would more than likely lose his license to practice law and that would be devastating. But her mother believed that he would get through it, so Joy would keep the faith as well.

Carmella stayed in her seat as Dontae and Joy went up to the front to hug their father before he was taken away by the guards. It was a sad sight to see, but Nelson Marshall's downfall had been put in motion the day he left his praying wife for someone as selfish as Jasmine Walker.

They hadn't received the total acquittal they had hoped for, but as they left the courtroom the Marshall family, nonetheless, lifted their voices and praised God for His mercy. Because they knew that things could have turned out a lot worse.

Lance approached just as they were leaving the building. He put his hand on Joy's arm and asked, "Can I speak to you for a second?"

"We'll see you back at the house," Carmella told her daughter as she and Dontae walked away.

Lance put his hand in Joy's and began walking with her toward the garage. "I'm sorry that we didn't get a full acquittal, but I promise you that I won't let this go until we can get him acquitted on this accessory count as well."

"You did your best, Lance. I wouldn't have been able to do anything more for him than what you did."

"You know what this means, don't you?" Lance asked with a big grin splattered across his face.

Those dimples of his drove her crazy. She wanted to run her hand down his beautiful face, just so she could touch one of those dimples. "What are you talking about?"

They made it to her car and then he said, "I'm talking about the fact that we don't have any more conflicts of interest between us. So, I'd like to pick you up tonight and take you out to dinner."

"It's about time," Joy just about screamed. "I was beginning to wonder if you were slow or something. I've wanted to go out with you for months." She pulled his head down toward her and kissed him like she'd been loving him for all of her life and had just found a way to show him.

"Whew," Lance said when they broke apart. "If I had known you'd act like this just because of a dinner date, I would have asked you out a lot sooner."

Shoving his shoulder, she said, "Shut up, slow boy. Just make sure you pick me up on time." Joy got in her car and drove off. Life hadn't turned out the way she had expected, but she was amazed at how God was able to break through the cloud of darkness in her life and enable her to enter into a wonderful new day. God was good and she would praise Him for a lifetime.

A Forever Kind of Love

THE PRAISE HIM ANYHOW SERIES

Prologue

Looking like a GQ model in his black Armani suit and his yellow tie with tiny black dots, with dimples on both sides of his handsome face, Dontae Marshall put the two-carat Princess cut diamond ring in his pocket. Dontae would have gladly purchased a five-carat ring if need be, but the woman he had fallen in love with didn't hunger and thirst for displays of wealth as the first woman he'd fallen for had.

Dontae was so thankful that his sister, Joy had admonished him to pray about his decision to marry Tory Michaels. He hadn't appreciated the way Joy butted into his business at the time. But after he took that hit on the football field and then had to deal with rehabilitation for his knee, while worrying over his doctor's recommendation that he give up his football career, Dontae discovered that Tory was not the woman for him. She hadn't been in it for the right reasons.

Tory didn't love Dontae Marshall the man; she loved Dontae Marshall the football star. And the day he decided to follow doctor's orders and hang up his helmet, was the day that Tory started bringing him all kinds of drama. In the end, Dontae cut his losses by letting Tory keep that big rock he'd given her and then they both decided to go their separate ways. Soon after Dontae put his full concentration towards building the new career he had mapped out for himself.

It had taken a few years, but Dontae had used the money he'd received as a signing bonus to open a sports agency. Even though he couldn't play the game anymore, he still loved sports, so he sat down and had a talk with Stan Smith, his agent. Stan offered to take Dontae under his wing and he taught him the sports agency business and just like that, Dontae found a new purpose in life. He was passionate about protecting young athletes from some of the nonsense that went on behind the scenes. Dontae believed that his job was to help navigate his clients around a system designed to favor the owners—and sometimes even coaches—rather than the players.

After learning as much as he could from his mentor, Dontae relocated to Charlotte, North Carolina and set up shop. It didn't take long for his agency to gain a good name among the athletic community and his business grew right before his eyes. Dontae's mom had told him that his success was due to the fact that God had been watching out for him. Whether it was God's doing or something much simpler, Dontae didn't care, all he knew was that life was good.

Dontae hadn't imagined that things could get any better, but when he met Jewel Dawson, he realized that God had been holding out on him. Jewel was everything he wanted in a woman. She was soft spoken, yet in command at all times. Jewel was a writer who had taken her career into her own hands and was making a pretty good living. She was daring, loving, beautiful and most of all, she made him smile... no, not just smile, with Jewel, Dontae had learned to laugh and enjoy life again. He picked up the manila envelope, grabbed his keys and headed out the door.

***

Dontae took Jewel to Villa Antonio, her favorite Italian restaurant. The ambiance was perfect for a romantic dinner. Jewel was wearing a sleeveless silk dress that crisscrossed in the back. The dropped waistline on the dress gave way to a skirt designed for twirling movements. Dontae definitely approved. As a matter of fact, he couldn't take his eyes off of her.

"I love this place. I'm so glad you got us reservations here tonight," Jewel said as they were seated in a dimly lit corner of the restaurant.

"I know you love it, that's why we're here."

Jewel leaned over and kissed Dontae on his full, luscious lips. "Thanks baby, you're always thinking about me."

The couple ordered their food and then spent the evening gazing into each other's eyes. Dontae knew with everything in him that Jewel was the one for him. He was ready to make a life with her and didn't want to wait a moment longer. However, getting down on bended knee wasn't an option for him. Oh, he had recovered quite well from his knee injury several years back, but the knee would act up on him at times. And since this was an important moment—one that he wanted Jewel to remember for a lifetime—he didn't want to spoil it by needing the maître d's help when and if he failed to get up on his own.

Jewel's hands were resting on the table. Dontae laid his hands on top of hers, still gazing into his beloved's eyes he said, "Jewel, I want you to know that I am happy when I'm with you. You have brought so much joy into my life and, and—"

"Aw, that's so sweet," Jewel interrupted.

That's when Dontae remembered the ring that was in his jacket pocket. His hand shook with nervousness as he pulled it out and gripped it like he used to hold the football when charging his way to a touchdown. "I just believe that you and I are a perfect match. We fit together, ya' feel me?"

Jewel nodded. "I feel the same way, Dontae. I think I started falling in love with you the moment we met."

That revelation brought a smile to his face, gave him the strength to do what he had gone there to do. He was seated across from Jewel, but suddenly felt miles away. Dontae got up and squeezed in next to his woman. He set the ring box on the table and opened it.

Jewel gasped.

"What I'm trying to say is..."

Jewel wrapped her arms around Dontae and screamed, "Oh my God. Yes, yes, Dontae, I will marry you."

In a joking mood after receiving such a wonderful response to his almost proposal, he waited until she held out her hand for him to put the ring on her finger and then said, "You didn't let me finish my question. How do you know I was going to ask you to marry me? Maybe I just wanted to give you a ring to celebrate our one-year anniversary."

A hint of sadness dimmed Jewel's normally bright eyes. She quickly covered her face and said, "I'm so embarrassed. I should have let you finish. I'm sorry, Dontae."

He couldn't carry the joke any further. The look on Jewel's face told him that he'd gone too far. "No, I'm the one who is sorry. Of course I want to marry you. I was just joking, but I didn't mean to upset you."

Jewel shoved him. "Boy, you play too much."

"I'm sorry about that. But you already agreed to marry me, so you're stuck with me." He took the ring out of the box. "Can I put this on your finger and make it official?"

Grinning from ear to ear, Jewel held out her hand.

Dontae put the ring on her finger; they then celebrated with several kisses and Tiramisu. When they finished off their dessert, Dontae kissed his soon-to-be bride and then grabbed the manila envelope he'd left on the other side of the table and handed it to Jewel. "I almost forgot to give you this."

"What's this?" Jewel asked, while opening the envelope, still grinning at her man.

"Just a little document that I need you to sign and return to my attorney." He leaned back in his seat and added, "At your leisure, of course."

Jewel pulled the document out and read, then stared at it as if the words were written in Greek. After a long silent pause, she turned to him and asked, "Is this a joke?"

Dontae swiveled his head in order to take a glance at the paperwork in Jewel's hand. "No joke, babe, I just need you to sign those papers and return them to my attorney."

"Are you serious?"

"What's wrong?" Dontae asked, not understanding Jewel's reaction.

While shaking her head, Jewel told him, "This is turning out to be the worst proposal in the history of marriage proposals."

Confused by her reaction, Dontae said, "I thought I did good. I brought you to your favorite restaurant. I picked out a diamond that I knew you would love and then I... I—"

"And then you had the audacity to hand me a prenuptial agreement." Jewel threw the document down on the table and yanked the ring off her finger. "If you're so worried that the marriage won't last, I don't think we should even bother getting married in the first place."

Dontae had been leaning back, relaxing and enjoying the moment. But as he watched Jewel take the ring he'd just given her off her finger, a feeling of panic overtook him and he bolted into action. Holding up his hands trying to halt her tirade, Dontae said, "Hold up... you don't need to take that ring off. We're engaged now. I want to marry you."

Jewel put the ring in Dontae's hand and stood up. "Take me home."

"But baby."

"Take me home this instant, Dontae. I don't even want to talk to you right now."

"Baby, be reasonable. Don't you want to discuss the wedding?"

Jewel picked up the prenup, threw it in Dontae's face and then shoved his shoulders until he got up so that she could make her way out of the restaurant.

Dontae could see that he had lost the battle, so he did as Jewel asked so that he would have a shot at winning the war.

1

Carmella Marshall-Thomas was in the kitchen putting the finishing touches on the desserts she had made for Ramsey Jr's coming home party. Her husband's oldest son wasn't moving back to Raleigh as she and Ramsey had hoped, but he would be in Charlotte with Dontae and that was good enough for her. Carmella enjoyed throwing dinner parties for her family, so the Marshalls and Thomases were all gathering together again today.

Raven and Joy were in the kitchen helping her with the meal, while Renee hung out in the family room with Ramsey and Ronny. Dontae was driving in from Charlotte and had promised to pick up Ramsey Jr. from the airport on his way to the house. So as usual everyone would be there except for Ramsey's youngest son, the one with the heart of gold. Rashan was a missionary and had travelled all over the world during his short twenty-eight years of life, helping out and doing the Lord's work wherever needed.

"Okay ladies," Carmella addressed Joy, her natural born daughter and Raven her daughter from her marriage to Ramsey. Carmella and Ramsey had been married for eight years now, and Ramsey's children, the kids with the *R* names, didn't seem like step-children to her anymore. They were family and that's all Carmella had to say about that. "Looks like we have taken care of everything in here. Now all we have to do is set the table."

"Why don't we make Renee do that, since she didn't bother to help us fix one thing today," Raven demanded.

"I second that," Joy said. "Renee acts like she's allergic to pots and pans."

"You two need to leave your sister alone. She contributes to this family in other ways. But one day she will come to understand and appreciate the value of spending time with us in the kitchen," Carmella told her girls even as she prayed for that wish to come true. She so longed to be as close to Renee as she was with the rest of the children. But Carmella had learned the art of patience, so she was willing to wait until Renee felt comfortable enough to have a mother-daughter relationship with her.

"You're just too nice, Mom, that's all that is," Joy told Carmella as she reached into the cabinet and pulled out the fancy china that Carmella only used for family events.

"Why do you always use your best china for us, but use the regular plates for other guests?" Raven asked.

Carmella smiled. She hadn't known that her family noticed her preferences until Joy pulled the right plates out of the cabinet and then Raven commented about it. "You all are the most important people in my life; I wouldn't dare offer anything but the best to my family." She grabbed hold of Raven's arm, looked her in the eyes and said, "And don't you dare accept anything but the best from the man you choose to marry. You let him know that you're treated like royalty at home and the only way he can get your heart is if he can do better than what your father and I already do."

"You didn't tell me to say any of that to the men I dated," Joy complained.

"Girl, you didn't date all that much and you know it. But by the time you met Lance, I knew he was the one and I knew he would treat you like a queen. So, I didn't need to give you anything to say. I just kept praying that you would wake up and see what was right in front of you." And besides, Carmella had other reasons for saying what she had to Raven. The girl was beautiful, talented and smart, but she had an insecurity about her that caused Carmella to worry that she might let any old riffraff in her life. She didn't want Raven mentally or physically abused by any man, so she kept praying for her daughter.

Smiling as she gazed at the band on her finger, Joy said, "You were right about Lance. That man is so good for me and to me. I'm just glad that I finally gave him a chance."

"Me too," Raven said joyfully, "Your wedding was one of the best I've ever attended, and certainly the best that I ever served as maid of honor for... wait. Did I mention that?"

"Yes, you did," Joy said as she tried to hold in a giggle.

"Forget I said that. I'm throwing all my bridesmaid dressing away. I hereby declare that I will never be another bridesmaid." Raven held her hand up as if she was testifying before congress.

"Here, here," Joy seconded.

Carmella said, "I've already spoken to the good Lord on your behalf; so, believe me when I tell you, Raven, your time is coming." Carmella then picked up the platter holding the roast she had made; roast was Ramsey Jr.'s favorite. "Now, will you ladies help me set the table?"

***

"Man, am I glad to see you. That flight had me calling on the name of Jesus and confessing all my sins," Ramsey Jr. said as he got into Dontae's Range Rover.

"Boy, quit lying. That was only an hour flight, hardly enough time for you to confess *all* the stuff you've done... Don't forget, I know you."

"Shut up and get me away from this airport."

Dontae pulled away from the curb and began driving out of the airport lot. "Flight was that bad, huh?"

"I'm telling you, Dontae, if your Mama wasn't the praying woman that she is, I'd probably be gone on to glory right now."

"Her prayers don't always work; you do know that, don't you." Dontae spoke like a man who'd had first-hand experience in the prayers-not-getting-answered department.

"Real talk... your moms has helped me get through some things these last few years. All of her prayers seem to be working for me." Ramsey Jr. spread out his arms and looked around at the tree lined scenery as Dontae continued driving. "I'm back in North Carolina, aren't I?"

"Where the pollen is high and the women want more than a brother can give."

"I feel a sneeze coming on now. But that's all right. It's only unbearable for about the first couple weeks of spring."

"At least flowers are blooming all over the place in Charlotte," Dontae commented.

"I can hardly wait to get there."

Dontae came to a red light. He stopped the car and turned to his step-brother. "I was thinking..." He hesitated, and then charged on in, "that since you'll be staying with me for a while, I want to introduce you to one of Jewel's sisters. We can double date or something."

Ramsey adamantly shook his head. "Not interested, bro. I just shook off a woman who I didn't know was bipolar until she came at me with a knife. I'm still trying to get my head together from that."

"Come on, Ramsey, I need your help."

With furrowed brows, Ramsey asked, "What are you talking about? Since when do you need help with Jewel? The two of you have been into each other from the moment you met."

Dontae wished he didn't have to talk about what happened between him and Jewel, but he was desperate to get her back and needed help from his brother to make it happen. "We broke up."

"What do you mean, you broke up? You just bought her an engagement ring two weeks ago."

"She gave it back. Got upset when I handed her the prenup."

"I told you it was a bad idea."

"Look, I love Jewel and all, but I'm not about to give her half my money if she decides to leave me for some other man twenty years from now."

"You are such a cynic," Ramsey said, laughing at Dontae's comment.

"No. I'm a realist. And Jewel needs to understand just how real things could get if she or I ever decide to divorce."

"Wow. You and Jewel haven't even gotten married yet, and you're already thinking about divorce."

"Hey, I'm just being a realistic."

"No," Ramsey said, "You're just being cynical and trying to make Jewel pay for something that happened before she met you."

Dontae knew that Ramsey spoke the truth. His father had caused him to be a bit jaded. But dealing with a woman like Tory had also caused Dontae to doubt the reality of happily-ever-after. Once things weren't going the way she wanted them to go, he wasn't hearing sweet nothings from her anymore... seemed like the love Tory had for him just got up and left. If Jewel ever flipped a switch and started acting like Tory, he'd be heartbroken, but he'd still have his money to keep him company, which was why Jewel signing that prenuptial agreement was so important to him.

"Not to bring it up like this, but you are going to be staying at my house rent free. So, I think that one good turn deserves another."

"I'll pay rent if it's that big of a deal. I'm only going to be crashing with you long enough to find my own place anyway," Ramsey reminded Dontae.

Feeling guilty for the unnecessary comment, Dontae back tracked. "I'm not trying to charge you rent. I shouldn't have said it like that. I'm just desperate, man. Jewel is the one for me, so I really need your help."

"Just drop the whole prenup idea and your problem is solved."

Dontae shook his head. The look on his face was set, as if he was thinking about Michael Jordan, Kobe Bryant and all the other brothers who gambled and lost without a prenup. Oh sure, Kobe's wife stayed, but if she had pulled the trigger on that multi-million dollar divorce, Kobe would have been out hocking shirts, shoes and soda to keep up with his standard of living. "I can't do that. Call me a fool. Call me jaded or whatever. But I just don't believe that people should go into marriage with their heart hanging out of their chest, without stopping to think about what could and probably would end up going wrong down the line."

"If I don't know nothing else, I know about things going horribly wrong," Ramsey said as he leaned back in his seat.

Dontae and Ramsey were both sinfully handsome and successful young men. But they had both experienced trauma that had changed their view of love, faith and God's ability to handle the things that concerned them. As smart as they were, neither man knew how to get out of his own way.

Ramsey popped up. "Ronny's traveling back to Charlotte with us. He's going to help me get my stuff set up in your house and in a storage unit."

"I can help you with that," Dontae said.

"Not with that knee of yours, you can't. I'm not going to be the one responsible for getting Carmella's boy all banged up again."

"What I mean is, we can pay a service to handle that for you."

"Naw, that's okay. Ronny just lost another job and I'd like to be able to put some money in his hands. And I'd like to spend some time with him before I start my new job. I told dad that I'd figure out what Ronny's next move should be."

Pulling into his mother's driveway, Dontae turned off the car and then asked Ramsey, "Do you think Ronny will help me out?"

Ramsey laughed. "Two women are involved, right?"

Dontae smiled at that. Ronny was definitely a ladies' man. "I forgot who we were talking about." Dontae nodded toward the front door. "You go on in, the family's waiting on you. I'm going to give Jewel's sister a call and tell her it's a go."

Ramsey put his hand on Dontae's shoulder. He had a sincere look on his face as he said, "I know we've only been brothers for the last eight years, but I just want you to know that I'm glad that we are family."

"Yeah, me too," Dontae said as he pulled his cell phone out and made a call to the woman he hoped would be his future sister-in-law.

The first person Dontae saw as he stepped into the house was Lance, his sister's husband. They shook hands and then Lance told him, "Man, am I glad you and Ramsey are here. I'm hungrier than a hostage and Carmella said we couldn't eat until you two rock heads got here."

"Stop." Dontae put up a hand. "I don't think I can handle all the love you're throwing my way."

"Don't get it twisted," Lance told him, "Family is good, but when you're hungry and your mother-in-law cooks like an Iron Chef, food is better."

The two men laughed as they joined the rest of the family. Carmella was busily uncovering the food as Dontae walked into the dining room. She turned and caught a glimpse of her son and then got the biggest grin on her face. "Come on in here, boy. I been waiting all day to give you a hug."

Even though his heart was heavy because of the situation with Jewel, Dontae yet and still smiled back at his mother. He could only remember one time in his life when his mother hadn't been there for him. With the horror stories he'd heard from other men about the things their mothers had done to them, Dontae wasn't about to dwell on one incident. "Hey Moms, I'm happy to see you, too," he said as they hugged. As he peeked over her shoulder, he added, "but I'm even happier to see that mac and cheese on the table."

"See Mom, I told you that I should be your favorite. This boy would take food over you," Joy said as she walked over and hugged her brother.

"Stop all that foolish talk, Joy Lynn. I have been blessed with seven children, two by birth and five by marriage and I love you all with a mother's heart," Carmella declared for everyone's hearing.

After that the family sat down to dinner. They talked, laughed and then played Trivia and Sequence. The ones who weren't playing either game got comfortable on the sofa and watched a movie. If anyone had looked into the Marshall household ten years ago, they never would have believed that all that sadness and dysfunction would one day turn into great joy.

As Ronny, Ramsey and Dontae stood, preparing to take that two hour drive from Raleigh to Charlotte, Carmella remembered something that she needed to tell Dontae. Ramsey and Ronny walked out to the car and Carmella grabbed hold of Dontae's arm and pulled him to the side. "Guess who I saw yesterday?"

Dontae gave her a blank stare. "I wouldn't know where to begin."

"Okay, okay... Coach Linden moved back to town. The school has hired him back and they are throwing an awards banquet for him." The excitement shone through with every word Carmella spoke.

Dontae didn't say anything.

Bringing her excitement down a notch or two, Carmella said, "I thought you'd want to know. I asked him to send the invitations to the banquet to my house because I thought you would want to attend."

A storm was brewing in Dontae's eyes as he said, "I don't want to attend. And I don't want you to go either." He turned and walked out of the house without further explanation.

2

"Oh no, that's not about to happen. Don't even worry about it. One hundred percent, I got your back." Dontae was on the phone with one of his clients while Ramsey and Ronny got themselves situated in the house.

"Thanks, Mr. Marshall. My dad was a little worried about me taking the meeting by myself, and he'll be out of town on business that weekend, so he can't attend."

"Your dad was right to worry. But I got this. I will contact Coach Jones and let him know that I will be making your hotel arrangements and setting the agenda for this meeting. Then if all goes well, you just might be the first round draft pick this year."

"That would be so awesome. I can't thank you enough, Mr. Marshall."

"Do me a favor. Stop calling me Mr. Marshall. In a year's time you'll be making so much money, people will be calling you mister. But the thing about it is, if you never forget what it felt like when you had to call others mister, you'll do just fine."

"I get it, I get it," his client said, then finished with, "Stay humble."

"Yeah, but don't be so humble that you end up missing the money being thrown your way." Dontae knew first hand that a career could end within minutes of getting started. But if a player was smart and grabbed hold of opportunities, he could make enough money to feed his family for a lifetime.

"I'll remember that, Mr.—I mean, Dontae."

"And no matter what happens next weekend, I'm getting you on a plane the minute the meeting is over. Under no circumstances do you agree to hang out with anyone for golf or anything else. You got me?" Dontae was firm on that. Owners and coaches tried to get over on kids fresh off the school bus. But Dontae made sure that his clients were protected from all the nonsense.

"Okay. My dad said the same thing."

"Your dad is a smart man." That made Dontae think about his own father. Nelson Marshall would be getting out of prison in about ten days. Dontae could only hope that he had finally wised up.

After hanging up with his client, Dontae walked into the family room where his brothers were resting. He made one more call; this one to his assistant. When Brielle answered the phone, he instructed her to contact his client's coach and inform him that he was the agent of record and would be attending the meeting. He then told her to make separate reservations for him and his client at the Ritz Carlton in Charleston, South Carolina for the following weekend.

"I love Charleston," Ronny said.

"And I love you for agreeing to help me out with my little problem. Unlike some other folk who shall remain nameless." Dontae pointedly stared at Ramsey as he switched from business mode to personal.

"Hey, we're family; why wouldn't I help you," Ronny said while leaning back in his seat on the family room sofa in Dontae's condo.

"Oh, yeah right," Ramsey Jr. scoffed, "And if Jewel's sister had been ugly, I bet you would have forgot all about this we-are-family moment you're having."

Ronny looked as if Ramsey had misjudged and falsely accused him. He put his hands on his chest. "I'm trying to take one for the team. At least I'm willing to help Dontae with his sad and pathetic love life."

"Hey, there's nothing sad or pathetic about my love life," Dontae objected. "At least I have a woman. I'm the one setting you up with a woman."

Ronny stood up, popped his collar as he strutted around the room. "Don't need help with the ladies. I'm doing you a favor."

Ronny was mostly correct. Being young and handsome, the three men needed little help where the ladies were concerned. However, what Ronny lacked was focus. He had an entrepreneurial mindset, but floated around from one idea to the next, never sticking with anything long enough to see it through to the other side of success. Dontae hoped that being around him and Ramsey this week would help his step-brother focus and figure out what he wanted to do with his life.

"Okay, you're right. You are doing me a favor and I thank you," Dontae conceded so they could get on with it. "Now, since you're such a ladies' man, help me pick out a restaurant where I can arrange for us to run into Jewel and Dawn."

"Hold on, Playa," Ronny took center stage again. "Didn't you tell us that Jewel threw those prenup papers in your face while y'all was at a restaurant? And you want to just simply bump into her at another one? What you want her to do at this restaurant, throw her drink in your face?"

"What's the man supposed to do, Ronny? He's got to run into her somewhere, because she's not taking his calls right now. And Jewel is a Christian woman, he won't find her hanging out at some rump shaking night club," Ramsey said.

"Just shaking my head." Ronny walked over to Dontae's laptop and turned it on. He then turned back to Dontae with confusion written on his face. "How do you use this thing?"

Dontae got up, walked over to the table. "You've never used a Mac before?"

"I'm a starving entrepreneur, where would I get the money to buy anything that comes out of the Apple store?" He pulled his cell phone out of his pocket and said, "I'm still using my flip phone."

Dontae and Ramsey had no problem laughing in Ronny's face.

"Laugh if you want to, but when Sprint told me I had a relic of a phone and tried to get me to upgrade, I told them I would wait until Beyoncé decided to upgrade me herself."

"You gon' be waiting a long time, bro. I think Beyoncé is happy where she's at. And anyway, you don't want none of that baby's daddy drama," Dontae said, laughing, but as he turned in Ramsey's direction to get a co-signer on his joke, Dontae caught a glimpse of sadness in Ramsey's eyes that took the fun out of the moment. Dontae was about to ask Ramsey if he was alright, but then Ronny got his attention.

"A notification of an email from Mama Carmella just popped up."

"Just ignore it, click on Safari and go on to the website you want me to see," Dontae told him.

Ronny shook his head. "Can't just ignore Mama Carmella's emails. She delivers some real nuggets." Ronny opened his flip phone. "If you're not going to check your email, I'm going to check mine so I can read her Praise Alert for the day."

Dontae rolled his eyes heavenward. His mother emailed her so-called Praise Alerts out to the family at least once a week. His stepfather's children all seemed to enjoy receiving the Praise Alerts; they even sent comments back. Dontae wished they would stop hitting reply to all because he wasn't really interested.

All these Praise Alerts were his sister, Joy's fault. About five years ago, his mother had given Joy a journal to write down her thoughts and to give God praise for things He had done in her life. At the time, Joy wasn't really feeling it. However, within a few months his sister had given her life to the Lord and gotten over some serious issues in her life. Ever since that happened, his mother decided that the entire family needed to be in on this praise thing. Hence the Praise Alerts.

"Get up, boy. Let me open my email so you don't have to strain your eyes trying to read it on that 1999 flip phone."

Ronny got up and then hovered over Dontae's shoulder while he opened his email account. Ramsey came and stood behind Dontae also. They each read the Praise Alert at the same time. Her Praise Alerts always began with a scripture out of Psalm 150:

Praise ye the Lord. Praise God in his sanctuary: praise Him in the firmament of his power. Praise Him for His mighty acts; praise Him according to His excellent greatness... Let every thing that hath breath praise the Lord. Praise ye the Lord.

After the scripture the praise alert went on to tell of God's goodness in someone else's life. This one said, '*For the past three years I have gone through so much. I went from being blessed and having everything, well at least materialistically (cars, homes, a great job), to having nothing, not even hot water to bathe—not that I wanted to because I was so depressed. My wife left me and my house was due to be sold on March 4th (foreclosure) and today I was approved for SSDI and they are working with me and Legal Aid to see how they can help to save my home. Imagine, the SS Administration trying to help. I don't know why God brought me so low, but I pray that it is for His glory. Oh and I also thank Him for giving me a fighting spirit that will not allow any demonic influences or energies to win. My wife said that my fighting spirit was what won her heart back... Praise the Lord!*

"Mama Carmella is something else," Ramsey Jr. said as he finished reading the Praise Alert.

"Tell me about it," Ronny added. "There have been days when I've been down on myself about my business and then she'd send one of her Praise Alerts and it just picked me right up."

Dontae wasn't as enthusiastic. He stood up, pointed to his seat and asked Ronny, "Can you show me the website you wanted me to check out now?"

"Oh, sure thing." Ronny sat back down and typed an address in the browser, hit enter and then pointed at the screen as the information materialized.

"The Sanctuary at Kiawah Island?" Dontae had a puzzled look on his face.

"Why you got your face all scrunched up like that? It's a five-star resort. What better place to win your lady back?"

"I'm not saying the place isn't nice. But it's all the way in Charleston, South Carolina. I just don't see why we have to leave Charlotte when both Jewel and I already live here."

"Just shaking my head," Ronny said again.

"What? What did I say?" Dontae turned to Ramsey for help.

Ronny said, "You're going to Charleston next weekend anyway. I just heard you book the Ritz for business. Why not schedule something with Jewel after your meeting."

"I'll tell you why," Dontae said. "There's going to be a ton of athletes in Charleston networking and cheesing for the camera that weekend. How can I concentrate on Jewel with all that going on?"

"That's why I'm suggesting The Sanctuary. Your meeting is at the Ritz. Once we check out of there... it's all about personal," Ronny said.

"I don't know, D, I'm kind of with Ronny on this one." Ramsey scrolled down, looking at the features the resort offered. "To me, if you just run into her at a restaurant in Charlotte, that doesn't seem like you put a lot of effort into it. But run into her at a swank place that this... and then she discovers that you set the whole thing up, now that sounds like a man who wants his woman back."

"How would I even get Jewel to agree to meet me at this resort?"

"You won't," Ronny said, then added, "Book the rooms for this weekend, then have Dawn tell her that she has a free weekend at a five-star resort. Jewel will bite because she's ticked with you and probably needs a little getaway right now."

Dontae took a moment to think it over, then said, "Actually, this isn't a bad idea." He turned to Ramsey and added, "So glad you invited Ronny out here this week. Looks like he's going to be helping both of us."

"He wasn't doing anything else. Might as well help us out," Ramsey said.

"Glad that my between-jobs situation could be of service to my brothers. But since we all know that I don't have any money... I might be charging for my services this week."

***

Jewel's eyes were just about popping out of her head as she and Dawn pulled up to The Sanctuary resort at Kiawah Island. The valet opened the car doors for them, then about two or three other employees said, "Welcome to The Sanctuary," as they made their way up the walkway. The front doors were pulled open by staff members as they approached. As they entered the large main entrance, Jewel couldn't help but be awed by her beautiful surroundings. Looked like a place where royalty vacationed.

As they walked through the doors, three more staff members welcomed them to The Sanctuary and then directed them to the registration desk. "Girl, this place is top notch. How on earth did you get a free stay at a resort like this?"

"Don't look a gift horse in the mouth. Let's just enjoy the weekend. Didn't you tell me that you needed to get away?"

"I had no idea that you would bring me to a place like this. All I can say is, you must really love me and I might need to break up with the love of my life about once a year if I get perks like this for my troubles."

Dawn took the room key from the desk clerk and as she and Jewel headed to their room she asked, "So you think this weekend will make up for your broken engagement?"

Jewel stopped, put her hand over her heart and shook her head. "Forget what I just said. I don't ever want to go through this kind of pain again in life."

"I'm sorry that I asked you that, Jewel. Please forgive me." Dawn put her arms around her sister and lovingly pulled her into an embrace. "I shouldn't have said that. Please just forget what I said and let's try to enjoy ourselves this weekend."

Jewel drew strength from the hug. She took a deep breath and then stepped back. "I'm good. I don't want to spoil our fun this weekend by dwelling on my problems with Dontae."

"That's the spirit," Dawn said as she they found their room and she opened the door.

Taking in the beauty of the suite, and walking from the living room, to the kitchen and then the bedroom, Jewel said, "The only way I can see you getting this room for free is if they think they are going to get about thirty grand off of you by suckering you into one of those timeshares."

"Girl please, I don't make enough money to even qualify for a timeshare."

Still walking around, taking in every facet of the suite, Jewel said, "Well you sure must be living right or something. God is in the blessing business and I guess he just decided to bless us this weekend."

"In more ways than one, my dear sister... in more ways than one," Dawn said without even cracking a smile.

3

"Man, you wasn't lying. This is hot," Dontae said as they stepped inside the resort.

As they walked to the registration desk, several staff members said, "Welcome to The Sanctuary."

"I told you that this spot was legit. Now come on. Let's hurry up and get the key to our rooms so we can get ready for our golf game."

Dontae stood flat footed and looked around the lobby area. "Why would you sign us up for golf? Jewel doesn't play and won't be anywhere near the greens."

"Will you stop thinking about your love life for a minute? We can do a little networking on the golf course and then we can do lunch on the beach at the Loggerhead Grill. They are supposed to have really good burgers and Dawn said that she'll have Jewel on the beach as we stroll towards the grill."

"All right, all right. That sounds like a plan." Dontae was anxious to see Jewel and make things right. But he didn't want to blow his chances. She'd been refusing to see or talk to him for two weeks now.

They went to their rooms to get changed. Dontae showered, threw on a pair of tan shorts and a white polo shirt. He pulled out his iPad to check his emails, never know when another endorsement deal might come through for one of his clients. Dontae didn't like to sleep on those types of things. His clients were pro-ballers, they made good money in the NBA and NFL; however, most of them longed for the big money that endorsements could bring, so he was always on the lookout.

While scrolling through his emails, Dontae noticed that someone from his old high school had emailed him concerning Coach Linden's awards banquet. Dontae deleted the email without opening it.

He then went through the rest of the emails, quickly answering questions and jotting down notes. As he was finishing up, he received another Praise Alert from his mother. Dontae was about to close down his computer without even opening it, but then he remembered how excited Ramsey Jr. and Ronny were to receive the Praise Alerts and he felt a little guilty.

He opened the Praise Alert and read from Psalm 150 again:

... Let every thing that hath breath praise the Lord. Praise ye the Lord.

The Praise Alert read, '*I found an article in a reader's digest when I was 13; it was a guaranteed formula for getting the results you want from prayer. So I said this prayer believing for a miracle, and it worked, and I heard the voice of Jesus in a dream, assuring me that everything would be okay. This would be the first of many miracles over a span of nearly two decades. You see, ever since that very first miracle, I never had peace, contentment or fulfillment in my life. In fact I was unhappy and depressed for most of that time because God was only in my life as a provider of material needs, like a year-round Santa. But I praise Him today, because He stayed faithful giving me miracle after miracle after miracle, because he never changes or writes us off, even when we deserve it. He is the same yesterday, today and forever and his word is infallible, claim it in faith and it never fails you. Mark 11:24 reminds us that Jesus never told a lie. Whatever you ask for in faith, you will receive. But remember that things can never take the place of God in your life. If you want the peace that surpasses all understanding, seek Jesus, not just as savior, but also as Lord.*'

Where does she find this stuff? Dontae wondered. But then he just put it out of his head. He'd read the Praise Alert. Now if one of his step-brothers mentioned his mother's Praise Alert at least he'd be able to say he read it also... read, but that's about it. Nothing in the email spoke to him or caused him to bless the Lord. Dontae had grown up in church, but sometimes he felt numb to it all.

He turned off his iPad, put it back in his suitcase and then grabbed his golf clubs. He was almost out the door when his cell phone rang. It was his mother. He opened the door to his hotel room as he answered the phone. "Hey Mama, what's up?"

"And how are you on this most wondrous day?" Carmella asked her son.

"I'm doing all right. Getting ready to golf with Ronny."

"That's good. Well, I don't want to hold you up. I was just calling to tell you that your sister said that your father will definitely be released on Tuesday."

"I didn't think he'd be out until Thursday. Thanks for letting me know. I'll try my best to get back there so I can see him next week."

"Good. Your father will need you and your sister even more than you know. And I'm proud that both of you have a mind to be there for him."

"Careful Mom, you actually sound like you care."

"Of course I care about your father. I was married to the man for over twenty years."

And then he left you for a woman who was barely in her twenties at the time, Dontae thought but wouldn't dare say to his mother. So he chose to say instead, "I just got your Praise Alert."

"What'd you think of that one?"

"Honestly Mom, I really don't know what to think. I don't even know why you send those alerts."

"You really don't know?"

"I really don't, but I wish you would enlighten me. And where do you get all those stories from?"

Carmella hesitated for a moment, then said, "Different people send me praise reports or I find them on the internet. But I sent them because I want all of you to know God."

Continuing down the hall towards the lobby, Dontae said, "Oh, well then you don't need to send those alerts to me, because I already know God."

"No," Carmella said with force, "you know about *my* God. I want you to come to know *your* God."

That sounded strange to Dontae. After attending church all of his life, how could his mother say that he didn't know God? He almost asked her for clarification, but then he ran into Ronny and decided to table the conversation for another time. "I'll call you back later, Mom. Ronny is ready to take his whoopin' on the golf course."

"Okay Son, I love you and tell Ronny I love him also."

"I'm not getting ready to tell a grown man that. But I will give him the phone so you can tell him yourself." Dontae passed his cell to Ronny.

Ronny gripped the phone to his ear, smiled and then said, "I love you, too, Mama Carmella."

Dontae took the phone back. "Love you, Mom. I'll see you next week." He hung up his cell and then he and Ronny headed to the golf course. Dontae proceeded to show everyone just how off focus his game was.

By the time they reached the fifth hole, Ronny was frustrated enough to ask, "What's wrong with you? You're not even trying to make us look good out here."

"I'm here aren't I?" He pointed at Micah and Drake, the two men they were playing against. "Go on back over there and continue telling them about your next get-rich-quick scheme."

"Oh it's like that, huh?"

"Yeah, it's like that," Dontae said as he lifted his club and prepared to swing and missed.

"Maybe you'd hit a few balls if you didn't have such a nasty disposition." Dontae scowled at him. Ronny shrugged his shoulders. "I'm just saying." He walked over to the other team and said, "Looks like it's y'all's turn again, since my partner can't seem to hit wind, let alone a little old golf ball."

That was it, Dontae had taken all he could from his younger brother. He threw down his gold club, swung around and charged at Ronny like he was still playing football. "I bet I could hit *you* with no problem at all."

Ronny's eyes widened. He held up a hand as Dontae approached. "What's with all this aggression? I'm not about to fight you. I'll fight the world with you, but I wasn't raised like this. I'm not about to come to blows with my own brother."

Dontae backed up, took a deep breath as he unclenched his fists. Dontae and Ronny hadn't been raised in the same household, but

Ronny was right. For almost a decade now, they had been brothers, and he was grateful for the new brothers and sisters that he now had. "I'm sorry about that, bro. I just don't know why I get so angry at times."

Micah and Drake both glanced at their watches and then Micah said, "Hey, we've had a lot of fun with the game, but we probably need to get back. Got a meeting scheduled in an hour."

"It's cool," Ronny said. The two men began walking away from them as fast as they could, as Ronny threw in, "Go ahead and chock this one up as a win for your team, Micah."

"Sorry about that, Ronny. I know you were trying to pitch to the investment banker. But my heart just wasn't in the game."

"Oh well. Easy come, easy go." Ronny slapped a hand on Dontae's shoulder and said, "Come on, let's go grab some lunch."
***

Lounging on the beach in her purple and tan bikini, Jewel felt as if she'd been swept away to a place of peace where the problems she had back in Charlotte didn't even matter. "Thanks for inviting me to this wonderful place. I feel so at peace here," Jewel said as she turned to her sister, who lay beside her.

"You're the only person I wanted to come here with."

Jewel laughed. "You don't have me fooled for a minute, Dawn. You are lying on the lounge chair right now, dreaming about Taye Diggs rounding that corner." She pointed towards the entrance over by the Loggerhead Grill. "And then walking by us, stopping as he catches a glimpse of you, and then dropping down on one knee and asking you to marry him."

Dawn waved the thought away. "Get real, Jewel. In case you forgot, Taye Diggs likes white women. He's been married to one for over ten years, so I don't have any illusions about him or anyone else getting all excited about seeing me."

Jewel sat up. She grabbed her sister's hand and pulled her up with her. "What are you talking about, Dawn? Don't you know how beautiful you are?"

Dawn averted her eyes.

"I'm serious. You always put yourself down about one thing or another. But you have got it going on and I think it's about time you accepted that fact."

"I know that I'm smart. But I'm just not as pretty as you and Maxine."

Maxine was their oldest sister and she was something to see. Long legs, slender body and a face that Halle Berry would kill for. But that didn't mean that Jewel and Dawn were throw-backs. "Okay, our sister is a model and we're not, but we are still desirable women. I know my worth, what about you, Dawn Henderson?"

"You don't know what it's like being a sister to you and Maxine," Dawn complained.

"And you don't know what it's like being a sister to a magna cum laude graduate both in high school and college. Then that same sister becomes this awesome engineer who helped design the car that I drive every day."

"Okay, okay. You win. Yes, I know my worth. I am fabulous. So, don't try to throw Taye Diggs off on me... now if Idris Elba came around that corner looking for a woman to love, I just might have to rescue that brother."

"Not if I see him first," Jewel said, giggling. She liked the sound of her laughter. She hadn't heard that sound in the past two weeks.

"Oh please," Dawn said, "You already have a man wanting to marry you, so you don't need to steal my Idris Elba dreams away from me."

Thinking of Dontae sucked all the joy out of Jewel's day. She stretched back out on the lounge chair and stared at the pool that was not more than a foot or two away from where she lay. She then turned her attention to heaven above, praying for answers that never seemed to come. She didn't understand the man she had fallen in love with, not one single bit. But she prayed that the love she had for Dontae Marshall would not torment her for the rest of her days.

"I'm sorry, Jewel. I didn't mean to make you sad all over again. I was just joking with you."

Jewel wished that she was at church so she could go down to the altar and lay herself prostrate before God and allow Him to heal her wounded heart.

Dawn cleared her throat. Tapped Jewel's arm and said, "Look, we're right here at the Loggerhead Grill. Why don't we grab some lunch and then go back to our room and get dressed so we can do some shopping this afternoon?"

Tempted to just lay there and wallow in self-pity for at least another hour, Jewel almost turned down her sister's game plan, but then she gave herself a silent pep talk and then slapped her hands together as she sat back up. "That sounds like a plan."

Just as two men rounded the corner, entering the pool area, Jewel bent down to pick up the straw hat she'd laid on the ground. She put the hat back on her head and then slid her feet in her shoes, bending to adjust the strap. As she rose back up, she startled as out of the corner of her eye she spotted someone close behind her—too close. She swung around and came face to face with Dontae.

Forgetting her close proximity to the pool, she moved back to allow more space between them, but losing her footing at the pool's edge, her arms began flailing. Dontae reached out and tried to grab hold of Jewel's arm, but she was, by then, too far out of his reach, so he leaned forward a bit to catch her. Jewel grabbed hold of Dontae about a second before she fell backward into the pool, taking Dontae with her.

"Dontae, what are you doing here?" Jewel asked as they wiped water from their eyes and then looked each other in the face.

"Looks like I'm about to go for a swim with you," Dontae said good naturedly.

But Jewel wasn't having it. She smelled a rat, and had a feeling that Dawn would be ordering a bowl full of cheese for lunch today.

4

Jewel toweled off and then walked a few feet away from the pool to sit down at one of the outdoor tables at the Loggerhead Grill.

Dontae pulled his shirt over his head, wrung it out a few times and then flung it over his shoulder as he joined Jewel and Dawn at the table. As Ronny sat down, Dontae said, "You remember Ronny, don't you, Jewel?"

Jewel gave Ronny a tight lipped smile. "Of course I remember Ronny. How is your travel business going?"

Ronny shook his head. "People just aren't traveling as much these days, what with the economic meltdown this country has gone through."

"Tell me about it," Dawn agreed. "This is the first time I've gotten out of Charlotte in a year."

Ronny held out a hand to Dawn. "I'm Ronny, Dontae's younger brother."

Shaking his hand, Dawn said, "I'm Jewel's younger sister... oh, my name is Dawn."

"Dawn." Ronny let the name roll off his tongue and he released her hand. "Such a beautiful name for an equally beautiful woman."

Before Dawn had time to blush, the waiter arrived at their table with their menus. They each studied the menus for a moment and then Jewel ordered the fish tacos. Her plan was to eat them and then blow all of her fish taco breath in Dontae's direction.

Dontae ordered the pulled pork; Ronny ordered a burger, while Dawn ordered the Cobb salad. As they handed the menus back to the waiter, Jewel pointedly asked, "So, what brings you two here this weekend?"

"Oh, just doing a little networking. We just left the golf course, talking with a few potential clients," Dontae answered.

"Is that right?" Jewel said while glancing at her sister.

Dawn fidgeted nervously. "Isn't this just wonderful that we all ended up here together?"

"Yes, isn't it just wonderful." Jewel decided to take care of her sister later. For now, she was just going to get through the lunch with Dontae and then go on about her business. But it really bothered her that he would spend so much money on this so-called "free" weekend resort getaway, while at the same time, he was worried that she was going to divorce him and try to take all of his money. He confused her.

They ate their meals with Ronny doing most of the talking. If she had learned nothing else about Dontae's step-brother, she knew that he was a talker. Jewel thought he'd make a great car salesman, could probably even do well enough to buy his own dealership. But who was she to tell him how to run his life. She couldn't even figure out what to do with her own life.

As they were finishing up their meal, the waiter came back to the table and asked, "Does anyone want dessert?"

Jewel wiped her mouth with her napkin. "No, thank you. Can you please bring the bill?"

"Not a problem," he said, then asked, "Will this be on one bill?"

Dontae said, "Yes."

Jewel quickly lifted a hand and said, "No." She then pointed to Dawn and told the waiter, "Make it two. I'll pay for her, and then you can give them," she pointed toward Dontae and Ronny, "their own bill."

When the waiter walked away, Dontae leaned toward Jewel, put his hand on her thigh. "Why won't you let me pay for your lunch?"

She removed his hand. "Don't you think you've paid for enough?"

Back in their room, Jewel gave Dawn an earful. "How could you lie to me like this, Dawn?"

"I didn't lie to you," Dawn protested.

"You most certainly did. I asked you numerous times how you were able to swing not just a hotel room, but a suite in this wildly expensive resort. You never once said that Dontae paid for our room." Dawn opened her mouth, Jewel pointed at her. "And don't you dare lie to me again. I know that you and Dontae planned this trip." Jewel wore out the carpet walking from one side of the room to the next. "He thinks he's got me cornered, but I'll show him."

Dawn flopped down on the bed. "Jewel, be reasonable. Dontae isn't trying to corner you. He just wants you to talk to him. The man really loves you."

"The man thinks I'm a gold digger," Jewel threw back at her sister. "I'm not putting up with being treated like that. My father never put a price tag on his love for Mama... and no man that truly loves me would do something as horrible as that either."

Jewel, I understand why you're upset. And you are right. Daddy has always told us not to sell ourselves short with the men we date. But I don't think Dontae meant anything by what he did. People in his circle have prenups drawn up all the time."

"Well then, maybe he needs to change his circle of friends." Jewel shook her head and lifted her hands. "I'm getting in the shower." She went into the bathroom and jumped in the shower. Walking out of the bathroom, Jewel threw on a sundress and was about to sit down so she and her sister could continue their conversation.

But Dawn had other plans. She grabbed her purse. "Let's just go shopping and enjoy the rest of our day.

Sighing heavily, Jewel put her purse on her shoulder and left the room with her sister. Jewel was trying her best to forgive her sister for what she considered a betrayal of sisterhood. She had told Dawn how Dontae had boldly handed her a prenuptial agreement, moments after she had joyfully agreed to marry him. He hadn't even let her enjoy the moment before shoving a document in her face, which let her know that he cared more about his money than he cared about her.

Why couldn't her family just stay out of her business and let her live her own life? But her parents thought that Dontae was a great catch. Both of her sisters gushed over how wonderful she and Dontae look together... the perfect couple they all claimed. But Jewel had her doubts because if they were so perfect for each other, why would

Dontae have his mind fixated on some divorce that should never happen anyway?

"Please don't be mad at me," Dawn said a second before they rounded the corner and entered the lobby.

Jewel was about to tell her sister that she would eventually get over her anger, after some prayer and fasting, but then she saw Dontae and Ronny standing in the lobby looking at her as if she had kept them waiting for some important meeting or something.

"Why are they waiting on us?" Jewel asked Dawn.

"That's why I asked you not to be mad at me," Dawn whispered, "Dontae called while you were in the shower. I happened to mention that we were getting ready to go shopping." When Jewel gave her the evil eye, Dawn said, "I'm sorry. I promise I won't tell him anything else."

Jewel wagged a finger at her sister, the traitor. "You better not."

"Ladies, just consider me your driver for the day," Dontae said as he bowed gallantly in front of them.

"Dawn drove, so we don't need your help." Jewel walked past Dontae and stepped outside.

Dontae rushed behind her. "Come on, Jewel, look," he pointed towards his Range Rover. "My SUV is already here and waiting on you. Dawn's car is still in the parking garage. And don't forget, if you purchase a bunch of things while you're out today, Dawn's little BMW won't have enough room to hold all your things."

"My car is pretty small compared to Dontae's SUV," Dawn said.

Jewel gave her the evil eye again.

"Just saying." Dawn hunched her shoulders.

"I'll trade you," Ronny offered.

"What do you drive?" Dawn asked.

"Ever since my car broke down, I've been driving these." Ronny lifted his feet to show what he was working with.

"And you think I would trade the Beemer I worked hard to get so that I could walk myself back and forth to work, church and the grocery store?" Dawn didn't even wait on an answer from Ronny, she strutted over to Jewel and said, "Do you want me to have my car brought out or are we going to ride with Dontae and the foot man?"

Throwing up her hands as if giving up, Jewel opened the passenger door and got in Dontae's car. "Let's just go."

Dontae climbed in the driver seat; while he put on his seat belt, Ronny and Dawn got in the back seat. "Which mall am I driving you lovely ladies to?"

"We're going to the outlet mall," Dawn answered.

Dontae turned to Jewel and tried to win some points by saying, "My baby don't have to shop the outlet malls looking for discounts. We can go straight to the regular mall, because I'm going to buy you whatever you want."

Jewel wasn't having it. The man shoved a prenup in her face and now he was acting like he wanted to buy her the world... if he did, she would take a shuttle to Mars. "I don't need your money. I'm just fine with shopping at the outlets and with spending my own money, thank you very much."

***

Dontae was tempted to call his Mama and ask her to pray for him because he was striking out right and left with Jewel. He had taken her to the outlet as she suggested, walked two steps behind her as she and Dawn explored each and every store they wanted to go into. He hadn't complained not even once about the three hours they spent going from store to store. But once they finished shopping and were back at the hotel, Dontae was starving so he invited Jewel and Dawn to have dinner with him and Ronny.

Dawn was getting ready to accept until Jewel said, "I wouldn't want to take up any more of your time or cause you to spend any of your precious money on someone like me."

Dontae put his hand on Jewel's arm and said, "I'm not worried about my money. I just want to take you to dinner."

All business like, she responded, "You're very kind to offer, but I'm going to do dinner with my sister tonight." Jewel grabbed Dawn's arm and began pulling her away. She waved at Dontae. "Thanks for taking us to the mall."

"Why does she keep harping on money?" Dontae asked, frustrated as he watched her walk away from him.

"Because you gave her that prenup, stupid," Ronny said as he put a hand on Dontae's shoulder. "You have really made Jewel mad. I'd say you've got a lot of begging to do."

Dontae removed Ronny's hand from his shoulder. "Get off me, man. I've been trying to make up with her. Didn't you see how she was today? She won't even talk to me."

"Why don't you just let her burn that prenup and then take her in your arms and show her how much you love her?"

"That all sounds wonderful when you're using your feet for transportation, but when you've got some real money to lose, not having a prenup doesn't make much sense." Dontae's dad had deserved what he'd gotten in the divorce settlement with his mother, because Nelson Marshall had cheated on Carmella. But even though Nelson Marshall was a cheater, a part of Dontae bled for his father, because he had to give up so much of his income in the divorce that the financial loss eventually became his undoing.

"If you love her, stop thinking about divorce and concentrate on how you can make a marriage with her work for a lifetime."

Dontae turned to his brother. The doubt in his eyes was evident as he said, "In this day and age, who can really last a lifetime in anything?"

5

"Mom, come on, I need your help," Joy whined as she sat in the kitchen with her mother.

Carmella's praise music was playing while she stirred the green beans she was cooking to go along with tonight's dinner. "I can't do it, Joy. Dontae told me flat out not to attend that awards banquet."

"Just because Dontae is ungrateful, doesn't mean that we can't go and celebrate a man who did so much for my brother and your son."

Carmella sat down next to Joy. "I agree with you, Joy. I think that Dontae not attending that banquet is rude beyond belief, but what can I do?"

"You and I can go in place of Dontae. Coach Linden will be grateful to see us, since he did send you an invitation as well as Dontae."

"I just don't know why it's such a big deal to you," Carmella said, eyeing her daughter.

"It's not a big deal to me. But Lance's law firm is in consideration for the school board contract. He wants to represent them in the worst way, and thinks that his showing up at this awards banquet might just give him the networking time needed to close the deal."

"So my son-in-law asked you to hit me up for the tickets?"

"Yes," Joy admitted. Then added, "But I need you to come with us, because I'm going to be bored out of my mind while Lance is floating around the room, collecting business cards and grinning at everybody."

Carmella tapped a finger on the counter, thinking how hard it was to please both her children at the same time. "Okay, I'll go. But I want to tell your brother myself, so don't go running your mouth."

"I couldn't if I wanted to. Dontae is out of town right now, and I'm not trying to bother him while he's on his mission."

"What mission?" Carmella had spoken to her son yesterday and he didn't act as if anything out of the ordinary was going on.

"Oh he didn't tell you?" Joy was practically giggling.

Carmella shook her head.

"I called Dontae's house so that I could tell him about his ungrateful self. I mean, who ever heard of not wanting to celebrate the very man who helped you get into the college of your choice, thereby allowing you to get drafted into the NFL. Essentially, Coach Linden is the reason Dontae is successful today."

Carmella held up a finger, stopping Joy for a moment. "I have to correct that, hon, because the God that this family serves is the reason me, you, Dontae and the rest of this family is successful."

"Okay, okay, you're right, Mom. So anyway, Ramsey told me that Dontae and Ronny were in Charleston trying to surprise Jewel and get her to take Dontae back."

One of Carmella's hands flew to her mouth while the other touched her heart. "Dontae really loves Jewel. And she is just right for him. I so hope that he is able to save that relationship."

"She's a heck of a lot better than that other one he wanted to marry. I'm just glad that Tory is out of the picture."

"You and me both."

***

Dontae and Ronny sat in the lobby trying to figure out where they would eat dinner. They had a few places to choose from, but Dontae wanted to make sure they picked the same restaurant where Jewel and Dawn would be dining that night. He'd tried to call Dawn to get that information from her, but Dawn wasn't answering her phone anymore.

"So what are we going to do, man? My stomach is growling."

"Go on to dinner without me. I can't get a hold of Dawn so I don't know where I should eat tonight. But I don't want to hold you up."

Ronny stood up, got ready to head out and then sat back down. "I can't just leave you like this. I'd never forgive myself if you went off and did something stupid." Slouching in his seat, Ronny said, "I'll just tell Mama Carmella that we spent the night fasting and praying; that ought to make her happy."

"I'm not praying. That stuff doesn't work," Dontae remarked.

Ronny gave Dontae a shame-shame kind of look. "Your mama would slap you if she heard what you just said. And anyway, who said anything about you praying. I'm the one over here praying for a nice thick steak, or a lobster... yeah, yeah, I'll just sit over here and pray for lobster."

Dontae rubbed his index finger around his chin while he took a moment to think things over. He turned back to Ronny and asked, "Do you think I should go up there and try to talk to her?"

Ronny laughed. "She has really got you all twisted up."

"Shut up, Ronny. If you're not going to help me, then why are you here?"

"I'm sorry about laughing. It's just that you're normally Mr. Got-it-all-together. I've never seen this side of you. Not even when you busted up your knee on the football field, and not even when you broke up with that girl, um..." Ronny started snapping his fingers trying to come up with the name.

Suddenly, Dontae stood up and said, "Tory..."

"Yeah, yeah, that was her name," Ronny was saying.

Dontae was looking at the woman in the flesh... well, not in the *flesh* flesh. Tory preferred to clothe herself in high end designers. And she wasn't slacking a bit that day. Had on an off white Sophie Theallet dress with a silk shoulder strap, coupled with the Gucci purse and shoes she was also rocking, he'd say that Tory had found herself another baller. Because she was definitely sporting at least three to four thou and Tory's credit was all jacked up, and since she'd dropped out of college, he knew that she couldn't afford those digs on her own. Matter-of-fact, his pockets were still hurting from all the money he'd laid out on her shopping sprees.

"What are you doing here?" he asked as she strutted over to him. She had a friend with her who was rocking Louis.

"Hanging out with friends for the weekend." She pointed to the woman standing next to her and said, "This is my girl, Diamond."

Dontae shook her hand. Ronny stood and shook hands with both women as Dontae introduced him.

Tory stood there for a moment, looking Dontae over as if he was a prized possession she had lost and then found behind the dresser or something. She then wrapped her arms around Dontae and squeezed him like she was in the fruits and vegetable aisle and was testing for freshness. "It's so good to see you." She then kissed his forehead, his cheek and was about to kiss his lips, but Dontae broke free and stepped away from her.

However, he hadn't broken free fast enough, because Ronny was tapping him on the shoulder and pointing toward the lobby entryway where Jewel and Dawn stood. Both women had their hands on their hips and fire in their eyes.

"Hey baby," Dontae said, as he stepped around Tory and rushed over to Jewel. He took her hand in his and walked her back over to where Tory and Ronny stood. "I don't think you met Tory before. But I told you about her. Remember... she was my—"

"I remember." Jewel pulled her hand away from Dontae and held it out for Tory. "I'm Jewel. How are you?"

"Honey, I'm always good, believe that." Tory shook Jewel's hand and then she and her friend began walking away. Before leaving the lobby, she turned back to Dontae and said, "Nice seeing you again. Don't be a stranger."

"Oh, I'm quite sure that he's going to be a stranger to you from here on out," Dawn said as Tory passed by her.

"Cat fight," Ronny said as he rushed over to Dawn and put his arm around her. "I'm going to keep you close to me, before you do something that will get your pretty little self arrested."

Stepping out of Ronny's embrace, Dawn said, "I'm not the one you need to be worried about." She walked over to Jewel and asked, "Are you all right?"

Jewel folded her arms across her chest as she glared at Dontae. "I'm fine."

"Look Jewel, I wasn't doing anything. Tory just showed up and before I knew anything she was hugging me."

"Looked like she was molesting you," Dawn said.

"Girl, you are quick on your feet. I think I'm falling in love," Ronny said while trying to lean closer to Dawn.

Dontae gave him the eye.

"Dontae is telling the truth," Ronny said. "He didn't do anything to provoke Tory to rub all up on him the way she did."

"Stop helping me, okay, Ronny?" Dontae said as he shook his head. He knew that he should have brought Ramsey Jr. instead of Ronny. His younger brother seemed to take pleasure in messing things up.

"Look Dontae, I think it might be best for Dawn and me to head back home."

"No Jewel, don't leave. I really wanted to spend some time with you this weekend so that we could talk." He looked around at a few of the people who were walking through the lobby. Dontae wanted to hold on to as much of his dignity as he had left. He wanted to play it cool, but the woman he loved was getting ready to pack up and walk out of his life again. He had to do something.

"What difference does it make, Dontae. We could talk all night long, but I don't think either one of us will change our minds."

Dontae wanted to pull out his eyeballs. Jewel was driving him up a wall. He grabbed hold of her arm and moved her toward the back of the room. He leaned in close to Jewel so that he could whisper in her ear. "Come on, baby, we love each other. Can't we work this out?"

"How can we work this out when you claim you want to marry me, but you also want an easy way out if you should ever change your mind? That's not the way it works with me. I have prayed for a forever kind of love, and I won't accept anything less."

Shaking his head, Dontae told her, "I don't ever plan to leave you." He averted his eyes a moment and then looked back at her and said, "But who knows, maybe one day you'll decide that you're not in love with me anymore... maybe you'll want to leave. Can you blame me for wanting to protect myself from that?"

"Yes," she said simply and then added. "I'm not going to say that you don't love me, because I believe that you do. But sometimes you are so distant that I don't even know how to reach you. Now if you can explain that to me, then maybe we have a shot."

When Dontae just stood there staring at her without opening his mouth to explain anything, Jewel said, "That's what I thought," and then walked away from him.

As Jewel and Dawn headed back to their room, Ronny turned to Dontae and asked, "So, does this mean the party is over?"

***

Carmella, Ramsey, Joy and Lance were all dressed up and seated at a table in the school gymnasium eating a chicken, rice and asparagus dinner that wasn't half bad. The dinner was in honor of Coach Linden and everyone seemed to be having a good time. Halfway through dinner, Lance leaned over to Joy and said, "The superintendent just walked in. I'm going to see if I can say hi."

"You go, boy, and bring back that contract so you can take me on that cruise you keep promising."

"You got it, babe." Lance leaned over and kissed Joy before he left the table.

As he walked away, Joy kept her eyes on her man. The love she had for her husband shone through her eyes as she smiled without even knowing that she was smiling.

"You can stop staring at him. I guarantee you that he'll be back," Carmella said as she nudged her daughter.

"I know, Mama. He's just so cute, I have a hard time keeping my eyes off of him," Joy said without an ounce of embarrassment.

Ramsey Sr. put his arms around Carmella as he told Joy. "I know exactly how you feel because I can't keep my eyes or hands off of your mother."

"TMI, okay... some things are just TMI." Joy put her hands over her ears as if she couldn't take hearing anymore.

"Oh please, you are a grown woman. And from the way you were just looking at your husband, I'd say that you know the deal," Carmella told her daughter.

"I'll never be grown enough to hear about my mother's love life."

"Okay, we'll leave you alone." Ramsey took his hand off of Carmella's shoulder and took the last bite of his chicken.

As the superintendent took the podium, Lance rushed back over to Joy and took his seat. "Did you miss me?"

"You know I did. I could hardly take my eyes off of you."

"That's enough, you two. If you don't want to hear my husband talk about our love life, I sure don't want to listen to the two of you fawning all over each other in public," Carmella said while giggling. She was actually ecstatic that Joy had finally found someone that she could love unconditionally. And she prayed that Dontae would soon come to terms with the love he had for Jewel and do whatever it took to hold onto that woman.

"It brings me great pleasure to introduce a great man... a man who has given of himself for over three decades... a man who has tirelessly worked to turn good players into great players." The superintendent stretched out his hand towards the coach and said, "My friend, Coach Linden."

Thunderous applause erupted throughout the room. Carmella stood and continued applauding the man who had helped her son break into the NFL. And then one by one people all over the room stood and gave Coach Linden the praise they thought he deserved.

Looking humbled by the applause, Coach Linden lowered his head in an aw-sucks kind of way. He then directed the crowd to take their seats. "Sit down, y'all. I am no one special. But I do thank you all for deciding to spend your evening with an old geezer like me."

The crowd erupted in laughter.

But just as Coach Linden was about to speak again, the double doors in the back of the gym swung open, banging loudly against the wall. Carmella and others turned in the direction of the noise and watched two police officers storm into the room. There was another man behind them. His face was filled with hatred as he yelled, "This man doesn't deserve to be honored for nothing."

The superintendent stood up and shouted, "What's going on here?"

"He raped my son," the angry man shouted back as he pointed to Coach Linden. "My boy trusted this monster and he took advantage of that trust."

The police officers were now standing on either side of Linden. The one with the handcuffs out said, "John Linden, You will need to come with us."

Linden didn't say a word as the handcuffs were placed on his wrists. The superintendent, though, was simply flabbergasted. He puffed out his cheeks as he demanded, "Uncuff him. We are having an awards banquet in his honor."

"Sorry Superintendent, you're going to have to find someone else to honor—because Coach Linden is on his way to a holding cell."

"Yeah! You're finally getting what's coming to your old lecherous self."

If Linden had looked humbled minutes before, he looked downright mortified now as the police officers escorted him out of the school building with the angry man screaming obscenities as he followed after them.

"What just happened here?" Joy asked as she looked around the table.

But Carmella wasn't so much worried about what had happened in the gym. She was more concerned with what might have happened ten years ago when Linden was Dontae's coach. Had she finally discovered the answer to why her son seemed so withdrawn and angry at times? She hoped to God that she hadn't.

6

Even though Dontae's weekend with Jewel had been a total bust, today was a good day, because his father had been released from prison. Dontae had driven from Charlotte to Raleigh to see him. His father hadn't wanted Dontae to pick him up at the prison site. He preferred catching the bus into town.

Dontae understood. Nelson Marshall had once been a powerful judge in the city of Raleigh. He'd had the goal of one day running for a seat in congress, but one affair had brought him low and he was now a slim measure of the man he once had been. Dontae had looked up to his father and feared his wrath. But today, he had come to restore some dignity back to the man who helped raise him.

Dontae had wanted his mom and sister to be with him when he met with his dad. He wanted them to see the look on Nelson Marshall's face the moment he realized that he didn't have to worry about starting over. But since they chose to go to Coach Linden's shame of an awards banquet last night, he really didn't want to talk to them right now.

Dontae pulled up at the Panera where he and his father had arranged to meet. He got out of his car, took a deep breath and then made his way into the bagel shop. His father hadn't been there for him at a time when he needed him the most, but Dontae was trying to forget about all of that now. His mother was always telling him that God gives out special blessings to people who stretch out their hand to give rather than to receive. Dontae was about to test out her theory.

Nelson was seated in a booth towards the back, waving like crazy as Dontae walked in. Dontae smiled and walked over to the booth. Nelson stood and hugged his son.

Dontae felt his eyes watering at his father's touch. He quickly pulled himself together, though, because they were surrounded by people and he didn't want anyone thinking he was soft, crying over a simple hug from his dad. Sitting down in the booth opposite Nelson, Dontae cleared his throat and said, "It's real good to see you."

Whereas Dontae was able to hold back his tears, Nelson just couldn't. He picked up a napkin and dabbed at his eyes. "Boy, you sure are a sight for these old eyes."

"You're not that old, Dad. You're still in your fifties."

"Yeah, well I'm closer to sixty than fifty and that's pretty old to be starting all over again." Nelson sighed, and then lifted his shoulders. "But I'm not concerned with that. I'm just thrilled to be home and to be able to see my family." With that said, Nelson dabbed at his eyes again.

"That's why I wanted to meet with you tonight, Dad... to let you know that you don't have to start from scratch." Dontae pulled an envelope out of his jacket pocket and handed it to his father.

"What's this?"

"Open it," was all Dontae said as an answer.

Nelson had this quizzical look on his face as he opened the envelope. As he pulled the contents out, Nelson's eyes widened and they filled with tears again. He looked like a broken man as he lowered his head and then passed the envelope back to Dontae. "I can't take this."

"Dad, what are you talking about? This is your money. I'm just giving it back to you."

Nelson looked up, hope springing forth. "What do you mean?"

"When you and mom divorced, you gave me the eighty thou you'd been saving for my college fund. But if you remember, I received a full scholarship, so I put the money in a CD and didn't touch it until yesterday when I cashed it in."

"But that check is for a hundred thousand."

"I made out pretty good on the interest," Dontae told his father as he handed back the check.

Nelson hesitated for a moment, but only a moment. He took the check and then asked, "Are you sure you want to do this? I know you received a scholarship, but I always assumed that you used the money for living expenses."

"Nope. Mama made me invest the money and wouldn't let me get an apartment with the money during my junior year when I wanted my own place." Dontae shrugged. "She was right, though. Because after busting up my knee, if I hadn't been able to keep most of my first year earnings, I would have needed that money real bad."

Nelson smiled then, but it was a bittersweet smile. "Your mom has always been the smartest woman I've ever met. And she can cook, too."

"The total package," Dontae said, not able to resist the urge to rub in that fact.

"Yeah, and I'm a total fool."

"You said it, I didn't." Dontae put his hand in front of his mouth to disguise the grin on his face.

"How are things going with you and Jewel?"

That wiped the grin off his face. Dontae said, "Not so good, Dad... like father like son, I guess."

Nelson shook his head, grief etched across his face. "Don't tell me you cheated on that woman?"

"No, nothing like that. She's just upset with me right now and I haven't been able to fix the situation yet." His phone beeped, letting him know that he had received a text. He looked at his phone. It was his mom asking him to call her. Dontae knew what she wanted to talk about, and he wasn't ready for that yet. So he ignored the text, just as he had ignored her calls earlier in the day.

"So where are you staying, Dad?"

"I'm at the Marriott down the street. Your sister booked me a room there for the week."

"So what's your plan after that?"

Nelson waved the envelope as he said, "This just made planning things a whole lot easier. I think I'll see if I can find a house to rent, one with a home office and then set out to find some consulting contracts."

"What kind of consulting will you be doing?"

Nelson had a light in his eyes as he spoke, "I thought about how I would build a career for myself every day that I spent behind bars. I worked in government all those years as a judge, so I know there is money to be made by helping businesses fill out government contracts. And with my law degree, I would also be able to review contracts for my clients."

"Sounds good, Dad. I'm glad you've got it all worked out."

"Now all we have to do is work out this situation you've gotten yourself into with Jewel," Nelson told his son.

***

"Don't you think you should give Dontae another chance?" Maxine, her oldest sister asked as she and Dawn hung out with her at an uptown eatery.

"You don't understand." Jewel took a sip of her iced tea and then said, "Dontae keeps part of himself hidden from me. I don't know from one day to the next who I'm going to be dealing with... the loving, attentive Dontae or the clouded and guarded Donate. He's got to change if he wants things to work between us and that's the bottom line."

"Okay, but you are going to lose that man if you don't hurry up and get over this attitude problem of yours," Maxine admonished.

Dawn shook her head. "I think you're wrong, Maxine." Dawn laid her fork on her plate. "I had been trying to get Jewel to work things out with Dontae also. I even tricked her into going out of town with me this past weekend so that Dontae could talk to her."

"You was wrong for that," Maxine said, laughing to herself about the things her sister had shared with her about their weekend adventure.

Dawn lifted her hands in surrender. "Okay, I was wrong. But I just wanted to help Jewel out... that is until I realized that she knows exactly what she's doing. Because I happen to believe that the divorce rate is as high as it is because people tend to look over the very things that bothered them about their mate even before they said, 'I do'."

Jewel nodded. "I have so many friends who have told me that they thought marriage would change their husband. So they put up with all his bad behavior until after the wedding. And all that did was cause more problems later on."

"Yeah, so leave her alone. Jewel knows what she needs from Dontae. And if he truly loves her like we think he does, then he's got to man up," Dawn said.

"Okay, you're right." Maxine put a hand on Jewel's shoulder. "We're here to support you, no matter what you decide to do."

But Jewel wasn't listening to anything her sisters had to say at the moment. Her concentration had been thrown off because of the picture of Dontae that had just flashed on the television screen above the bar area. She stood up and walked over to the bar as a close up of another male filled the screen. This man was in court being arraigned.

Jewel looked at the bartender as she pointed at the television and asked, "What's that about?"

The bartender looked up toward the television and said, "Oh, that's Coach Linden. He just got arrested for molesting the boys that he coached years ago."

"That's awful," Jewel said. "What school does he coach at?"

"He's a high school coach out of Raleigh."

Dontae grew up in Raleigh, was all Jewel could think as she went back to the table and grabbed her purse. "I've got to go," she told her sisters.

"What's wrong? You look like you just watched a murder or something," Dawn said.

"I need to call Dontae and make sure he's okay," was all she said as she left the restaurant.

***

Lance's cell phone was ringing. He sat up in bed and answered. Joy could only hear her husband's side of the conversation, but from what she could make out, the superintendent of schools was on the other end and Lance was arranging a meeting with the man.

When her husband hung up the phone, Joy said, "You're not still considering taking them on as a client, are you?"

"Why not?" Lance asked as he got out of bed, heading for the bathroom.

Joy jumped up. "That man might have done something to my brother, that's why."

"You don't know that for sure. Dontae hasn't said anything about Coach Linden," Lance said.

"We haven't talked to Dontae since Coach Linden got arrested the other night. So we can't confirm that Dontae wasn't one of his victims."

Lance lifted a hand. "*Alleged* victims."

"Don't you dare talk to me about being innocent until proven guilty." Joy was pacing the floor now. "And to think that I was against Dontae for being so rude to Coach Linden. But now I know why he didn't want to have anything to do with the man." She turned back to Lance. "And now my husband wants to represent that monster."

"Calm down, Joy."

"I'll calm down when you show some family loyalty. And it's not just Dontae that we need to be concerned with. Unless you've forgotten, my stepfather was the principal at that school for two years of the time that Coach Linden was there, so Ramsey could also be sued before all this is over."

Lance put his arm around his wife, trying to soothe her. "If I'm able to get these charges dropped, then nobody will be able to sue anybody."

Pushing her husband away from her, Joy asked, "What about my brother? If Coach Linden did something to him, shouldn't he be able to sue?"

Hunching his shoulders, Lance said, "I don't know what you want me to do."

Throwing up her hands, she turned away from him. "Go get in the shower and go to work, Lance. I don't even want to talk to you right now."

She sat back down on her bed and called her mother. When Carmella answered the phone she asked, "Have you talked to him?"

"I wish I had. But he's not returning my text messages or answering my calls."

"What are we going to do, Mom?"

"We're going to pray, and put this in God's hands. There is a reason why Dontae is avoiding us and it's all going to come to light."

Thinking about Lance representing the school against Coach Linden's victims put a knot in her stomach. "I really need to speak with him, Mom."

"Sunday is Mother's Day. Everyone else is going to be here, so I don't think Dontae is going to miss celebrating Mother's Day with me."

"Okay, so do you think we should ask him about this in front of the whole family?"

"We probably need to take him to the side, but let's pray about it."

"Okay Mom, I'll see you on Sunday. And hopefully we'll find out if Dontae is one of Coach Linden's victims."

"I hope not, Joy. Because if that is true, I just don't know what I'm going to do."

7

Carmella was having a banner day. Since she now had seven grown children with jobs, well... Ronny was between jobs, but Carmella believed that something was going to turn up for him soon. As far as Carmella was concerned, her heart was full because she would have six of her seven children in her home today. Rashan was still on the mission field and wouldn't be able to attend her Mother's Day brunch, but she and Ramsey had done Face Time with him earlier that morning.

Ramsey had somehow gotten all the men in the family to agree to cook the brunch. Carmella didn't have high hopes for the meal they were about to consume, but she would eat it with a smile on her face, just at the thought that the men in her life loved her enough to do this.

"I am so glad that we didn't have to slave in the kitchen today. It's about time the men do something productive around here," Renee said as she kicked her feet up on the lounge chair like the princess she thought she was.

"Since when have you ever slaved in the kitchen?" Raven scoffed at her sister's proclamation.

"I used to help Mom in the kitchen when we were kids all the time," Renee reminded her sister.

"You were Mom's little helper then," Raven agreed. "But you won't even come in the kitchen to help us now." Raven pointed towards Joy and Carmella when she said the word us.

Carmella saw the sad look on Renee's face and quickly came to her rescue. "Renee doesn't have to spend time with us in the kitchen. We spend time together other ways, don't we?"

Renee nodded and then as she looked intently at Carmella, she added, "But even though I don't cook with you... you do know that I love you, right?"

"I sure do, honey." Carmella reached over and gently touched Renee's arm. "And don't you ever feel bad for wanting to hold onto the memories you shared with your mother. Lord knows, I treasure every memory that I had with mine, and even though she's been gone from this earth for many, many years, there's still not a day that goes by that I don't wish she was here with me."

When Renee's eyes filled with tears, Joy, Carmella and Raven surrounded her and the four women group hugged. When the women parted, Renee wiped her eyes, shook her head as she mumbled, "Mother's Day... for the longest time, I didn't have anyone to spend this day with. But you know what?" she said while looking at Carmella. "If I can't spend this day with my birth mom, I sure am happy to be spending it with you."

"I understand exactly what you're going through," Joy told her. "It's kind of like how I felt at my wedding; I wanted my father to walk me down the aisle, but he was in jail. And then, Ramsey, being the wonderful step-father that he is, walked me down the aisle."

"Daddy was so proud. He told me that you were the first child he had the honor of walking down the aisle," Raven said.

"Don't get me wrong, Raven, I was truly grateful that Ramsey was there for me... but it didn't stop me from wishing it had been my dad."

"And I with you... with all of you," Carmella said as she kissed her girls' foreheads. Life was good, even when you had to struggle to get to the good part.

"Hey, what's going on in here?" Ramsey asked as he and the boys came out of the kitchen carrying plates and bowls of food.

Carmella glanced over at the men in her life. Ramsey was so open, honest and loving towards her. Ronny had a bright future in store, once he could figure out what the Lord put him on this earth to accomplish. Ramsey Jr. and Dontae already had their careers in order, but both men were nursing some wounds that were long overdue for healing. Ramsey had asked her to leave them alone. He said if they wanted to talk to their parents, they would come to them. Even though she mostly agreed with him, she couldn't allow Dontae to go another day without taking some of the burden off his shoulders.

Just as she was silently praying about how to approach the subject of Coach Linden—since it was obvious to everyone that Dontae did not want to talk about the man—the doorbell rang.

Carmella hopped up, thankful to have something to take her mind off of what she would have to do to her son before he walked away and just began ignoring their calls again. Looking out the peephole, Carmella was surprised to see Jewel on the other side. She had come to family events with Dontae before, but not since she and Dontae had broken up. *Lord, is this your answer to my prayers?*

Carmella swung open the door and said, "Bless the Lord, my son is going to be so happy to see you."

"Who is it, Mom?" Joy asked as she entered the foyer. When she saw Jewel, she began to smile. Joy hugged her and said, "I'm so glad you could make it."

"You knew she was coming?" Carmella asked with a puzzled look on her face.

Joy nodded and then whispered, "She's been trying to talk to Dontae about Coach Linden, too. I was hoping she could help us get some answers out of him."

"Dinner is on the table, so you two need to get back in there so we can eat and—" Dontae was saying as he entered the foyer. He stopped short as he caught sight of Jewel. "What are you doing here?"

"You haven't been answering my calls, and we need to talk," Jewel told him like a woman determined to get answers to mysteries that had troubled her for too long.

***

Looking at the women in his life, Dontae could see that each one of them wanted answers from him, but to give those answers he'd have to open himself up to things he didn't want to deal with or ever think about again. He put his hands in his pants pocket and felt his keys. "I'm going for a drive. Go ahead and eat without me."

"Don't do this, Dontae. Don't run out on the very people who love you and want to help you," his mother admonished.

"I'll be back. Just give me a little time to myself." He rushed out of the door before anyone could stop him. He just needed to get away. To be alone... to feel safe. But as he sped down the street his mind wouldn't let it go, wouldn't let him forget. So Dontae once again went back with that seventeen-year-old kid, away from home at a summer football camp. The football camp that Coach Linden had talked his parents into letting him attend. It had been ten years ago, but Dontae was reliving it as if it had just happened to him last night.

"Good game, boy. We are heading out of here with the championship and do you know who we have to thank for that?" Coach Linden strutted in front of the team like a man on his way to the Super Bowl. He answered his own question, "Our team MVP, Stevie Wallace and the boy wonder who scored the winning touchdown tonight, Dontae Marshall."

The locker room erupted in cheers.

Coach Linden then said, "So, you guys go on out and party and have yourselves a good time tonight. Be back by midnight." He held up a room key. "And Dontae and Stevie get to stay in the suite tonight. There's two bedrooms and plenty of room in the living area to throw another party."

All smiles, Stevie grabbed the room key with excitement dancing in his eyes. "Thanks, coach." Stevie turned to Dontae and said, "We're picking up some girls tonight."

Dontae smiled, thinking that he was about to score and Coach Linden had made it all possible. The boy hung out, getting a little rowdy at times, but mostly just having fun and celebrating their win. Their fake ID's weren't working, so a bunch of them decided to go back to the hotel and get into the liquor that Coach Linden had stashed in the suite that Stevie and Dontae would be staying in. They ran into a few girls who wanted to hang out with them, so they all went back and got their party started with booze and music and dancing.

Around midnight Coach Linden opened the door and came into the suite. He turned off the music. Everyone turned and stared at him. His hands were on his hips and smoke was coming out of his nose as he yelled, "Do you know how many complaints I have received about all the loud music coming out of this room?"

"But coach, we were just having fun like you told us to," Brad, one of the football players said.

"I didn't tell you all to disturb the entire hotel." Coach Linden pointed towards the door. "Party over, get to your rooms."

"What about us, coach? Do we still get to sleep here tonight?" Stevie half asked and half slurred because he had drunk more than his fair share of the booze.

"You and Dontae can stay, but it's lights out for everyone." He pointed at the girls. "I'll call you a cab, so that you can get home safely."

Feeling ill from all the beer he'd drunk through the night, Dontae was ready to lay it down. He went to his room, closed the door, took off his jeans and threw them on the floor. He didn't have the energy to do anything else, so Dontae fell face first onto the bed. He heard himself snoring as his head hit the pillow.

Dontae didn't know how long he had slept before he felt someone lying in the bed with him. At first Dontae thought he was dreaming and imagined that one of the girls from the party had snuck into his room. But even in his drunken state, something didn't feel right. The hand that was moving down his back and then touching other parts of his body didn't seem girly. It was more like the touch of big, clumsy man hands. Dontae jumped out of bed and fumbled around in the dark until he found the light switch. Coach Linden was lying in his bed naked and smiling up at him.

"What are you doing? Get out of my bed," Dontae said in a low voice. He wanted to yell at his coach, but Stevie was in the next room and he didn't want anyone to know what Coach Linden had just tried to pull.

"What wrong?" Coach Linden asked. "I just wanted to sleep in here with you tonight."

Coach Linden was married. Dontae never imagined that the man was gay. But the world was full of people who went both ways... maybe that was how Coach Linden lived his life. But Dontae's parents had brought him up in church and had taught him right from wrong.

They'd opened the Bible to the book of Romans and showed him where God spoke of men and women who became lovers of their own kind, and how the word of God said such acts were unseemly and would be judged by God.

"You'll have to kill me before I get back in that bed with you," Dontae told him and prepared to fight to the death. But then his stomach lurched and the illness he felt earlier erupted as he vomited all over himself and the floor.

"Clean yourself up," Linden growled as he got off the bed and pulled the boxers he'd left on the side of the bed back on. He flung open the door and stormed out of the room, looking as if Dontae disgusted him. Dontae ran over to the door, quickly closed and locked it. Looking down at his shirt, Dontae saw clumps of vomit splattered over it. He wanted to go and wash himself off, but the bathroom was across the hall and he'd left his duffle bag full of clothes in the living room; there was no way he was going out there tonight.

Dontae took his shirt off, wiped his mouth and neck with it and then threw it on the floor. Looking at the bed where Coach Linden had been laying with him made Dontae feel ill again. He couldn't get back in that bed. He wanted to call his dad to find out what he should do. After all, his dad was a big time judge; he'd know how to fix Coach Linden. But it was too late to call his house. The team was heading home in the morning, so he would just tell his dad what happened when he got home.

Dontae pulled the blanket off the bed and sat down in the chair across from the bed, put the cover around him and slept off and on. Every time he thought he heard a noise, he would jump and try to keep his eyes open, until his lids would close on their own.

By morning Dontae's eyes were red and sleep deprived, but he didn't care. He'd made it through the night without Coach Linden coming back to his door. Now he just needed to get on that plane and get home. Someone knocked on his door and Dontae practically jumped out of his skin and then shouted, "Go away."

"I'm leaving your duffle bag in front of the door. Get dressed so we can all get to the airport on time," Coach Linden said through the door.

It took Dontae five minutes to gather up enough nerve to open the door to get his duffle. But the simple fact that he couldn't go home until he got dressed and left this hotel room was the one thing that set a fire under him. Coach Linden wasn't standing at the door waiting to pounce on him, so he pulled his bag into the room and quickly got dressed. Throwing the bag's strap over his shoulder, Dontae rushed out of the hotel room and made his way to the lobby where some of the other team members were already waiting. He hadn't thought about Stevie at all that morning. Not until he saw him walking towards them and noticed that Stevie wouldn't make eye contact with him. At that moment, Dontae realized that after leaving his room, Coach Linden must have snuck into Stevie's room.

When Dontae had made it home, he'd discovered that his father had left his mother for another woman. The following week, Stevie dropped out of school and tried to commit suicide. Everyone assumed that the anger Dontae displayed when he came back from camp stemmed from his parents' break-up, but year after year as he'd kept Coach Linden's secret, Dontae felt as if he was, in effect, sending that monster to the more defenseless Stevie's room.

Now his family wanted answers, but how could he tell them that it wasn't just what Coach Linden did to him that ate at him, but the fact that he hadn't yelled out that night and exposed Coach Linden. If Dontae had run into the room that night, maybe Coach Linden would have been too ashamed at being caught to try the same thing with Stevie, who had been so wasted that he probably hadn't been able to fend the man off.

8

"I'm worried, Mama. Do you think I made a mistake by inviting Jewel? Maybe, Dontae won't come back because he wouldn't want her to hear what he has to say." Joy was wringing her hands as she stood next to her mother.

Carmella shook her head as she exhaled. "If he's going to marry that girl, he owes her the whole truth and nothing but the truth. Time out for married couples keeping secrets from their spouses."

"Amen to that," Joy said and then added. "I wish you would say that to my husband."

Carmella looked concerned as she asked, "Has Lance been keeping secrets from you? Is something going on with you and Lance? Is that why he's not here today?"

"He's celebrating Mother's Day with his own mother today. But you're right, there is something between us."

Brunch had been eaten an hour ago, now everyone was in the family room watching television while Joy and Carmella hung out in the kitchen. Carmella sat down on the stool next to her daughter. "What's wrong?" She held her breath, praying that whatever it was, it was something that could be fixed.

"Lance has been meeting with the school board. He's very close to striking a deal to represent them."

"But isn't that what you wanted? You asked me to attend that awards banquet on Lance's behalf, remember. You told me that he wanted to become the lawyer of record for the school systems," Carmella reminded Joy.

Joy hung her head in misery. She couldn't decide what was more important in this instance... loyalty to her husband or to her brother. "It's just that with the way Dontae has been acting, I truly believe that

Coach Linden did something to him. So, I think Lance should stick by his family and not represent people who have brought harm to us."

Carmella rubbed Joy's back. "I can understand how you feel. But whether Lance decides to represent them or not, he's still the man you fell in love with and he's still the man you promised to spend the rest of your life with. So your job is to love him, even when you don't agree with him."

"I don't know if I can do that in this situation, Mom."

"Then you had no business getting married. He's your husband, Joy. Stand by him."

"How can you ask me to do that? That coach may have done something despicable to your son and you want me to stand by my husband if he decides to represent those people for his own selfish reasons?"

Carmella pointed at her chest. "I can be mad at Lance all I want to be. But I will not ask you to bear my burden. You took vows with your husband before God. Just because the road gets a little rough, that doesn't change the promises you made."

Joy wanted to argue her point, but she knew she'd never win this argument with Carmella Marshall-Thomas. So she simply said, "Mama, sometimes I think you are just too saved for your own good."

Carmella shook her head. "You can never be too saved." She stood and said, "Come on, let's get back in the family room with the rest of the family."

Nodding as if she was coming to terms with something, Joy stood and followed her mother. But just as they were rounding the corner for the family room, the front door opened and Dontae walked in with Nelson following behind.

Stepping towards his mom, Dontae said, "I'm only telling this story once, so Dad stays or no go."

Carmella looked at Nelson. She had spent twenty-three years of her life with him. During those years of her marriage, Nelson had seemed little "g" godlike to her. He had been a wonderful provider and a great father to his children. She never dreamed that Nelson would cheat on her and had been caught off guard and thrown for several loops when she discovered the truth. But that was then and this was now. The man standing before her now had been humbled by life and the mistakes that he'd made; she could see the difference in him by the sadness in his eyes and the slight slump of his shoulders. "You're welcome to stay, Nelson. How have things been going?"

He stepped forward. "I'm looking for an apartment and making contacts so that I can get my life back on track."

"I've been praying for you. And if your children have anything to say about it, you'll be back on track before you know it."

Joy hugged her daddy. "I was going to stop by the hotel to check on you tonight, but I'm glad you're here with us now."

They went into the family room. Dontae rushed over to Jewel and took her hand. "I'm glad you're still here."

"I wanted to wait for you. I knew you'd come back." She gave him a weak smile and squeezed his hand.

Carmella whispered in Ramsey's ear and he nodded, then got up and shook Nelson's hand. "Good to have you back home. The kids have missed you."

"I missed them something awful as well," Nelson said and then added, "And thank you for allowing me to come in here so I can hear what my boy has to say."

"Not a problem." Ramsey turned to Dontae. "Do you want me to clear the room so you can talk with your mom and dad in private?"

Dontae shook his head. "You're all my family. I've been holding this in so long that I just want to say it once and be done with it."

"All right, in that case, the floor is yours," Ramsey said before sitting back down next to Carmella.

Dontae glanced around the room. One by one he took in the faces of his brothers and sisters, his parents and then Jewel. He studied her face the longest because he wanted to know if she would look at him differently after he opened himself up and exposed his wounds. There might not be a need for a prenup at all after this day was over, because Jewel might just decide she didn't want to marry someone like him.

Dontae knew that he wouldn't be able to tell his story if he kept looking at Jewel, so he turned to safer territory. He looked at his mom as he opened his mouth and confessed everything that happened that last night at football camp. He finished up by telling them about Stevie. To Dontae's surprise, he told his story with dry eyes. The tears hadn't come until he started thinking about Stevie again.

Carmella quickly came to his side. "It's not your fault, Dontae. Don't torment yourself like this."

"You don't understand, Mama. If I would have hollered and even tried to alert Stevie to what Coach Linden tried to pull with me, then he might not have gone into Stevie's room that night and Stevie would have kept playing ball and he certainly would have been recruited before me. He was just that good."

"You were victimized by Coach Linden, Dontae. Most victims don't holler out, or tell anyone what their victimizer is doing." Renee stood up and went to Dontae also. "When I was in the eighth grade a girl bullied me unmercifully. But it wasn't until the end of the school year that I finally confess to Dad what I was going through. That's why I work as a youth counselor now. I want to give kids a place to turn, when they think there is nowhere to turn."

Dontae leaned on Renee's shoulder and cried through his sorrows. He wished he'd had someone like his little sister in his life back then. But then his mother started crying and Dontae turned from his little sister and took his mother in his arms and tried to soothe her pain.

The entire time Dontae was telling his story, Nelson had been like a ticking time bomb. He'd held his peace so that Dontae would be able to get everything out that was bothering him, but he could take it no more. He stood with fists clenched. "I'm going to kill him."

Joy put her hand on her father's shoulder and said, "You just got out of jail, Dad. We can't have you going back so soon. I'm going to kill him. And then maybe my husband won't have to decide who to represent."

The rest of the evening turned into an, I'm-mad-as-H-E-L-L-and-I'm-not-going-to-take-it-anymore episode. The men were all ready to ride out. They wanted to go bail Coach Linden out of jail and then drive him to a wooded area, let him out of the car and then hunt him down. They'd tie him to a tree and whip him until he begged for his life. Then they would just go on and kill him anyway.

The women's thoughts weren't any better. Instead of tying the man to a tree, they wanted to string him up by his toes, let him hang there while they took turns stabbing him in the heart. For what else would you do with a monster, but drive something through his black heart?

A house full of Christians and nobody thought to pray, not that night anyway. The wound was too fresh and too devastating. Tears brought them comfort and anger and thoughts of revenge became their friend.

Once things had quieted down in the house, Dontae and Jewel went out on the porch and sat for a while. When he finally mustered up enough nerve to look at her again, he was thankful that he didn't see anything different in her eyes. But he had to hear her say it. "So, I guess you're thanking God that you gave me back that ring now, huh?"

"Why would you think something like that?"

"Well, now you know why I'm so messed up in the head."

"If I'm thanking God about anything, it's that you made it through the horrific part of your life and that I now know you a little bit better." She put her hand over his and looked at him with compassion showing on her face. "Thank you for sharing that with me."

Dontae poked himself in the head several times. "I just wish I could get it out of my head. I've been so angry for so long that I just want it all to stop."

"You know how the Bible tells us that God casts our sins into the sea and remembers them no more?"

"Yeah," Dontae answered wondering what that had to do with what Coach Linden did to him and to Stevie and to countless others.

"I sometimes wish that we could cast the sins that people do to us in some sea of forgetfulness and that way we wouldn't have to ever give them the satisfaction of thinking about them anymore."

"Yeah, me too," Dontae said as he looked off into nothingness. The street was dark now and it was getting late. With the two hour drive he had ahead of him, he would have normally been gone by now. He noticed Jewel's car parked across the street. "You don't plan to drive back tonight do you?"

"I hadn't planned on staying so late. I'm on a deadline and need to get back to work."

"You work from home, so there's no need for you to get on the road tonight." He turned to her. "Look, just stay here with my parents; I'll bunk with my dad for the night and then I'll follow you back to Charlotte in the morning, okay?"

Hesitating for a moment, she finally said, "I can see that you're worried about me. And you already have enough on your mind, so I won't get on the highway tonight. I'll wait and drive back with you in the morning."

"Thank you." He lifted her hand and kissed it. "I wanted to tell you about all of this a while ago, but I kept worrying that you'd think that I was gay or something and then not want to be with me."

Shaking her head, Jewel put her hands on his face and gently told him, "You are not what was done to you. Don't confuse the two. An evil monster molested you, that doesn't make you gay... just makes you a victim."

"I don't like thinking of myself as a victim."

"Nobody does." She kissed his forehead as she said, "But as long as evil is in this world, there will always be a monster out there victimizing someone."

"I think I managed to convince myself that since he didn't do anything but touch me, I hadn't been molested. But you're right, that's exactly what he did to me."

"What he tried to do was steal your future. But look at you, Dontae you made it, despite what Coach Linden did. You beat him; don't you know that?"

Dontae stood, walked to the edge of the porch and then turned back to face her. "To tell you the truth, I'm not sure what I believe right now. I just know that I need you in my life... I need your love."

"You never have to doubt my love for you, Dontae."

Looking at her ring finger he asked, "Then why aren't you wearing my ring?"

246

"I want to wear it," she admitted with surprising ease. "But I don't think you're ready for a lifelong commitment yet. But when you are, please come find me. I'll be waiting." With that she stood up and went back inside the house.

Dontae wanted to go after her and deny her assertion about his marriage readiness. But deep down he knew she was right. She had him pegged. Something was holding him back and he would be spending the night with that person, so maybe he'd try to figure some things out about himself.

***

At the hotel with his dad, they both tried to put up a front like everything was normal between them. But as Dontae lay on one double bed and his father on the other, they both knew it wasn't true. Nothing would ever be normal between them again, but they could still move forward in this new normal that they would somehow create.

Dontae turned to his father and asked, "So Dad, how did you like being at the house tonight with mom and her new family?"

Nelson had no words, just shook his head.

But Dontae saw the regret in his eyes. "Why couldn't you make it work with , Mom? I don't understand how Jasmine got to you in the first place."

"I had lost my way, I guess. In pursuit of my career, I had stopped going to church on a regular basis and just became consumed with what I wanted and I wasn't thinking about what was best for my family. Cheating became easy after that."

They were silent for a long while after Nelson's confession then Nelson asked, "Why didn't you tell me about Coach Linden trying to make a move on you?"

"I wanted to. The whole ride home all I could think about was how powerful my dad was and how you would make Coach Linden pay for what he'd done to me and Stevie. But when I got home everything had changed. Mom was falling apart and was trying desperately to pick the pieces of her life back up and you had moved on with Jasmine. You didn't have time for me anymore."

"And then I let Jasmine call the police on you, so you thought that I wouldn't hear anything you had to say, huh?"

Dontae nodded.

Nelson found that he hadn't shed the last tears over how much his affair had cost his family. He'd lost a career, done prison time and almost destroyed his family. And for what? Some woman who wasn't even in his life anymore, nor did he want her in his life, for that matter. "I'm sorry, son. I'm so sorry. All I can do is promise to be there for you from now on. I'm going to make this up to you... you have my word."

"That's all I need, Dad. Now stop crying and get some sleep." Dontae hit his pillow to fluff it up a bit so he could get a good night's rest. He was drained from having to comfort his mother earlier and now watching his dad fall apart over his revelation was just too exhausting. "This has got to be the worst Mother's Day Mom has ever had."

"Without a doubt," Nelson agreed while wiping the tears from his face. "But at least she had Ramsey to help her get through this."

9

Three days had passed since Dontae had told them what Coach Linden tried to do to him. Like the others, Carmella hadn't taken it well. But unlike the others, Dontae was her son, and it felt as if her heart was bleeding. She hadn't gone in to work on Monday or Tuesday. That morning, Ramsey had gone in to do the bookkeeping for her while her clerks handled the baking.

But now it appeared as though Ramsey had had enough of her moping around the house. He stood at the end of the bed with hands fisted on his hips. "How much longer, Carmella?"

Playing dumb she asked, "How much longer, what?"

"A few of the kids called me this afternoon. They're worried about you because they haven't received the Praise Alert you normally email out to them."

Guilt crossed her face. "I forgot to send that out." She sunk further into her pillow. "Would you mind scouring the internet to find a praise report for me and then send it to the kids?"

Sitting down on the bed next to his wife, Ramsey gently told her, "I can do a lot of things to help you get through this difficult time. I can hold your hand, love you... I can even go down to the bakery and help the staff make those scrumptious desserts that you are so famous for. But I cannot praise the Lord for you. That's an individual thing and something you will have to do on your own."

Tears flowed down Carmella's face as she accepted Ramsey's word as truth. God would not settle for a substitute praiser. Everyone must give God His due out of their own hearts. But right now Carmella's heart was so heavy, and she was so ashamed at the condition she'd found herself in that she didn't even feel worthy to praise God.

Ramsey lifted her into his arms and held onto her. "Dontae is all right, baby. He survived. The enemy didn't tear him down, so don't let it tear you down."

"I was supposed to protect Dontae, and I allowed him to go somewhere with that monster."

"I was Dontae's principal at the time, and I hadn't recognized what was going on. And evidently, Coach Linden was doing all this right under my nose."

"But I'm Dontae's mother, I should have paid more attention to what was going on."

Ramsey shook his head. "You didn't know, Carmella. This is not your fault and I'm not going to sit here and let you carry this all on your shoulders. The blame and the shame belong to Linden and Linden alone."

"You just don't understand, Ramsey. None of this was ever supposed to happen. Grown men aren't supposed to molest teenage boys." She put her hand to her heart as the tears kept coming and said, "And now I feel so much hatred in my heart towards Coach Linden that it scares me."

"It happens, Carmella. I was so livid when I found out about Renee getting bullied for an entire year that I wanted to hurt that kid."

"I've never felt like this before, Ramsey. Not even when Nelson and Jasmine were sending me through all kinds of drama, never once did I feel hatred towards them. But I am feeling so much hatred for Coach Linden right now that I don't even know… how can I praise God when I'm feeling like this?"

Ramsey held on tighter, as he told his wife, "You praise Him anyhow. Isn't that what you've always told me? Through the pain, through the grief and even through the hatred. You keep praising God until He moves the thing that is hindering you out of the way."

***

On her knees, with hands steepled, Jewel cried out to the God she had known since she was fifteen and called out to Him in the back of her grandmother's church, asking Him to come into her heart. Since that day, Jewel had always trusted that God would look out for her and make her into who He wanted her to be. She believed that God was powerful enough to bring the man of her dreams into her life and that He was able to keep them together. Today she was adding something else to the things she believed God was well able to do.

"Thank You, Father, for always being here for me. I thank you for keeping me and for blessing me over and over again. You've even blessed me with things that I don't know about. Things that I don't readily see... so I just want to thank You for everything. Because I know that if anything good has ever come into my life, You were right in the midst of it.

"Dontae was one of those good things that You sent my way. I know we've had our differences lately, but that's only because I'm trying to get him to understand this concept of forever love the way You have shown it to me. But in the meantime, Lord Jesus, I'm asking you for a special blessing for Dontae. I'm asking that You renew his mind and even erase part of it. Make it so that he is able to forget the man who tried to destroy his life, even forget the very act. I believe you can do this, Lord God, and I will keep praying this prayer until the day it manifests for Dontae. Thank You, in Jesus' mighty, can-do-anything-but-fail, name I pray this prayer."

***

"Welcome to my humble abode," Dontae said as he opened the door to let his father into his home. Nelson had called at about seven in the morning and asked Dontae to stay home from work that day. "So, I guess you're ready to tell me why you decided to drive all the way to Charlotte and why I had to take the day off of work?"

"I came to see my favorite son," Nelson told him as he walked in, looking around the house.

"Funny... I'm your only son." Dontae stopped, thought about it for a minute and then said, "At least I thought I was your only son. But feel free to correct me if I'm wrong."

Nelson slapped Dontae on the back. "You thought right. I was just joking with you."

"Are you hungry?" Dontae asked as he headed to the fridge.

"Naw, I picked up a breakfast sandwich on the way down." Nelson sat down on the stool in front of the kitchen island. "Where are your step-brothers?"

Dontae took out a jug of orange juice, poured it in a glass and took a sip. "Ramsey's at work and Ronny is out picking up some material for this new business he's all excited about starting."

"Oh really, what's he working on?"

Putting the jug of juice back in the fridge, Dontae said, "He won't say. Claims he wants to present it to us once he has everything in order."

"I hope it works out for him."

"If this doesn't, something will. Ronny is destined for success, just needs the right project."

"I'm searching for the right project myself... can't see myself going back into law. But this old dog still has a few tricks left."

"You'll find something, Dad. I have faith in you."

"Well, one thing is for sure; I still have connections. And those connections have brought me to your door this morning."

Dontae sat down with his father. "What's up?"

"I found Stevie Wallace."

Dontae looked at his father like he had grown two heads. "Why were you looking for Stevie?"

Nelson put his hand on Dontae's shoulder. "Listen to me for a minute, son." Dontae nodded, giving his father the floor, Nelson continued, "When I was in prison, I sat in my cell every night thinking about one thing and one thing only... redemption. I told God that if He would give me another chance, I would never neglect my family again in life. And God has given me another chance with you and your sister and I'm so thankful for that."

"What does Stevie have to do with you receiving redemption?" Dontae asked.

Nelson's throat was getting dry. "Can I get a bottle of water?"

"Sure thing, Dad." Dontae hopped up and grabbed a bottle of water from the cabinet below the sink. He handed it to his father and sat back down.

"I know you contacted the DA and agreed to testify against Coach Linden, and I think that's a good step forward. Putting Coach Linden away will stop him from hurting any more kids that have been placed in his care. But Stevie... that's where your redemption lies."

Dontae was silent as he thought about what his father was saying to him. In a way it made sense. He had always felt guilty for not warning Stevie about Coach Linden and for not helping him while he was being attacked. That night, he'd denied himself the knowledge of what was going on in the next room. Because if he had acknowledged that the sounds were Stevie calling out for help, then he would've had to do something. And Dontae had just gone to sleep, hoping that he, himself would not be further victimized that night.

Dontae had avoided thinking about Stevie for so many years, but indirectly, Stevie had always been on his mind. He saw him in every young recruit with all the potential in the world that he signed to his agency. Dontae guarded his clients and shielded them from the things in the sports industry that could do them harm. He had taken to his career change like a fish to water, because with each new recruit, he had been subconsciously looking out for Stevie. Now it was time for him to look Stevie Wallace in the face and go hard for the redemption he now needed so desperately.

"Maybe you're right this time. It's way past time for me to man-up and face Stevie."

Nelson stood, pulled his keys out of his pocket. "Let's go."

Dontae hesitated. "You want to go right... right now? How do you even know where Stevie is?"

"When you mentioned that Stevie had been arrested, I figured he might be in jail right now or at least on parole. So, I made a few calls and found out that he's been out for about six years and has kept his nose clean. He's married with three kids, but because of the felony on his record Stevie has been bouncing around from job to job. He's working at a gas station in South Carolina, just fifteen minutes away from your house."

When Dontae first moved on the southwest part of Charlotte, he'd thought it strange how he could be driving down the street and be in North Carolina one moment but then in South Caroline the next. The two states probably needed to drop the whole 'north' and 'south' business and just go on and be plain old Carolina. But he wasn't in government, so he wasn't going to tell them how to run their business. And anyway, he had bigger things to concern himself with, at least that's the way Dontae saw it. "You took the time to find all of that out?"

Nelson nodded and then said, "The way I see it, your mom made out pretty good when she married Ramsey. He's a good guy and I'm glad that she's happy. But I'm still your and Joy's daddy, so it's my job to take care of you two."

"Some more of that redemption, Dad?"

"Yeah." Nelson shook his keys and then said, "Now, let's go get you some redemption."

Dontae had seen the gas station numerous times as he drove down this street, but he'd never pulled in. It was one of those mom and pop service stations that also did car repairs. He got out of the car, looked back and noticed that his dad was still in the driver's seat. He started to say something, but then Nelson lowered the passenger window and said, "Go on. I'll be right here when you get back."

Squaring his shoulders, Dontae pulled up his big-boy britches and walked into the gas station to handle his business. No customers were inside and no one was behind the counter. There was a note taped to the counter that encouraged customers to tap on a small bell for service. Dontae figured that they probably didn't have a lot of customers, so they were able to run the shop with one clerk at a time. He tapped the bell and waited.

"I'm coming."

Dontae heard the deep baritone voice and immediately recognized it from back in the day when Stevie had the ball in his hand and was headed down the field shouting, "check him, check him" or "I got this" and then, "touchdown".

Stevie stepped into the business area of the gas station. He was wearing overalls and wiping some black substance from his hands that Dontae assumed was oil. He hadn't seen Stevie since high school, so he still remembered him as the touchdown-kid. But Stevie wasn't just a scorer, he had an uncanny ability to read his opponents. He could spot their weaknesses and their strengths and he'd use them to get inside their heads.

"What can I do for you?" Stevie asked without looking up.

Dontae waited. He wanted to gauge Stevie's reaction once he realized who was standing in his place of business. Dontae didn't have to wait long. Stevie put the rag down and glanced up. He did a double take. His face went through several different emotions and then he held out his hand. "Dontae Marshall, how've you been?"

"Some days good." Dontae shrugged. "Others, not so good."

Stevie acknowledged that he understood how Dontae was feeling with a head nod. "I watched the game that night. I felt like it was me they were pulling off the field."

"I got through it," Dontae said as he held his chin up like a boy who'd been told, after scraping his knee, that a man has to be strong.

"So what brings you here?" Stevie asked.

Now that he was there looking Stevie in the face, Dontae was struggling with how to best approach the topic. He tossed a couple conversation starters around in his head and then finally landed on, "I just wanted you to know that I'm going to be testifying against Coach Linden when his case comes up."

"Good for you," Stevie said as if he couldn't care less. He picked the rag he'd been wiping his hands with back up and said, "I need to get back to work."

Dontae tried another approach. "Look, if you don't want me to mention your name, I won't."

He averted his eyes as he said, "Why would you mention my name in association with Coach Linden?"

Dontae was taken aback by the way Stevie was playing this. He never expected Stevie to deny that anything ever happened. "Stevie, I was there, remember? Coach Linden tried to attack me first."

"It was nice seeing you, Dontae." Stevie started walking away.

Dontae reached into his jacket pocket and pulled out a business card. "Take this." He handed Stevie the card. "I'm in Charlotte now, so if you ever want to talk, I will make myself available to you."

Stevie nodded as he put the card in his pocket and then headed back to work.

"How did it go?" Marshall asked when Dontae got back in the car.

Dontae shrugged. "Not really sure. He pretended like nothing happened. I got the impression real quick that he wanted to be anywhere but in that small space with me, so I gave him my business card and told him to get in touch if he ever wanted to talk."

"Well, that's all you can do then. Now, hopefully, you can put everything about Linden out of your mind," Nelson said as he drove his son down the street.

"That's one thing that I can't do." Dontae pointed at his head. "As hard as I try, I just can't get it out of my mind."

10

While Dontae was trying to figure out how to get things out of his mind that never should have been there in the first place, Joy was on the phone with Jewel trying to get her to accept Dontae just the way he was. "You know, when you love someone, you sometimes have to put up with things you wouldn't normally put up with," Joy said as she watched Lance stroll into the kitchen and pour himself a cup of coffee.

"I know, Joy. And I truly do love Dontae, but I don't want to help him get into something that he might later regret getting into."

"Dontae would never regret marrying you. And I promise that I will stop butting into his business if you will just take that ring back." Joy prayed that Dontae would never find out that she made this call. But even though they were both grown, she was still his big sister and felt an obligation to look out for him.

Joy had no idea what had been tormenting Dontae all these years. She thought all of his issues stemmed from their parents divorcing after twenty-three years of marriage. But clearly, Dontae had been battling a different demon altogether. Joy had been the one to invite Jewel to her mother's house on Mother's Day, so if the fallout from that day caused Dontae and Jewel to drift further apart, she'd never forgive herself.

"I am here for Dontae. He knows that. I just don't think we should be making wedding plans at a time when he needs to be dealing with other issues."

Lance was leaning against the kitchen counter, sipping his coffee and staring at her. Joy conceded. "Okay, I'll give you that. But as long as I know that you're still in Dontae's corner, then I'm satisfied with that. And I'll get out of your business."

"I know that you're just looking out for your brother, so I'm not offended or anything. You can call me any time," Jewel told her.

Joy thanked her for understanding and then hung up.

"It really does mean a lot to you, doesn't it, babe?" Lance asked as he set his mug down and approached his wife.

"What means a lot to me?" Joy had been trying her level best to do as her mother instructed her. But having just hung up with the love of Dontae's life and accepting the fact that the wedding was, at best, postponed, she really didn't know if she could do this stand-by-your-man stuff right now... especially if he was about to start up another conversation about that case.

"That we be supportive of Dontae." He was only a whisper's distance from her now.

How should she take his question? Was he finally hearing her or was he just going to start another debate? She didn't have the energy to try to figure her husband out, so she just decided to go with the truth. "Dontae is important to me. So, yeah, it's also important that I support him, especially in light of what he went through, and what so many others had to endure at the hand of Coach Linden."

Lance put his wife's hand in his. "I've done a lot of soul searching this week."

"Oh yeah?" was all she said to that.

"I had to ask myself if my ambitions were more important to me than my family. And do you know what I decided?"

She couldn't get the lump out of her throat so she could speak. Joy was terrified of the answer, because in that moment she would discover if her husband loved her enough to do something that would cost him dearly, career-wise. She well knew that the exposure that this court case would receive alone, would give Lance more notoriety than he'd ever had on any case before. Could he walk away from that for her?

"When I married you," Lance began, "I knew that I would have to give up certain cases because you're a prosecutor and I couldn't agree to defend anyone who you were prosecuting. But it never entered my mind that I might also have to give up cases that our family members might be involved in."

She leaned in and touched her forehead to his. "I never thought we'd have to face a situation like this either. I'm sorry if I've been difficult to deal with these past few weeks."

"Thank you for saying that." He kissed her forehead. "But you were right. The superintendent wasn't all that excited about me until he realized that Ramsey was my father-in-law and Dontae my brother-in-law. I don't even think they knew about what Coach Linden had done to Dontae, because they wanted me to get Dontae to be a character witness for Linden. I laughed in their faces at that."

"No honey, you didn't laugh in their faces. That's not professional at all," Joy said, but she was thrilled that Lance had too much integrity to approach Dontae with something like that.

"I didn't have to worry about being professional with them, because I told them that I couldn't take the case."

She screamed. "I am so happy right now. Thank you, Lance. You don't know how much this means to me."

"I hope it means a whole lot, because my earning potential just got a bit lighter."

"Oh ye of little faith. The God I serve knows how to reward us for unselfish acts of kindness," Joy told him before wrapping her arms around him and thoroughly kissing him.

***

Dontae was in his office reviewing some contracts when he received a call from Ronny. "What's up?" Dontae asked when he picked up the phone.

"I know you're busy so I'm not going to hold you, but I was just wondering if you'd noticed that we didn't receive a Praise Alert from Mama Carmella last week or this week either."

Dontae had noticed, but he didn't want to say anything, because his mom was probably still upset over his confession and needed a little break. The Thomas men hadn't been around when Carmella Marshall had fallen apart after his father asked for a divorce. But Dontae had. And he'd witnessed his mother lean on God for the strength to pick herself back up. She would be all right. "Do you think we should head to Raleigh to check on her this weekend?"

"I'm going to call Dad and see what's going on. We might need to ride out though. Ramsey's been tripping over it, too. We need those inspirational stories. Mama Carmella can't just quit on us."

"I hear you."

"Well, get back to work. I'll let you know what I find out after I talk to Dad."

"All right. I'll be home late tonight. Jewel wants me to take her to that new Tyler Perry movie."

"Why don't you call Dawn? I wouldn't mind double dating."

Dontae laughed. "Thanks anyway, bro. But I got this." They hung up and Dontae continued reviewing the contracts for his clients.

Around three in the afternoon, his assistant buzzed him. "A Mr. Steven Wallace is here to see you. He doesn't have an appointment, but he assured me that you will see him."

Dontae jumped out of his seat. "Send him in."

It had been a couple of weeks since Dontae saw Stevie, but as he walked into his office, Dontae noticed that he had on the same greasy overalls he'd had on the day Dontae visited him. "Good to see you, Stevie. What brings you on this side of town?"

Stevie plopped down in the chair in front of Dontae's desk. "I got fired today. Business is slow, so as usual, I had to go."

"I'm sorry to hear that."

Stevie waved Dontae's concern away. "I'll find another job. Might even start my own lawn care business or something."

Dontae was reminded of his father saying that Stevie had a hard time holding onto a job due to the felony on his record. Dontae found himself thinking, *But for the grace of God, there go I.*

"I sat in my car for about an hour having a real pity party about my lot in life. I felt awful about losing another job and didn't know how I was going to tell my wife. But then I thought about a time when I felt worse... much worse and I suddenly knew that I had to speak with you."

Intrigued, Dontae leaned forward. Put his elbows on the desk and asked, "Just tell me how I can help. Whatever you need, I'm here for you." *Unlike the time that I just wussed out on you.*

260

"Five years ago when I was in prison, a prison ministry team preached one Sunday. I didn't have anything else to do so I went and I listened." Stevie touched his heart as he continued. "I felt something that day, but I had so much anger built up in me that I rejected it. I remember praying in my seat while tears rolled down my face. I told the Lord that day, that if He could tell me why Linden picked me rather than you, then I would serve him."

Dontae felt some kind of way about Stevie's confession, because he had wasted so much time when all the while, this man had been waiting on an answer that only he or Coach Linden could have given him. But Dontae had been too busy avoiding the truth to be of help to anyone. Time to stop avoiding and just tell it like it was.

"He came after me first, Stevie. But I was so drunk and scared when he came into my room that I threw up all over myself. He had the audacity to leave my room looking as if he was disgusted by all the vomit on me and the floor."

Shaking his head, Stevie said, "I kept thinking that even though I knew that I liked women, I must be gay deep down or he never would have come at me like that."

"I wondered the same thing about myself. How a man could even approach another man like that... but a very smart and beautiful woman recently told me that I am not what was done to me. Linden didn't care what either one of us wanted. He is a selfish and sick man and that's why I have decided to testify against him. It's my way of apologizing for not being there for you that night."

"Look man, we were both drunk that night. I probably wouldn't have been able to help you either. All I remembered was going to that room and stripping down. Back then I always slept in the nude. But I haven't done that since that snake snuck in my room. Even with my wife, I have to put on my pajamas before I go to sleep."

"When I travel, and I'm in hotel rooms, I sleep with the television on. Just can't deal with the darkness like that when I'm in a strange place."

"I should testify, too. My family has always wondered what happened to all my potential. I think it's high time that I told them."

Stevie looked as if three tons of steel had been lifted off of him. After ten years of torture, he was finally coming alive again.

"With both of us standing behind the other accuser, Linden won't be able to walk away from his crimes. He's going down."

"I'm trying not to wish for the worst of the worst for Linden, especially since I'm getting ready to call my wife and tell her that I'll be attending church with her this Sunday."

"I think I'll attend with my—" he almost called Jewel his fiancée but then he remembered that she'd given back the ring, "girlfriend."

"All right man." Stevie stood. "Don't be a stranger; I don't live far from Charlotte, so we're practically neighbors."

Dontae stood and walked around his desk. He hesitated for a second, but only a second. "What kind of work are you looking for?"

Stevie smiled, "I'm a jack of all trades. I do whatever puts the food on the table."

"I might have a job for you," Dontae said.

"Hey, I'm not looking for a handout. You don't owe me anything. I reached up and grabbed that room key and I drunk my own self into a stupor. It wasn't your fault, so you don't owe me anything."

"I'm not offering you a handout. I remember how good you used to be at spotting winners and losers. I'm looking for a scout to help me grow my business. Does that seem like something you'd be interested in?"

Stevie got excited. Then he caught himself, like someone who had been told over and over again not to expect anything good out of life. "You for real?"

"As real as real gets."

"I've been watching high school and colleges games for the longest, picking out the players that I thought could go the distance. I could do that job in my sleep." Stevie held out a hand to Dontae. "You got a deal, man. Thanks."

"See you on Monday," Dontae said, after giving him the location of his office. When Stevie walked out the door, Dontae sat down and exhaled... redemption sure felt good.

11

Ramsey had been praying for her, her children had been praying and Carmella had also spent much of her time in prayer, asking God why bad things happen to good people. She'd been tempted to just lie in bed for a month to protest this horrible thing that her family now had to endure. But Carmella had committed her life to God a long time ago, so she knew she couldn't continue moping around as if Jesus had come down from the cross and refused to die for the sins of the world.

Her son had been violated, that was a fact. But so many other things in Dontae's life were beautiful and blessed of God. Her son had been drafted into the NFL, and even though he'd hurt his knee the first year in, Dontae had still been able to keep his signing bonus, which enabled him to start his own business. Dontae was now a millionaire in his own right. If Carmella didn't know nothing else, she knew that God was in the work-it-out business. Some things might take a little longer to get worked out, but in God's good time, it would all be sorted out.

Like the problem Dontae was having with trusting God for a lifelong marriage. Carmella had prayed that Dontae would soon come to realize that love only lasts when two people are willing to work together, and defend their love against the whole world. Dontae was so stuck on how things had ended with her and Nelson that he had totally missed the fact that he was not his daddy and that through the power of Jesus Christ he could break the curse of divorce off of his life. She prayed that for Dontae and for the day that he would be able to remove from his memory even the thought of Coach Linden.

Since Carmella believed that God was a prayer-answering God, she forced herself to stop crying and to praise God even though things didn't turn out the way she'd expected. Sitting in front of her computer, Carmella turned on her radio. Fred Hammond was singing *Running Back to You*. She cranked it up as she began her first Praise Alert since Dontae's awful news.

As always, she began the alert, which went out to Ramsey and their seven children, with her favorite scripture in Psalm 150: *Praise ye the Lord. Praise God in His sanctuary: praise Him in the firmament of His power. Praise Him for His mighty acts: praise Him according to His excellent greatness. Let everything that hath breath praise the Lord. Praise ye the Lord.*

Today she noticed something in those scriptures that she'd never paid much attention to before. The verse didn't say praise God because everything was wonderful in her life, or because God had answered all her prayers and she had need of nothing. No, this verse simply admonished her to praise God just because of who He is... and that's what she intended to do. "Thank you, Jesus," she whispered as her fingers danced in praise over her computer keys.

She began writing: I normally send out praise reports that other people have written. But today I want to share with you some things that have been on my heart. First off, my prayer is that none of you ever have to deal with anything in life that causes you to lose your ability to praise God. In my fifty-plus years on this earth, I have dealt with two issues that almost stole the praise from my lips: The divorce from my first husband and the molestation of my son. I couldn't understand how people in this world could be so evil and how things like this could happen. But these last few days I have spent most of my time studying the Bible. And as I was reading the twenty-fourth chapter of Matthew, it all became clear to me.

In the beginning of that chapter, one of the disciples asked Jesus to tell them what signs to look for so they could tell when the end of the world was near. The answer that Jesus gave sounded a lot like the world we are living in now. He said,

Ye shall hear of wars and rumors of wars: see that ye be not troubled: for all these things must come to pass, but the end is not yet. For nation shall rise against nation, and kingdom against kingdom:

and there shall be famines, and pestilences, and earthquakes, and divers places. All these are the beginning of sorrows.

Then shall they deliver you up to be afflicted, and shall kill you: and ye shall be hated of all nations for my name's sake. And then shall many be offended, and shall betray one another, and shall hate one another. And many false prophets shall rise, and shall deceive many. And because iniquity shall abound, the love of many shall wax cold. But he that shall endure to the end, the same shall be saved.

And the gospel of the kingdom shall be preached in all the world for a witness unto all nations; and then shall the end come.

After writing those verses, Carmella grabbed a tissue and dabbed her eyes a few times. She then continued her email to her children...

I'm in tears as I am writing this to you all because I see it so clearly now. Evil is running rampant in this world because the devil knows his time is short... he knows that God is about to sound the trumpet and all those who have endured the hardships of this wicked generation and kept the faith will one day see the glory of God revealed. So I'm asking all of you, the Marshalls and the Thomases, to keep the faith and never lose your praise.

As for me and Ramsey, we will always praise and thank the Lord for the seven beautiful children we now share. You all are so precious to us and we continually pray blessings over your lives, even knowing that the evil one will try to block your blessings. But be of good cheer, because the God Ramsey and I serve has overcome the world and the evil one. But Ramsey and I will not always be here to pray over you or to praise the Lord for you. These are things that every one of you must learn to do for yourselves.

So from this day forward, I am challenging each one of you to find your praise. I will email you praise reports from time to time, but I will also be looking for your individual praise reports. Time is short and no one knows when the end will be. But one thing I do know... I intend to make it to heaven, and I want to see all of you there with me.

And remember, if God never does anything else for you, He's already done enough.

***

Holding hands as they strolled down the streets of a strip mall, Dontae and Jewel seemed at ease with each other after a night of dinner and a movie. "I like this."

"Like what?" Jewel asked with a raised brow.

"Us... you and me." He stopped walking, turned to her and while gazing in her eyes, trying to communicate all the love he felt, he said. "I want us to be together, Jewel. I feel as if a part of me is missing, with the way things stand between us."

Jewel put her hand on Dontae's face as she told him as gently as possible, "And I want you to fight for our love."

That comment angered Dontae. He stepped away from her and lifted his hands heavenward as he tried to rein himself in. He'd been doing everything he knew to do for months now, trying to get back into her good graces. If that wasn't fighting for their love, then what was it? Turning back towards her, Dontae demanded, "What do you think I've been doing?"

"Oh, you've got a lot of fight in you right now." She crossed her arms and stared at him for a long moment. "But what about five, ten or even twenty years from now? What happens when we've been married so long that we can't even remember how it felt to be young and in love anymore... will you fight for our love then?"

Dontae really wanted to say yes to five years from now, yes to ten years from now and even yes to twenty years from this very day. But it was always in the back of his mind that his mother and father divorced after twenty-three years. His parents didn't have a prenup and therefore his father found himself being raked over hot coals in the divorce proceedings... not that he didn't deserve it, but dang.

They got back in the car. Dontae turned to her and said, "Real talk?"

Jewel nodded.

As they sat beside each other, in the parking lot of one of their favorite shopping centers, Dontae felt it was time to say what truly troubled him. "I love you with all my heart. But I don't know what the future holds. Who's to say that I won't turn out to be just like my father and decide that twenty years is enough with one woman and then want a divorce so I can marry someone else?"

"Real talk?" she asked of him.

It was Dontae's turn to nod.

"If you could do me like that after I spent all those years loving you and making a home for the family I hope to have with you... then you deserve to lose your money."

"You would take all of my money?" Dontae asked incredulously.

"If you could cheat on me and then trade me in for some teenager, I certainly would take all—" she paused, then corrected herself, "half your money. I think that's a fair price to pay for breaking my heart, don't you?"

Dontae didn't know what to say to that. Jewel hadn't gotten herself injured on the football field and she didn't go in to his office every day and bust her butt for his clients. He did all the work and he really didn't think it fair that he'd have to split the spoils if their marriage should come to an end. But he also knew that Jewel wasn't a gold digger. She wasn't looking for an easy paycheck. She truly believed that not having a prenup would make Dontae want to stay and work things out. Whether that was true or not, Dontae couldn't say.

He drove Jewel home, walked her to the door and when he tried to kiss her good night, she stopped him. "I think we first need to figure out what we are going to do before we cloud the issue any further."

Dontae nodded, then asked, "Do you still want me to pick you up for church in the morning?"

"I would like that very much," Jewel told him.

"Okay, well I'll be here at eight in the morning, so we can do breakfast before church." With that said, Jewel went into the house leaving Dontae standing on the porch looking lost and alone.

12

When Dontae arrived home Ramsey Jr. and Ronny wanted to know how he felt about the email his mother had sent out that night. Since he'd been busy pouring out his heart to Jewel, he hadn't seen the email yet. His brothers seemed to really want to get his feedback, so Dontae went to his room and turned on his computer. His mother hadn't sent them a Praise Alert in a few weeks, so even though Dontae wouldn't admit it to his brothers, he was kind of excited about reading what his mom had to say.

As he opened the email and read the first few paragraphs, Dontae didn't know whether he should be angry with his mother for putting his business out there or if he should feel sorry for how hard the knowledge of what happened to him hit her. He double checked the "sent to" area and was comforted by the fact that the email was only sent to their immediate family... since his brothers and sisters already knew the story, Dontae wasn't upset with his mother.

Even though he didn't like thinking about that horrible incident, he decided to continue reading to discover what else his mother had to say. He was totally caught off guard by the statement about the end times. But ever since he was a little boy, his mom had always talked about something called the rapture, when the people of God would suddenly disappear and then God would judge the ones that had been left behind. Dontae seriously doubted that the world was about to come to an end, but the more he read from the twenty-fourth chapter of Matthew that his mother had mentioned in her email, he began to wonder if she wasn't right. The world did seem a lot more evil these days, with people doing whatever they pleased no matter how it affected anyone else.

When he was a kid, Dontae used to trust in God and people in general. But things happened that destroyed his trust in mankind and those things had even rocked his faith. He'd never told his mom that his faith wasn't where it used to be, but somehow she had known. And now she was asking him to keep the faith that he'd laid down a long time ago. "How can I praise God when," Dontae poked his forehead with his index finger, "my head is still all messed up?" Dontae was talking to the computer screen as if his mom was on Skype or doing FaceTime with him and she could answer his questions.

Dontae's life had been affected by a man who thought he could use and abuse young boys and never face any consequences. Dontae had tried his best to move past the pain and humiliation that night caused him. But there was another man in his life who had caused him pain that had not been so easy to sweep under the rug. The way his father left his mother after claiming for years to be so in love with his wife, had stunned him.

To be honest Dontae wished that he could just open his mouth and praise the Lord for doing this or that for him. But right now things were so jacked up that he just wasn't going to be able to do that. He turned off his computer and even though he knew his brothers were waiting for him to come out of his room and discuss the email with them, he just couldn't face them right now either. So he turned off his laptop and went to bed hoping to drown out the cares of life.

But his troubles seemed to meet him in his sleep as tossed and turned, this way and that way, trying to figure out what was going on and why he couldn't seem to find anyone. His mother was gone, his brothers and sisters were gone. Dontae became frantic in his dream-like state of mind. He worried that something terrible might have happened to the people he loved and then his heart felt as if it was about to jump out of his body as Jewel's face appeared before him.

She said, "I tried to wait for you."

What did that mean? Had Jewel given up on him and found someone else? Not his Jewel. She wouldn't have left him like everyone else had. He rushed over to her house and pounded on the door. He pounded on that door until his fist started to bleed. "Open the door!" he screamed.

"She ain't there," Dontae heard someone behind him say.

He turned around and saw an unkempt bearded man. "Where is she?"

The man didn't say anything, just looked up and pointed heavenward.

"What do you mean?" Dontae mimicked the man by pointed heavenward. "I asked where is she... do you know or not?"

"They're all gone. My family, Jewel, and even old lady Maggie down the street. My wife kept warning me, but I wouldn't listen... I wouldn't listen," the man said again with much sorrow in his voice as he walked away from Dontae, looking as if he was heading nowhere in particular, just out roaming the earth.

Then other people came down the street looking as if they were aimlessly roaming the earth also, but they were all headed in the same direction. As Dontae stood there watching, hundreds, then thousands, then tens of thousands of zombie-like people walked past him. Curious, Dontae began following them.

The walk was long and hard. Several people got in fights. Dontae witnessed one stabbing after the next, but the zombie-like people would just get back up after bleeding out and start walking again. "Where are we going?" Dontae screamed. The world had gone mad, and he needed answers.

The next thing Dontae saw was his dad and Coach Linden in front of him. His dad took out a gun and Dontae shouted, "Don't do it, Dad. You'll just end up back in prison."

But Nelson didn't seem to care about prison or about the fact that it was broad daylight. He lifted his gun and unloaded it into Coach Linden's body. Dontae watched the man fall to the ground. Even though Dontae knew that Coach Linden had to be dead after being shot so many times, he was still tempted to kick the man. But as he approached, his dad reached out a hand to stop him.

"You're a better man than me, son. Let the Lord fight your battles, just like your mama taught you." After saying that Nelson drifted into the crowd. Then Coach Linden got back up and continued roaming the streets with the rest of the zombies.

Dontae was so confused by everything he was witnessing. All types of evil and degradation was going on. People were being murdered left and right, but none of them were able to stay dead. What in the world was going on?

All of a sudden everyone seemed to stop and lift their heads, staring into the sky as the heavens seemed to open up and a booming voice said, *"Why do you seek Me now? Why do you long for what you cannot have?"*

At those words the people around Dontae began weeping. Then they started clawing as if trying to reach the sky.

The booming voice said, *"Depart from me. I never knew you."*

Suddenly Dontae realized who was speaking. It was God and Dontae didn't like the fact that he was being included in the same boat with all these zombies. Dontae lifted his eyes to the Lord and asked, "What about me, Lord? Don't you know me?"

"I once knew you. But you refused to trust Me."

That's not fair, Dontae wanted to shout and scream at the Lord. Of course he didn't trust God... he didn't trust anyone. How could he be held accountable for that? *"Don't You know what happened to me?"*

God simply said, *"Don't you know who I am? I am the God who wanted to heal you. But you chose not to come to Me. And now I will not come to you."*

"No!" Dontae reached out a hand, hoping and praying that he could stretch that hand long enough to reach heaven. But the heavens had closed up and darkness descended upon the earth. And everyone he loved was gone; he couldn't even find his father anymore, since he had taken off running after shooting Coach Linden. Dontae was alone, but he didn't want to be alone. He wanted to live, love and laugh. But his mom's words kept coming back to him... the end of days... the end of days.

Dontae turned from one side to the next, watching all of the horror and confusion that was unfolding right before his eyes. His mother had told him that after God pulled his chosen people out of the earth and the ones that had been left behind realized that there was no longer any hope for them—that they were doomed to die without

Christ— the people would cry out to God, but would not be heard. He was witnessing that now. As the heavens had shut up to them and no one was able to get an answer from the Lord, the people's eyes grew hard with hatred and they began shaking their fists toward heaven.

But Dontae didn't blame God for his fate. As he stood there in the midst of the lost, knowing that he was one of them, he remembered his mother telling him that he didn't know God for himself, that he only knew about her God. And he realized that he needed to spend the rest of his life, no matter how miserable it would be, getting to know God for himself.

Tears drifted down Dontae's face as he got on his knees, steepled his hands and began praying to a God that wasn't interested in hearing from him anymore. But at that moment, Dontae had nowhere else to turn and since he knew that God was merciful, he figured he'd give it a shot.

But as he was praying, the angry mob all around him noticed and they didn't like what they saw. One of them hollered at Dontae, "Get up! Don't you know that prayer is for fools? There is no God."

Another proclaimed, "Can't you see all the destruction around us? Doesn't that tell you that God is just some mythical being? Stop wasting your time, get up and help us find the families we have lost."

But Dontae ignored them and just kept praying, telling God that he didn't want to live in a world without Him. That he would hold on to his faith and trust and believe that God would one day come back for him. As Dontae continued praying and continued to believe that he would one day be rejoined with his family, he felt a kick to his back and a blow to the head. He unsteepled his hands and opened his eyes, wondering what the devil was going on.

The mob had turned on him. From every which way he looked, people were picking up sticks and coming at him with knives. They were foaming at the mouth, as one blow and then another assaulted his body. Dontae tried to get up and run, but the assault was too brutal; he couldn't get away. He felt helpless, just as he had that night Coach Linden had entered his bedroom. But this time, instead of throwing up all over himself, he called on the name of the Lord to free him from the attack... and the funny thing was, now that God had left the earth to its own kind, Dontae actually trusted that God would and could deliver him.

***

"Wake up, man... wake up."

Why were they still pulling on him? Didn't they know that the Lord was coming for him? Maybe he needed to shout louder. "Jesus! Jesus!" Dontae was shouting at the top of his lungs, calling on the only help he could turn to. Because even though his father had been lost with him, and even though his father had finally slayed the animal who'd attacked him, that animal didn't stay dead and Dontae hadn't seen his earthly father since Linden had gotten back up and continued to roam the earth. But his heavenly Father was another story. Dontae now knew that he could always turn to Him for help.

"Wake up, bro. And stop hitting me before I hit you back."

That was Ronny's voice. His eyes popped open and he saw that Ramsey Jr. and Ronny were standing over him. "Y'all got left behind, too?"

"What?" Ramsey had this puzzled look on his face.

Then Dontae got a puzzled look on his face as he familiarized himself with his surroundings. "Am I in my bed?"

"Of course you're in your bed. Where did you think you were?" Ronny asked.

Dontae sat up, rubbed his eyes. He hadn't been left behind. It was all just a horrible nightmare. "Oh, thank God."

"Might we ask what you are thanking God for this morning? Maybe we can put it in a praise report and send it out to Mama Carmella," Ramsey said with a smirk of laughter on his face.

Ignoring the question, Dontae asked, "What time is it?"

"Almost nine in the morning," Ronny reported.

Suddenly Dontae remembered his promise to Jewel. They were supposed to do breakfast before church. He jumped out of bed. "I'm late. I've got to go." He jumped in the shower, threw on one of his suits that had already been to the cleaners and was nicely pressed. But before he ran out of the house, he pulled two things out of his top dresser drawer and put them in his jacket pocket.

By the time he got to Jewel's house it was too late, she had already left. He stood on her porch paralyzed for a moment, waiting to see if that bearded man would walk by and tell him that Jewel and a bunch of her neighbors had just disappeared. But no such man approached him, so he breathed a sigh of relief as he jumped back in his car and raced over to her church.

The praise and worship team was singing *How Great is our God*. It was an old worship song, but it did the trick. Dontae raised his hands and sang along, because after the horrible dream he'd endured the night before, he realized that God was great and mighty, even if He didn't do anything else for him... as long as He didn't leave him behind after the rapture, Dontae would praise Him. So, that's what he did, all through that worship song and the next. Dontae smiled at himself, wishing that his mom was there to see him, somehow he knew that she would be proud. Even though it took a nightmare to show him the way, Dontae finally realized that God was worthy to be praised, just because of who He is.

After praise and worship and the offering, the pastor stood behind the podium and read from John 16:32-33

Behold, the hour comes, yea, is now come, that ye shall be scattered, every man to his own, and shall leave me alone: and yet I am not alone, because the Father is with me. These things I have spoken unto you, that in me ye might have peace. In the world ye shall have tribulation: but be of good cheer; for I have overcome the world.

After hearing those verses, Dontae wasn't able to concentrate on anything else the pastor had to say, because it was as if God Himself had spoken those words to him. In his dream last night he had felt as if he was scattered, and tossed to and fro and so, so very alone. But even with all the things he'd witnessed in that horrible dream and in his own life, he still felt as if he could somehow reach God. Coach Linden trying to take advantage of him didn't matter anymore, Tory only wanting him for his money was a non-issue and his father leaving his family at a time when they needed him most didn't matter either—because God Himself would help Dontae overcome all of his tribulations.

By the time the altar call was made, Dontae was ready. He lifted his hands and walked down to receive Christ, *his* own personal savior. And as he was rejoicing, he turned and saw Jewel. Tears were flowing down her face and he could see the love of God all over her as he hadn't seen it before. This was the woman for him, not just today or tomorrow, but for the rest of his life. She was heaven sent, and he would never let her go.

He walked over to the woman that God had placed in his life to have and to hold forever and a day and he took the prenup out of his jacket pocket and tore it up. He then took the ring out of his pocket and held it out to her again as he said, "I don't need a prenup, Jewel. With God's help I promise you, I will fight for our marriage until the very end."

"That's all I wanted to hear," she said as she kissed him and then allowed Dontae Marshall to slide the ring back onto her finger, where it would stay as a symbol of their forever kind of love.

Epilogue

Six months later, Dontae testified against Coach Linden. He felt good about his part in helping to put a predator just where he belonged. But it was Stevie's testimony that really did Coach Linden in. Stevie was a new man and he and his family seemed to easily move beyond the pain of his past. Dontae decided is time for him to do the same. At the sentencing, when Dontae spoke, he looked Coach Linden directly in the eye and said, "After this day, you will most likely spend the rest of your days in prison, but I will not allow you to imprison me any longer. If I've learned anything from this experience, it's that I can't change the past and I don't have to dwell in it either. So, I will forget about you and move forward. I will have a happy life. What you do with the rest of yours is your business. But I pray that you allow God to work on your heart and to deliver you.

After that Dontae left the courtroom not even needing to hear just how many years Coach Linden received as his sentence. They were running late and a limo was outside the courthouse waiting for Dontae and Jewel. They had gotten married the week before and were now headed to the airport to begin their two week honeymoon in Paris and Italy. As far as Dontae was concerned, his bride deserved no less. She was a Godly woman who taught him to love, so he was about to show her some serious love in a place that was made for lovers.

But as they pulled up to the airport, Dontae remembered something he forgot to do. Now that they were at the airport, it would have to wait. He got out of the car and waited as the limo driver handed their bags over to the porter. He tipped the driver, grabbed his wife's hand, then rushed into the airport. After going through the check point and racing toward their terminal, they made it to the gate just as passengers were boarding the aircraft.

Dontae kissed Jewel as they sat down in their first class seats, but he kept reminding himself about what he forgot to do. He didn't have his laptop because he refused to take it on his honeymoon. But he did have his iPad. Dontae took it out of his carry-on bag and quickly opened his email. It was time for him to send his first Praise Alert.

Before typing his praise report, he added Jewel's email address to the circulation. She was now part of the family and should take part in their little praise-a-thon also. Dontae then began to type.

Hey Family, I'm on the plane getting ready to start my honeymoon, but I didn't want to leave the country before I sent out my very first Praise Alert. There was a time in my life when I didn't think I had anything to praise God for, but I now know differently. God has done so much for me; I hardly know where to begin. But I would first like to thank and praise God for the loving family that I have. You all have meant so much to me and I doubt I'd be where I am today without your support.

But the thing I am most thankful for is how God kept on blessing me even when I didn't deserve or appreciate Him for doing it. My mindset has totally changed and I can now praise God just for waking me up this morning, but not only that... I woke up next to the most beautiful woman in the world... sorry sisters, you all have to take a backseat to Jewel. But I think all of you are beautiful, too.

God has been good to me. I even thank and praise Him for allowing me to be able to give my wife the honeymoon of her dreams... isn't God good? He sure has been good to me. I will forever praise Him for leading and guiding me all of the days of my life, and for renewing my mind.

Now I have given you my praise report; I'm sure as time goes by I will have many more. But I'd like to hear from some of you. So whose next... what do you have to praise God for?

Dontae smiled as he wrote those words, because he knew his brothers and sisters loved God, but a few of them had lost their praise. Now was the perfect time to get it back.

The stewardess said, "Please turn off all electronic devices."

Well family, it's time for me to go, but before I sign off, I'd like to reiterate what Mom always tells us. No matter what trials or tribulations we go through in life, just go on and praise God anyhow. The end

Author Bio

Vanessa Miller is a best-selling author, playwright, and motivational speaker. She started writing as a child, spending countless hours either reading or writing poetry, short stories, stage plays and novels. Vanessa's creative endeavors took on new meaning in 1994 when she became a Christian. Since then, her writing has been centered on themes of redemption, often focusing on characters facing multi-dimensional struggles.

Vanessa's novels have received rave reviews, with several appearing on Essence Magazine's Bestseller's List. Miller's work has receiving numerous awards, including "Best Christian Fiction Mahogany Award" and the "Red Rose Award for Excellence in Christian Fiction." Miller graduated from Capital University with a degree in Organizational Communication. She is an ordained minister in her church, explaining, "God has called me to minister to readers and to help them rediscover their place with the Lord."

She is currently working on a For Your Love trilogy for Kimani Romance. The first book, Her Good Thing, releases in September 2012. She is working on a historical set in the Gospel Era for Abingdon Press. First book in Gospel Series, How Sweet the Sound releases in 2013, and a My Soul to Keep series for Whitaker House.

Praise Him Anyhow Items

PHA Journal   PHA t-shirt

Order Form:

Product	Price for (1)	How many	Size	Total
Praise Him Anyhow Volume 1	$13.95			
Praise Him Anyhow Journal	$9.99			
Praise Him Anyhow t-shirt (s - 1X)	$15.95			
Praise Him Anyhow t-shirt (2X)	$17.95			
- Sales Tax (7.25%)			Add Tax	
Total				

Mail to: Praise Unlimited * 13000 S. Tryon Street * Ste F-228 * Charlotte, NC 28278

CPSIA information can be obtained
at www.ICGtesting.com
Printed in the USA
BVHW042113090320
574584BV00008B/128